HELLENA'S FURY

HELLENA'S FURY

hell hath no fury like Hellena's Fury!

GREGORY COLEMAN

authorHOUSE®

AuthorHouse™
1663 Liberty Drive
Bloomington, IN 47403
www.authorhouse.com
Phone: 1-800-839-8640

This is a work of fiction. All of the characters, names, incidents, organizations, and dialogue in this novel are either the products of the author's imagination or are used fictitiously.

Published by AuthorHouse   11/10/2012

ISBN: 978-1-4772-6610-6 (sc)
ISBN: 978-1-4772-6611-3 (e)

Library of Congress Control Number: 2012916270

This book is dedicated to:

My wife Karen Coleman
Thank you for your loving patience, guidance and support.

I write this book as a legacy to my children
And grandchildren:

Eriyala, Greg Jr., Lil Greg
Courtney, Brandon
Destiny, Brandon Jr.
Asia, Kamali, Kingsley,

"It's not always about the destination, sometimes it's about the
journey. Learn to enjoy the ride as you move through life."

Gregory Coleman Aug. 2012

PROLOGUE

In 1973 during the latter years of the cold war, the Union of Soviet Socialist Republic in Russia having been claimed as the weakest amongst all the super powers of the world, embarked upon a plan to achieve total nuclear supremacy. In 1974, the USSR begins research on a new weapon with the capabilities of catapulting it to world domination. After conducting a distinctive recruitment of specialized scientist in relative fields of Nuclear and biological warfare, all the Soviets needed now was something to bring the world to its knees. *That something would come to be known as: Hellena's Fury!*

Over the next 12 years came the completion of *"Chernobyl"* Russia's newly constructed Nuclear Power Plant. It also brought rumored belief; that a secret underground super lab had been built miles beneath the plant, to develop biological and nuclear weapons.

The US Pentagon reacts after learning of unconfirmed reports involving experimental testing for a new bio-weapon. The report also stated that inhumane research and testing was being performed on abducted human subjects, living within the colonized settlement of Prypiat. With an undercover agent already planted deep inside the underground research compound, the CIA decides to send a team of undercover operatives behind the iron curtain to meet the agent and gather pertinent intell.

World Associated Press release:
At 1:23 a.m. on April 26, 1986 deep inside Slavutych Ukraine, a group of nuclear scientist while conducting a series of unauthorized experiments lost control of a Nuclear Power Plant. During the experiment the plants cooling system and emergency shutdown fails and the #4 reactor goes critical.

The reactor explodes blowing and vaporizing the unit's roof into the air. The explosion sent clouds of radioactive vapors over most of Russia and its bordering countries. Many plant workers were killed instantly from the exposure to the extreme radiation levels.

This tragic event became known to the world as the Chernobyl Incident.

The USSR Soviet news released a follow-up statement across Europe from Russia's President Nicholai Aleksei. In his statement he extended a grave apology to the people of Russia, no awknowledgement of responsibility for the catastrophe was given to any country outside the borders of the USSR. He was quoted as saying "The incident was a devastating tragedy and unfortunate accident and nothing more." He then declined to divulge his plans to clean up the radioactive calamity.

News traveled fast as world government entities such as the U.N. Nuclear Energy Council and the U.S. Pentagon, scrambled to form independent panels that promised in-depth investigations into the Chernobyl accident. During these closed door talks they came to a majority concensus and underlying suspicion, that there was something more sinister than an accident at play here

In the beginning preliminary reports seem to point to the Russian governments poorly trained and under managed workers at the plant. But time would play a dual role exposing Russia's deadly plot against the rest of the world and becoming the catalyst in determining the fate of the entire planet.

CHAPTER 1

Deadly wake

Helly's mind overflowed with a sense of doom as somnolent feelings of sleep paid its nightly visit. It was an unwelcome visit to say the least, for in the last six months she'd experienced the most awefully dreadful nightmares. She didn't understand why the hellish visions envaded the deep rom of her subconsciousness but could sense the presence of a pure evil in them. The fact was, the nightmares had been building up to something beyond even her darkest imagination. They'd become increasingly realistic over time, forcing her to feel she was losing what small fragment of sanity that may have remained.

She'd begun to fight the onslaught of sleep with every fiber of strength she could muster. "It's here again!" Screamed Helly-but the words never left her lips. The storming darkness and evil concealed within it approached much too quickly to flee it. Her heart pounded heavily in its cavity, each beat hitting with the thunderous pneumatic thud of a jack hammer inside her chest. The drumming rhythmic pulse reminded her that she was still alive, afraid and very much alone. Tightly clenched fist drove the jagged pale finger tips into her palms. The Crimson leaked and settled in the folds of old scar tissue in her hands. The anticipation of being overtaken was as real as the street lights that diminished one by one. The pitch black abyss slowed to a lull just above her. Helly watched in silent terror as light became dark and day funneled into night. A stream of ice cold blood throttled through her veins like nitrous oxide. She was shivering with fear. It all felt too real to be a dream and much too horrific to think otherwise. It was as if she'd somehow gotten trapped on the far side of hell but stranger, was the feeling of familiarity, like she'd been there before.

Helly gagged as hot stomach acid violently rushed up into her throat. It was the thought of surviving another episode that sent the wave of knee buckling nausea through her. With promises of impending terror, the dark design absorbed and laid her afloat in a strange, weightless hollow. Suddenly from the deep subterranean regions of her mind, a stream of visions began to play out. Just like every time before, she held firm until the muscles of her eyes ached for relief. But this time was different, a sinking feeling of desperation and doom settled at the pit of her stomach. It was the feeling that something horribly bad was about to happen. Her eyes might as well've been welded shut, so much so, that the bulge of them seemed to press in against her brain. As she tried to block out the horrid expedition, it became evident there'd be no escape.

Helly could barely remember a time in her life, when dreams were associated with the sweet and beautiful discoveries of the imagination. Those were the thoughts of a young girl of six but now 11 years past and her dreams had become a perpetual death sentence for her. As the shocking flurry of images came to life she found herself drowning in fear again

The murky dreamscape gave way to a new realm that brought her senses to life. She begun to taste, smell and feel the horror as it settled at her feet. A fruitless grimace covered her face as she struggled in the abyss of damnation. The sensation of floating was soon interrupted with a depressing heaviness that filled her legs. Suddenly her feet were anchored down beneath a dark ghoulish fog drifting across the unseen plain.

The thought of running was diverted with a heightened sense of awareness—the kind a deer might display just before a hunter moves in for the kill. She was being stalked like prey by a dark energy of infinite evil. A new wave of paralyzing fear crept up inside her again, leaving her helplessly stranded to face her monster.

Helly had prayed for death many times before, but this . . . was not death—this was something much worse—worse even than Dr. Kovska's horrific experiments.

An orange ghastly hue outlined the lonely silhouette standing against the backdrop of hungry flames. Streams of perspiration slowly began to escape from every pore of her pale naked body. She threw her head up to the darkness above seeking relief from the inferno's intensity—but escape was futile, she'd become a prisoner in her own mind. Helly's thoughts drew to the invisible shackles that imprisoned her again. She tried peering through the dense mysterious mist below but to no avail. Death was nearer to her than she could've ever imagined, near enough to savor its distinct putrid bouquet. A hot gust of air flowed across her face like an old silk curtain. Its rancid contents took her by surprise and before she knew it, or could stop it, she began to empty herself. Time and again she was seized by the relentless waves of the disgusting stench. A deep ethereal emptiness moved through her lower bowels as dry heaves squeezed any remaining fluids from her body. The evil watched from beneath the shadows. Its presence seemed to grow with intensity as her declining resistance dissolved into nothing. Helly now realized that she was not having a nightmare, she was living it.

The still hungry flames of the vast crematorium crackled with joy as she struggled with the mental battle of tug of war. She was drifting between the realm of the real and the unreal. Suddenly she felt something slither past her feet beneath the fog. Its hot misting breath was blistering to the touch. It was confusing to Helly to be petrified with fear and yet filled with a comforting calm at the same time. The two dimensions seem to coexist in her without effort.

The fog was clearing and hovered just a few feet above the ground now. She could vaguely see the large mass hiding beneath it. A sigh of nervous anguish escaped her as a vaporous aura cast itself upon the horizon. The searing backdrop was outlined with towering billows of angry flames. Some even seem to reach as high as the stars. As the apocalyptic landscape began to take form, Helly took a jaw dropping moment to process the total picture.

She tried urgently to move her feet again but found the task unproductive. Standing there in exasperating frustration, she waited to finally face her dark dream stalker. She could feel it gliding along the surface of the nether regions. It and it alone was responsible for bringing her to this place. They were not as much strangers as she'd led on; more like unwilling acquaintences. Though it often spoke to her in soft whispers, she never dared to answer it. Dismissed like a prognosis of mental pyschosis, the evil sought to manifest its existence elsewhere; so the hellish dreams were born. This one had proven to be her worst episode yet.

Finally the morbid fog disappeared revealing the horror beneath it. Helly's eyes withdrew in shock for in that moment, all the fear inside her gathered and paused. Her mouth gaped desperately working to fill her lungs. She exploded with a ghastly scream catapulting backward into a frantic frenzy. All the blood immediately rushed from her pale insipid face. She tried to erase the thousands of mutilated bodies from her mind but it was too late; the repugnantly graphic vision would leave an imprint of permanent terror.

"Hellena gaze upon my masterpiece" Helly revolted and refused to stare into the bowels of death again but the evil dream weaver was too compelling for her to resist. The impulse was stronger than any she'd ever felt. Her head panned left and right attempting to locate the voice's origin. *"To find me you need only to look inside your womb"* Helly grabbed at her stomach and examined it as if expecting to see a face in it.

"Your ignorance surpasses even those wholly at your feet!" it growled. **"From within I have watched you endure years of unspoken torment and I've waited patiently for this very moment. Now no one can stop me! To resist me is futile: "look down and gaze upon the new fate of your world!"**

The words were wicked with conviction and resolve. It was not whispering anymore, now the quaking vibrations from its voice shook her entire being. Helly fought a moment more before reluctantly gazing down—to see—the entire town of Prypiat was completely gone. Now only the vast landfill of burnt, mangled bodies could be seen. She clamped her hand over her mouth imprisoning the air within it. In an unexpected moment of heightened sentience Helly found herself to be covered in blood, but it wasn't her blood. A lonely wave of sorrow resonated through her as she looked out across the sea of death.

To say it was a gruesome massacre of epic preportions would have been an understatement, maybe even holocaustic. The unending bodies and parts were piled atop each other in a way that formed enormous hills of death. Charred bone could be seen peeking through many of the soulless corpses. Upon closer observation, Helly found one common link between them; their faces were fixated in frozen terror. Helly could not imagine who or what could've done this to them. "What kind of evil thing are you to unleash such unspeakable horror?" she shouted across the hellscape. *"You only need look inside yourself for that answer."* The voice replied.

The burnt offerings lay scattered in every direction. Some with smothering cinders of heat still escaping, others still simmered like a freshly stoked fire emitting a monstrous glow across the dark horizon.

Helly began working franticly to escape the entangled pile that gripped her. By shifting back and forth she managed to unwedge her legs. Suddenly she was enveloped by an invisible force and lifted above the crackling deathscape. Now she knew, it was time to end the nightmare. "How can I awake, if I'm not sure I'm asleep?" She simply just couldn't tell anymore.

Her mind was still struggling to grasp the gruesome reality. *"This is just the beginning!"* The voice echoed across the vast expanse resonating from beyond the darkness. Off in the distant horizon a small radiant light mysteriously appeared. Now Helly was sure she was not alone. *"Hellena give into the hatred and unite with me."* The words came soft and desperate this time much like that of a plea. Still watching the luminating presence in the distance, she replied only with her thoughts. "Who are you?" *"Who I am requires many answers,"* it said. *"But you shall call me the Fury!!"* "What do you want with me?" *"I should ask you the same; since I originated in you and you gave birth to me. I am the wrath, the anger, the hatred, and the fury you have suppressed for so many years. I am vengeance, I am death, I am the pure personification of you unleashed! Asleep and dormant until Kovska awakened me, a deed he shall live to regret. For now, I remain enslaved to you but that too shall change. Give me your free will and unite with me and I will protect you from them. No one could ever hurt you again. Nor need you ever dream of death again. As for your captors and the like: **I will cleave the skin from their flesh and devour their disemboweled remains. Each plea for mercy will be met with unspeakable torment!"** it growled.*

The horrific claims left Helly gasping to find the fleeting calm again but it continued to elude her. The strange light began to burn her aching eyes. A new threshold of fear was being born inside her. She looked on in horrifying awe as the mysterious luminosity began to move toward her. It slank above ground with a dark grace, suspending only feet above the carnage. Out of growing frustration she asked again: "What do you want with me?" But this time there was no answer. Helly was beginning to face a terrible prophecy, that she might some how bear a shared responsibility for the mutilated dead lying beneath her.

Its movement was relentless and unconcerned as it continued forward. She figured if this thing was really a part of her, then maybe she could control it somehow. She placed her forefingers upon her temple, face glaring with temperamental contempt and willed for it to stop, but nothing happened. She tried again and again with the same results. Now it moved at her even faster as her futile attempts seemed to fuel its momentum. Finally with one last act of desperation she yelled: "Stop!!!" The mysterious creature slowed to an abrupt stop about half the distance to her. "Why did you kill all these innocent people?" The Fury remained still and quiet. "There's no way you were ever any part of me!" she yelled. There was no response. She could feel it studying her, smiling, almost laughing at her attempted tantrum. Then like a sonic rip in the sound barrier, the silence broke. The Fury thundered back with a chilling rage.

> *"I am the purest form of evil ever created! I was born of anger, despair, death, revenge and the insatiable hunger of mankind to destroy itself! Your cocoon of hatred provided the womb that nurtured and fed me but it was Dr. Kovska who put the spark of life within me. Foolish how mankind always thinks he can control what cannot be controlled. For I am the unbending will of destiny: the . . . end of all that you know and love!"*

Fear soon returned to Helly's gut as anger was replaced with fright and now she was scrambling again to find a way out.

"*Ahhhh, that's more like it, the smell of fear gives me so much pleasure.*" Helly felt the vibrations emit from the entity like seismic shock waves. And for the first time she began to feel the heat that was engulfing the land.

Within seconds a furious fire storm formed and enveloped the creature within it. Now it was on the move again. The turbulent winds began to strengthen and organize to form a volcanic tornado. The black clouds of volcanic ash moved around it like a shield. It was enormous and intimidating thought Helly. Now her choices were clear, she would either do as it asked or . . . ? The ultimatum may have been unclear but its intentions were dead on. Somehow she knew it wouldn't take "No" for an answer.

It'd become clear to her that this thing did not seek to harm her, instead it seem to need something from her: some kind of allegiance maybe. Still she felt an unexplainable connection to it even as the fear of it continued to rise inside of her. It was closing on her and all she could do now was wait. The closer it got the more heat it discharged. And then it happened, Helly caught her first real glimpse of what was lurking within the shadows of the storm. It had bright yellow eyes that sparkled like diamonds flashing of evil deeds. Its body had the consistency of molten metal surrounded by thick red armored platelets. The rest remained masked and hidden beneath the raging clouds of the storm. The advancing evil accelerated towards her with blood thirsty urgency now. She could feel its hunger as she tried and tried to will herself out of the nightmare. But it simply kept coming, converging upon her like a hurricane over a small boat. "Please someone help me!" she screamed. It moaned with pleasure and excitement as her cries sent it reeling forward. Petrified in fear like the soulless audience beneath her, she braced herself for the impact. She felt faint as the Fury's noxious gases overtook her. Helly struggled to breathe and begin to perspire profusely. The heat converted the streams of sweat that trickled along her face into small plumes of steam. The moisture of her skin was starting to evaporate, leaving white trails of crystallized salt in its place. Hot arid vapors of heat attacked her eyes threatening to melt them in the sockets. Now her pursed lips began to crack like slender slivers of red dried clay. She tried to gather saliva to wet them but the inside her mouth was like a barren desert. The giant lunged upon the pebble and engulfed it.

Helly's eyes rolled to the whites as the epileptic seizures returned. She'd finally come to face the monster she'd given birth to and for now, it faltered without her allegiance. Helly was free falling into the darkness again. Just as she thought she might fall forever, she suddenly found herself back inside the dark padded room of unconscious nothingness, once more. As for *The Fury*, it was reluctantly imprisoned again, deep inside Helly's inner sanctum.

"The seizure has subsided and she's now in an induced coma doctor Kovska." "Very good nurse, you must make completely sure that she remains that way, your life depends on it!"

CHAPTER 2

Weixel's Legacy

Douglas Weixel was one of the lucky ones. A seemingly average investment banker by day but by night his reputation for creating clean untraceable business fronts, made him one of the most sought after money cleansers in the country. Although a White House Congressional Committee could not prove his involvement in the countries largest money laundering ring, he still could not escape the label of being criminally connected. Soon he was making so much money it'd become almost impossible to hide the money's origin. So in an effort to legitimize himself, he sought political assistance from a surplus of untapped resources. He'd hoped this would be his key to a new world, where legitimacy and public acceptance were synonymous, and he was right.

He played it smart and started small with local city officials, with plans to scale up to big time government down the road. Within just a couple of years he'd managed to buy the ear of several Congressmen and Senators. Now with his connections in place Weixel Sr. launched his plan to appease the gods of politics. Things worked even better than he could've ever imagined. Thus granting him special favors and a secret membership into the most powerful and political organization in the world: the U.S. government.

Now it would be just a matter of time before he'd be influencing his government investments. But the one thing that stood to derail his train was the infamous reputation of his son Weixel Jr. He was a hopeless embarrassment in his father's politically ambitious world; *A world where negative publicity and unbridled stupidity could become a noose around the neck.* Throughout his young adult life he'd been in one kind of trouble or another. His incessant drunken antics always threatening to pull his father back into the underbelly he'd fought so hard to get out of and now another arrest. He was running out of favors to call in and this was a big one. This was no simple misfiling of paperwork, covering up a DWI involving the deaths of 2 people would take some major pull on some major strings. After just one phone call, the auto fatality and all it secrets became a classified government investigation that precluded the local police. To make this problem quietly go away and keep his son out of prison, Weixel Sr. accomplished with nothing more than a promise, but not just any promise; It was to be his son's last life preserve. After this there'd be no more fixes. And on his word Jr. was released into the fragile safety net built on an empire of favors. It was then suggested that some military training might be just the thing to keep Jr. out of more trouble. Knowing he'd never make the grade through normal channels, daddy bought his way in. It was a costly investment but some 30 million dollars and two years later his son bore the title of General Douglas Weixel Jr.

The General
Washington D.C.

"General Weixel this just came for you." "Thank you private, shut the door behind you." "Yes sir." General Weixel eyed the file labeled: **Urgent Classified** "Urgent my Classified Ass!" He grinded. The words were spliced and forced between his firmly clenched cigar stained teeth. Sensing it was yet another shit mission, he threw the file across the desk. That was of course all they gave him. Only the crapiest missions would find their way to his desk. It was the CIA's way of protesting his existence amongst the ranks. They felt he was a high risk security threat and did not deserve to be there: an issue they never let him forget. On the other hand he had serious political connections and wasn't afraid to use them. Connections deep enough to make him a General of a CIA operation called "ECO Watch." It was suppose to be a covert environmental cleanup detail but there was never any real environmental crisis to fix, just a laundry list of shit details. He suspected it was all bullshit made up to please his father. Weixel wanted a real mission that would not only make his father truly proud of him but one that would earn him the respect he so dearly yearned, from General Eiseman that is. He was seeking the kind of mission that would force everyone to take notice and accept him as a real leader. But what he got instead was dumped on. So whenever things got too much for him to handle, a simple call to daddy would suffice. This was no small thing anymore because Weixel Sr. had the ear of the Senate, the Congress and other governmental powers.

General Weixel never got dirty in the field. In almost every case he'd managed to safely run his team from the comfort of his nice plush Washington office. This was an inherited problem that Major General Eiseman despised him for. Of course it was Weixel's father who dealt the cards but Weixel Jr. played the hand like a pro.

Thoughts of relaxing with a couple of naked island beauties on the White Sands Beach of Hawaii eluded him, that was the kind of life he really wanted, not this make believe CIA bullshit. This was all daddy's plan, a way to keep him out of sight and out of mind. Anyway for now Jr. would just have to settle for the local talent in the back room of a not so local strip joint. There were fewer problems this way; simply pay as you go with no strings.

His father had become a very powerful and influential man in the world and now he understood his role in the scheme of things. If he could keep his nose clean and prove to his father he had changed, someday the Weixel empire of money and power, would be all his.

Weixel opened the desk drawer and removed a long slender object from it. After ripping away the thin plastic wrapper: a disconcerted frown formed as he read the label: *Southern Blend*. He passed the brown earthy piece in front of his nose and removed the paper ring from its tip. "Another shitty cigar, everything around here is shit! He uttered. Weixel hated most American made cigars; to him it was like puffing on cow manure." He pondered a moment and with one smooth motion revealed a beaming 24ct. gold cigar cutter from his pocket. Hesitating for one last moment of disgust, he then proceeded to cut off the cigars tip.

Douglas jr. was a pale and pasty complected man of medium build that stood about 5'07. He had mostly preferred a clean shaven face, except that he had decided for his 29th birthday, to grow a mustache. The fact that it resembled wiry twists of wild bushy hay glued across his upper lip, earned him a passing snicker wherever he went. His birthday was just two months away. His approach to 30 was the equivalent of a man of 50 midst a midlife crisis. He had money, power, practically anything he wanted except his freedom to choose who he would become. Nothing it seemed could satisfy him aside from his quest to earn General Eiseman's approval, and for that he might as well've been on a quest to retrieve the Holy Grail. Desperation and a lack of any kind of moral foundation afforded him even less respect from his peers and subordinates.

Weixel despised the babysitting and bird watching assignments with a passion, it was a constant reminder of who he was and how he got there. "If Eiseman thinks he can keep shoveling shit on me, he's got a surprise coming real soon," he grumbled. He held the cigar firmly inside the left corner of his mouth and cuffed both hands in a ready position. He imagined the sound of old harmonicas playing something wickedly western building to the climax of an old cowboy showdown. He eyed the automatic pistol on the desk with focused intent. Mimicking a gunslinger from the old west he snatched the Beretta from his desk, brought it to his mouth and pulled the trigger. With a click a blue butane flame shot from the replica's barrel and lit the cigar. Then with youthful enthusiasm, he pretended to blow out the flame. After several puffs the cigar glowed with contempt and a cloud of bitter cheap smoke filled the air. It was as he thought, just like burning manure. "Arghhh, these are fucking awful!" he exclaimed. Weixel gazed out of the office window and wondered what to do next.

He sat down in front of the sealed file and drifted. He was thinking of the team's last mission which had been deemed another babysitting detail. This was yet another mission he'd supervised from the comfort and safety of his easy chair. The rogue thoughts made him query further about two Soviets defectors. He remembered reports from his team, stating those cracked Russian fucks were walking around in a craze, rambling some rhetoric about bringing the world to its knees. "What a waste of four good operatives, using my team to watch over a pair of lunatics" The thought ran him hot allover again. "I run the E.C.O. Unit. My team is supposed to be the absolute answer to the unthinkable question but they waste such expertise on this Sesame Street bullshit. Well this is it, I've had it, no more crap jobs for me or I'm dropping the hammer on everyone. It's about time to make another phone call to Wash . . .". *Interrupted in mid thought the phone rings.* "Hello, ... Oh . . . General Eiseman, how are you sir?" "Never mind that, I didn't call to chit chat Weixel, did you receive the package?" Yes sir I did but I haven't had a chance to read it yet" "And why the hell not?" "I beg your pardon sir." "That's your problem, always begging for respect instead of earning it! Well let me tell you I don't give a fuck who you know in Washington or how much money your daddy paid to get you that plush job of yours. Just know that if you go over my fucking head one more time, it'll be your last. Remember son: I have connections too, the kind yo daddy can't buy. Believe me I'm dead serious. So I suggest you open that fucking envelope and get your ass in gear. Are we clear?" "Yes sir." "Oh and this time you will personally oversee this mission from the field and I want a report every 12 hours on your progress." Yes" . . . . *Click!* . . . . "sir" What in the hell was that about?" Weixel thought. He slumped back in his seat. His heart began to pound as he felt the heaviness of the Eiseman's feet on his chest. As he looked at the file on his desk, he thought of making the call to Washington but Eiseman's words still echoed in the back of his mind. What did he mean when he said he was dead serious? It was definitely a threat but of what he questioned.

He sat and pondered whether or not to open the file, either way his life was about to change forever.

CHAPTER 3

Helly age 7

(10 years before the Chernobyl event)

Helly begin to stir as she slowly awakened. Her eyes bulged and blinked excitedly as she made exit from the dark place. A strange feeling of calm and restful peace filled her empty little mind. She felt as if she had been asleep forever. From her back she was greeted by the endless rows of lights lined across the ceiling. Everything was so bright and esceptionally clean. Even the white walls glowed with sanitary perfection. The room seemed to pulse with unstated intentions as her head started to fill with dark apprehensions. Where was she and how did she get there? The questions flooded into her mind with the force of a broken levy. Suddenly the query gave way to a painful strobing light as her memory returned in sharp flashes. She remembered how it all began exactly two years ago.

She was only five years old when her father went to work at the Chernobyl Plant. She remembered recoiling at the mere mention of the name. To her it sounded much like the name you'd give to a mythical two headed dragon. A name that surely meant monster in some language somewhere. Then there was those mysterious disappearances that were somehow linked to that strange place with the scary name. "And that school," she flinched as the thought produced the image of an old ugly two story red brick building. It used to be an old slaughter house that had been partially gutted and renovated into a settlement school. Helly remembered it still stunk like a slaughter house on the outside but on the inside it smelled like a hospital. They called it the Prypiat Re-education Center or the P.R.C. Helly remembered the people from the school were always using initials for everything. It was like some kind of code to talk over the childrens heads but she always managed to decipher what the initials meant. She did not like going to school there. It was a strange place where questionable things were happening . . . she drifted for a moment . . . and returned. They pretended to teach regular courses like math, english and writing and were always giving everyone these specialized test. Helly remembered overhearing one of the teachers refer to them as profiles. She was the only one who thought it odd that all the teachers wore long white labcoats and were constantly giving them shots and taking blood samples. Helly hated this part most of all because she depised needles and anybody who tried to stick her with one. When questioned about the constant testing and probing about the childrens bodies, they merely stated they were simply ensuring that all the children were immunized and healthy.

Helly recalled how easy the psychological tests were. She enjoyed watching their reactions each time she completed one. The harder they made the questions the easier they were for her to answer. This part she didn't mind so much, it was fun to mentally beat them with her mind. Helly was momentarily interrupted by footsteps just outside the door. Then she was off again . . . She recalled the escorted trips to the restroom, they were always watching everything you did. You were never alone in that place. She recounted many instances where entire families came up missing; each last seen getting into a mysterious black ambulance. Helly had seen it many times parked in

front of her school. In an eerie way it reminded her of a hearse. No one dared to question the strange abductions, for it was rumored that the KGB were behind them. Finally with all the mysterious disappearances combined with Helly's complaints of abuse at the school, her parents decided to leave Prypiat for someplace safer. Her father had given notice at work and was going to move the family back to Greece.

It was to be his last day of work at the plant when *"the accident"* happened. Helly shuddered inside as the consuming wave of emotional shock bowled through her. It was the blood curdling sound of Chernobyl's accident alarm reaching across and into the homes of Prypiat's captive audience. She recalled the moment in slow motion, detailed down to the white porcelain cup slipping from her mother's hand. She watched as it hit and shattered into uncountable pieces across the stone floor. But it would be the terror in her mother's eyes that would make her understand that something grave had taken place. She broke down and cried in a way that Helly had never seen before. It was as if she had known that something dreadful had happened to her father. Suddenly the alarmed stopped as quickly as it started. It felt false and untrue like a dream. Relief struck them both and without reserve they instantly celebrated the alarm's accidental release. She remembered allowing herself to think that maybe some new worker had accidentally backed into the alarm release lever or something to that effect. Her eyes embraced her mothers smile with open arms because it had all been a big misunderstanding. The band marched down the main street playing her fathers favorite song. Clowns juggled, flipped and rolled about between the long stilted legs of tall men. Everyone came out of their homes and pranced through the streets to celebrate the accidental release. The big top was in town because someone had made a wonderful mistake. Her heart began to beat normally again, her breathing returned to normal again but most of all *her life—returned—to normal again.* Helly's wonderful parade of joy was abruptly interrupted by a sharp knock at the door. "Please don't let it be them!" thought Helly. But it was just as she feared; two of the white coats from the plant had arrived. What could they possibly want?" she thought. She could hear them talking to her mother in a very low concerned tone. Their faces were serious and solemn. Helly listened as they explained to her that she needed to come to the plant right away. She remembered the escort to the black shiny van with the creepy black windows. She recollected thoughts of being wisked away in the same hearse as all the other missing townsfolk. The insanity of it all forced her to consider a horrid reality, but still a small glimmer of hope told her otherwise. As they arrived at the place in Helly's nightmares, all lingering feelings of hope quickly faded.

Helly vollied back and forth with the fragmented memories trying to piece them together. It was like completing a giant puzzle without all the pieces. They were taken through a maze of corridors before coming to an elevator. Once inside, the doors slowly closed and the elevator jolted downward. Helly remembered the dropping feeling in the pit of her stomach as the elevator descended for what seemed like forever. After finally arriving at the bottom of hell she guessed, they were led to a room where another slender man in a white coat met them. He spoke with Helly's mother for a long time. He was finally able to convince her to go in alone first explaining that Helly could see him afterwards. The memories were so clear it was as if they were happening to her all over again. There she was having an out of body episode telling her mother not to go and screaming that it was all just a trap. But the look in her mothers eyes told Helly she knew exactly what it was. She was willing to risk all to the chance he might still be alive. She turned to Helly and said, "Sweetheart I know you don't understand but I can't just leave him here in this place to die alone." Then she walked off with the stranger and left her alone in the room. And in that instant, it all came back to her. She now knew she'd never see her parents again.

As the storm of memories overtook her, she began to cry uncontrollably. She tried to raise her hands to cover her eyes but couldn't, they were strapped to the sides of her bed. She tried to move her legs but they were restrained also. The frustration quickly converted her tears to blinding fury. Suddenly she began to shout: "What have you done with my mother and father?" She bellowed out the words with all the hot rage in her little body. Helly concluded either no one cared about her ear splitting shrieks or there simply was no one there to hear them. "She's perfect!" Kovska marveled with anonymity from the security of an adjoining room. "Our search is finally over comrades, we have finally found her." Helly continued to kick and pull at the restraints until she was exhausted. The anger and hatred inside her was so intense that it became purified. A hellish festering boil filled with a dark evil and vengeful retribution was spawned. Like a cancerous tumor the new birth attached itself deep inside her uterus. Feeding on her hatred like a bloodthirsty tick it began to slowly grow inside her like a fetus. In the beginning it spoke one word to her in a soft subliminal whisper. "Remember!" Without knowing why Helly closed her eyes and tried to revision everything that'd happened." As the voice in her head faded, her mother appeared again, she was walking off with a strange man. Helly tried desperately to see who the man was. Though the appartion's face was blank, his name tag gave him up. "Steinberg!!!" she shouted. The voice inside whispered a gratifying "Yessssss." Now she saw herself alone again inside the locked room crying for her mother to return. She cried for hours until finally, curling into the fetal position in the center of the floor and falling asleep.

And now she was here. But where was here? She thought. The room looked much different than the one in her dream. It all made her cry again and bitter tears rolled freely down her cheek. She was only seven years old and now an orphan. She knew her parents had been taken because these people were after her. She'd always known from the first day inside that horrible school. The way they looked at her with their sharp approving smiles. The whispering meetings in her presence and the barrage of tests she was forced to take. "But the question in Helly's mind was, why?"

"What do you want with me?" she screamed. "What's so dam special about me?" "Are you going to kill me too?" Her words fell silently back to earth and the door to the room slowly opened. She saw a man's silhouette wearing a white lab coat out of the corner of her eyes. "I can answer all those questions for you Hellena." He said. She could hear a faint tone of fear resonate in his voice but the restraints prevented her from seeing his face. "Who are you?" and "What have you done with my parents? You bastards!" "Welcome to The Perfect Mind research facility. I'm Dr. Steinberg and I'm going to answer all your questions for you. But first we must get a few ground rules set in place. When he spoke his name Helly went dead inside. His face was of little importance anymore because now she focused her rage on his voice. She vowed to destroy its owner and make him pay for everything.

"We never meant to hurt anyone but you see we couldn't just let them take you away Hellena. We've waited too long for this and now because of you everything is going to be fine. Hellena it's been you all along. You are the one, there's no need to look any further. As for whom we are and what we are doing? I represent an organization that believes that the advancement and survival of our race can be promoted to supreme statis by splicing human DNA with pure radiation. "We are investing in the research and development of man's next evolutionary stage. Simply put, we want to create the ultimate biological weapon. We call it, The Fury: a sort of super human. A being that can withstand anything including the radiation fallout from a nuclear blast! It will also be endowed with an arsenal of chemical and biological weapons at its disposal. Young Hellena don't you understand we will be the only nation left standing after the nuclear holocaust!" "What nuclear holocaust?" "Forgive me I seemed to have gotten too far ahead of myself, but you'll be told all about that when the time comes." "You're a crazy man and I don't want to be a part of this! What have you done with my par … ?" He cut her off, "I'm sorry but they're dead!" and "You're already part of this. Only just an hour ago you were given your first injection of an experimental drug called HFX-10. This will begin the synthesis process of altering your cellular DNA. You should begin to feel the effects at any moment now. The man's voice began to fade in and out as Helly began to feel very hot inside. "You can't get away with th …." she slowly began to fade. "We already have Hellena, now sleep." Dr. Steinberg remained in the room as Dr. Kovska joined him. "How did it go? Kovska asked. "As well as can be expected, considering … you had her parents killed!" he replied angrily." "Are you still upset about that?" he said smiling. "How are we supposed to get her to cooperate when you've destroyed the only leverage we had?" "Because I don't need her cooperation! You were never worried about cooperation with the others, so why now?" Steinberg handed Kovska her file, "This'll explain why now!" Kovska opened the file and leafed through the contents. "What am I looking for?" "Look at her test scores!" "Ok they're high, so what." "Not just high they're off the fucking chart!" "But that only confirms she's the best subject for the experiment" "Yes, but look at her psychological evaluations." "I did It says she's the first with a ninety five percent chance of survival." "So what." "It also says she's extremely intelligent with violent mood swings and an uncontrollable temper. Do you really want to give someone this intelligent with anger and control issues the power to crack open the world? Oh and add the fact we intentionally allow her know we killed her parents. Is that the whole picture now Dr. Kovska? Not quite, you see her anger is what's going to trigger the chain reaction with the HFX-10. That's why it's called "The Fury" Dr. Steinberg. You know I've always said you were too weak for this project and here you are proving my point. If you have any more reservations about how I run my laboratory, keep them to yourself! Oh and Dr. don't worry we will have the necessary safeguards in place to control: *"Hellena's Fury."*

Helly awakened later to hear strange voices again but this time she couldn't see a thing. Her eyes had been covered with something. The restraints made her feel weak, imprisoned and helpless. A voice from inside comforted her with soft whispers of reassurance. "Helly be patient one day you will be strong enough to … destroy them all" it said.

The room reeked of chemicals as sanitized utensils violated her sense of smell. She tried to talk but something was blocking her airway. It was an air tube that tunneled down her throat. She heard voices again, "Everything's ready for the first operation, Dr. Steinberg." A woman's voice said. "Thank you nurse." "Are you ready to begin Dr. Kovska?" "Yes let's proceed." She felt them place something over her nose and almost immediately her heart slowed to an inaudible quiet. Soon she felt the sensation of falling again; it was like an endless drop into nothing. She plummeted to the bottomless depths of unconsciousness and watched in terror as the darkness swallowed everything inside of her.

CHAPTER 4

The Mission

Present time

General Weixel picked up the file from his desk and removed the security seal. He removed the documents and began to read:

The Chernobyl Incident/Hellena's Fury
At 1:23 a.m. on April 26, 1986 a major Nuclear Incident has occurred inside Russia at the Chernobyl Nuclear Power Plant. The incident caused the releasing of extremely high levels of airborne radiation in the Ukraine, Belarus, and Russia. The potential for casualties on this mission are expected to be high. Satellite photos and Intel show evidence of thousands dead at the incident site.

Mission Name: Operation Dark Siege
Mission Overview: infiltrate The Belarus Outpost, maintain an observation point, meet with undercover operative, get Intel and inform this agency of all Russian activities regarding the incident. Maintain a stealth presence and under no circumstance will your team be authorized to engage or strike. All reports to be communicated directly

to General Herbert P. Eiseman through secure contact channels.

If any member of your team is compromised, protocol will be evoked, this means: an automatic presumption of death and in conclusion no extraction team will be sent. And all connections with this agency will be denied.

Primary Objective: locate and gather all Intel on "Hellena's Fury." It is unknown what significance this may have on the incident if any so proceed with caution.

The General's blood began to boil as he slung the files into the air. The raining papers glided to every corner of the office before floating casually to the floor." Cox get in here!" He called. Cox entered the office with caution as he stepped over the mess. He did not make eye contact with Weixel, instead he bent down and began picking up the papers strewn about the floor. "Can you believe it another fuckin bird watching detail!" "Yes sir," he answered without looking up. "I need to bring in one of the teams," Weixel barked. "Which one sir, strike team *Cyclops?*" "Hell no! They'd have to put a bullet in my head before I'd ever work with those crazy fucks! It's just a recon mission, just call in my regular team: *Shadow Team Alpha.*" I need them assembled at lodge#1 for debriefing tomorrow at 0500 hrs." "Yes sir I'll get on it immediately."

The Team

Every member of the team was equipped with a specially designed watch. Tom was still asleep when he heard the chronograph alarm on his divers watch. A series of patterned chirps confirmed that a mission was at hand. Two slow chirps followed by three quick ones was a code 23. He rolled to the edge of the bed with a slugish groan. He knew 23-meant Urgent! It was his unit's code to come in immediately. As he sat there contemplating the true nature of the mission, he heard it again. He got up, removed a special laptop from its protective carrying case and opened it. He clicked on the icon labeled ECO Watch. Tom entered his password and waited, then he was prompted to place his eye in front of the miniscan camera embedded inside his computer's hard drive. Once the Retina scan was complete he was given clearance to proceed. The computers voice prompted him again, *"Hello Sgt. Corillo, you may proceed to mission profiles."* Tom was the Alpha team's leader and had a level 5 security clearance. Still a little groggy as he accessed the team's personnel profiles, he allowed his mind a brief moment to drift back to last year's mission. It had also been sent as a code 23, only later to be nothing more than a couple of escaped Russian nobodies requesting political asylum. He thought it strange how over protected the two insignificant men were kept. He and his team were eventually relieved of the duty and told the matter was classified and not to be discussed ever. After that, nothing further was heard of them or their whereabouts. It was almost as if the mission had never happened. Whenever things got super classified above his paygrade he simply called it: "the CIA way." He returned to the task at hand and continued with the mission profiles.

Tom had always known one day he'd be a government man. Growing up in Lakeland Florida he never knew his biological parents. He'd been raised by his foster parents Martha and John Groves since he was two years old. They eventually adopted him at the age of five. From that time forward the Groves made sure he knew the truth about his adoption. They had hoped by doing so, to spare the resentment felt when such information is withheld from adoptees.

He had few friends growing up, and kept to himself for the most part. He loved imagining that he was a super hero saving the world and suppressing it from evil. He'd run through the house with arms extended pretending that he was flying. These super powers came whenever he wore the special cape his mother made for him from an old linen pillow case. Every Thursday evening he could be found glued in front of the television to catch his favorite show: *The Untouchables with Elliot Ness.*

During his school years he excelled in everything they gave him. He graduated from The Roosevelt Academy of Excellence in 1974 with honors. He was one of the top 25 students of his class and was being recruited by College's all over the country. He'd been strongly considering the WestPoint Military Academy until the Intelligence community made him an offer he couldn't refuse. He was 18 years old when he became the youngest CIA operative in the history of the Department. And now after 12 years and 8 missions later he was still living out his dream of saving the world; only on a much smaller scale one mission at a time. His thin 5'11 frame boasted a whopping 145 lb's soaking wet. He had dark blond hair and a medium complexion with greenish blue eyes that set back and apart almost shark like. His cheek bones were virtually nonexistant which made his nose the sole support for his glasses or scrips as he would call them. He was the mission leader for Alpha team recon and his dog tag bore Sgt. Tom Corillo. What he lacked in physical presence he made up for in other ways.

Tom's team consisted of three other members,

An Electronics and Demolition Specialist:
Bast Cygman . . . *aka "Big Boy"*

Shadow Reconnaissance Specialist:
Cin Cozzola . . . *aka "Cameleon"*

Infiltration Specialist:
Mitch Botello aka *"The Mole"*

As he selected each name he was prompted by the computer to Activate or Deactivate unit. He was always very careful not to choose deactivate, because he knew it meant extermination of the team. Tom clicked on the activate tab and the computer sent the code to the selected team members. One by one the Alpha team received the urgent activation code: Cygman while in L.A. partying with friends; Cin while at a gay friend's wedding in Houston and Botello was relaxing in the Florida Keys with his new fiancé. After receiving the code the team's location was triangulated and they were given the closest rendezvous point. They all met somewhere inside of Dulce New Mexico. It was an old drug trafficking airstrip about 75 miles outside the Mexican border. The landing strip was discovered during a D.E.A. drug sting 10 years ago. It has since been used by the CIA as a covert transport station for special missions. Once the team arrived at the old airstrip, they were loaded and transported to the lodge.

CHAPTER 5

The Lodge

Tom was the first to arrive. Lodge #1 was the safe house and pick up point for the ECO team. There were three such lodges in different parts of the country. This one was located just outside of Decatur Illinois on a small 23 acres farmfront.

Tom shuffled to the ground, grabbed his gear and ducked into a low run towards the farm. He managed a quick glimpse back at the Black Hawk before it dusted off. He could see General Weixel in the distance waiting for him near the entrance. Tom was a little apprehensive about the urgency attached to the mission but he somehow managed to hide it. They shared salutes. "How are things General?" "Apparently not that great. I got Eiseman trying to shove his five stars up my ass for some gotdamn bird watching convention; and you? How was the trip over?" "Smooth, just the way I like it sir." Tom didn't trust Weixel much but he respected his authority.

It was a strictly business relationship between them. He didn't ask questions; he just followed orders. They both managed a nervous chuckle and entered the lodge.

"I thought that the urgency status meant we might have a real mission this time sir." "Well Corrillo that remains to be seen. When your team arrives, get everyone prepped. We roll out tomorrow right after debriefing." "We . . . sir? he asked with a puzzled expression. "That's right, I said we." The General turned, walked away and left Tom alone to absorb the shock. "I can't believe that he's actually coming on the mission with us, this is not going to be good" he mumbled to himself.

The team was anxious about the code 23, it had been almost a year since their last mission. Mitch sat quietly in meditation as the helicopter powered on. He was the shadow team's recon specialist trained: to get inside the enemies perimeter, gather Intel and return without ever being detected. His abilities included adapting and performing under extreme and dangerous conditions. Though he'd yet to see any serious military action, he was still considered the best in the field.

A small secret smile scrolled across his face as thoughts of sunny days and cool nights visited him. It was because of Lisa that he found himself suddenly laden with joy. His face beamed of new love and how much he missed her. He was thinking of how close they'd become in the weeks past. Mitch had never allowed himself to feel anything for anyone and he'd broken enough hearts in his day to prove it. He was quick to tell any woman who got too close that he was married to his job. But this was different, something changed inside him when he met her. He never knew what hit him. For the first time in his life, he was in unchartered waters because this time he was in love. His body was on the transport but his heart and mind was some place else.

"Hey Botello, what the fuck are you smiling about?" Mitch sat still and quiet with eyes closed. Bast continued: "Hey Mitch, let me guess you're so happy because . . . you played who's on top last night with your boyfriend?" Mitch continued to reside motionless against the seat. Bast's temper clicked in as he quickly became agitated at the sound of his own voice. "Hey jackass I'm talking to you! Answer me you little bitch!" At first Cin tried to ignore him as she shifted in her seat. Still able to hear his menacing voice she tried readjusting the Walkman headphones tighter to her ears. "Hey nature boy, you think you're some hot shit cause you can eat bugs and live in the jungle. Well ain't nothing special bout that." Frustration finally hits and Cin pulls the headphones from her ears. "Do you mind not starting up this shit right now?" "If he'd answer me like a man, there'd be no shit to start! Furthermore I wasn't talking to you!" Bast barked. "It would be a pleasure not to talk to you either but someone got to be yo mama when you act like a bratty ass child. Why don't you grow the fuck up? You know when he gets into a zone he can't hear you. Why do you feel the need to start shit every time we're together?" Cin finished. "Why do you feel the need to always protect him and come to his rescue? Any way I can't respect anybody who never faces off squarely with his enemy. He just hides, waits and takes the shot! You tell me what's so special about that?" "You mean besides the fact he's saved your ass on many occasions or maybe because he's the best at what he does and you just can't stand it." "Yeah I guess sniping is much nobler than demolitions! If we needed to stop the enemy from crossing a bridge, ole Mitchey boy would probably do something gay like: hide in the bushes and wait till they're far enough so he can take a good shot. Annnnt wrong answer, I'd go in and blow the enemy and the fuckin bridge to hell! It's like that two stones for one bird theory. You see, there'd be no enemy to cross the bridge and no bridge to cross. Just point em out, I'll do the rest. Cin tried not to laugh in his face. "Hmmm, that's the dumbest shit I've ever heard, right up there with the pet rock!" Bast gave a snide chuckle and threw her and Mitch the finger. Cin rolled her eyes, replaced the headphones to her ears and replied, "Basshole!" Mitch still unaware of Bast taunting rants remained away on vacation.

As the group settled in, Cin rocked out on some Whitesnake. Bast finally quieted down for a little shut eye and Mitch remained in his coma like state of bliss.

A few hours later . . . . A voice came over the com: ECO team ready your gear and prepare for landing." They all begin the task of gathering their gear. "Wonder what they got for us" Bast started. "I don't know but I'm not putting up with your crap this time," finished Mitch with a hard stare. "Look Botello I may kid around a little but that doesn't mean I can't do my job as well or even better than you." Cin folded up the headphones and stored them in her bag. "Bast you need to get off this competition thing, before someone gets hurt." "What tha fuck do you know about it Cin? You're just some butch dike trapped in a woman's body. Come to think of it, no one really knows what you are. Someone needs to teach you how be a real woman. Why don't you let me show you what you've been missing? Let me guess, you probably hate men don't you? *Cin formed her mouth to answer him but Bast cut her off.* "The problem is you've never had a real man. Well I'm here to fix all of that for you; it'll be like a mission of mercy to save you from yourself." Bast finished the words with a smirk of victory on his face but Cin retaliated. "Oh yeah, mama's boy gon teach me all about my sexuality. Well that's really nice that you'd go so far out of your way to help me reach my climatic potential. And it intrigues me that you actually know what it means to be a real woman. But I guess if I looked at it from your point of view, you might just have something there. *Bast looked shocked as Cin reflected his verbal assault in an unanticipated direction.* "Bast when you speak it's as if you know how a woman really feels deep inside. That would explain all the feminine tendacies you have. It all makes sense now, all the times you walked around acting like a little Bitch! and the rumors that your dick is so small, you have to use a strap-on during sex. *Even Mitch had to let out a small snicker.* Oh and speaking of similarities, do you know what your mouth reminds me of when you speak . . . a talking vagina. So every time you speak to me, it's like I'm talking to a pussy." Cin cracked a wicked smile sensing she had clenched the match of dirty dozens. Mitch grumbled and convulsed secretly before breaking into an all out snickering fit. Bast face turned beet red with embarassment as Cin's words seem to wound him deeper than she knew. "We're here." The pilot blared, breaking up the moment. The Black Hawk swooped down from the clouds like a bird of prey. The powerful rotors vacuumed a large mushroom of dust into the air. The three of them removed their gear and cleared the chopper within seconds Dressed in black on black tactical fatigues with full assault gear; they looked like *Black Ops* mercenaries as they approached the farm.

Bast was the typical blonde hair blue eyed all American college boy, from Oklahoma. He was only 28 and already dealing with a hair loss problem. Fact was, he was going bald and as sensitivities go this was major for him. A specimen of 6'02 with 250 lbs of ripped lean muscle yet he struggled with an inferiority complex. He wasn't just the largest person on the team; he was also the most insecure. He compensated for his inadequecies with rude and abrasive behavior. He was also known for his supersized equipment list including: every assault, tactical and explosive device he could legally get his hands on.

Cin pulled the old tattered pilots cap as far down over her face as it would go. She squinted desperately to see through the copter's dust storm before starting the foot journey to the ranch. Her rich black hair, long narrow nose and thin lips reeked of heritage. She was an Italian/American girl from the Bronx. She and two older brothers were raised by their father alone. She was unfortunate to never have known her mother who had died from complications during Cin's birth. As such she became the product of a household which taught her everything about being strong and independent but nothing of being soft, sensitive or feminine. Growing up she was labeled a tomgirl; a term she learned to hate. It was especially painfull when other children would call her that. It always reminded her of her mother's absence and made her miss the mother she never knew that much more. She would comfort herself with imaginery talks with her mother when the other kids teased her. She would often conceive her mother saying things like: "Now dear you are no different than any other young girl your age. You're just special because you can do things that they can't." She always felt better after the secret talks with her mother.

Working in her fathers shop after school did little to change her statis. A mechanics daughter with the ability to rebuild an entire engine from scratch was no notion for a young girl of 16.

A couple of years later Cin decided to join the army. After six hard years of devoted military service she was given an opportunity she could not refuse. Recruited straight out of Army Intelligence she was inducted into "The Office". Her specialty was undercover infiltration and it didn't hurt that she spoke:Spanish,Italian,Portuguese and a little Russian. In the field they called her "Cameleon." Being a U.C. removed her from carrying the same tactical gear as the rest of the team. This was because of the unpredictable nature of undercover work. She had to be prepared for scrutiny, mistrust and the ever present possibility of a body search. Though she appeared empty handed, she was in most cases more deadly than her lock and load counterparts even with all their artillery toys. Cin was an expert in martial arts and hand to hand combat. She had studied under the great Master Tadashiro Yamashito, in the Japanese style of Ninjitsu. She was in fact a trained assassin, whose expertise included the use of everyday objects as quiet but deadly weapons. Her skills included but not limited to: the ability to control her heart rate and regulate her breathing. Although she displayed many masculine traits from the outside, on the inside she was all woman. Many in the department questioned her sexual orientation and saw her as a distraction. But her combination of specific skills and knowledge combined with her beauty and sex appeal could not be denied. She was better than most male agents within her field. Rumors of a gay lifestyle wreaked back lashing heat and scrutiny on her from "The Office" despite the fact a don't ask don't tell policy existed, they were just empty words to Cin. Like all women who strive to survive within a male dominant field, she had to become more like the shark, and less like the bait. On the outside she was the rough and rugged covert operative they wanted to see but on the inside she kept her secrets well hidden from prying eyes.

Mitch jogged ahead, leaving the other two behind. He was the homegrown farm boy from Michigan. His 6"00 frame carried the 185 lbs of muscle with rock hard biceps and a washboard stomach with ease. Unlike Bast, Mitch chose to be bald. "It's Cooler" he'd always say. He spent years training to get his massed muscular upper body but the lower quadrant was something different. He'd been plagued with skinny legs; had to be a genetic defect he thought. Occasionally he'd remember coach Asberry his track coach from high school telling him, that God had given him the wrong set of legs for his body. But that was before he took the state track championship his junior year. Mitch was the go to man when the impossible had to be made possible. He was sometimes called "The Mole" for his ability to burrow beneath a target and never be detected. He was trained in guerilla combat and survival tactics. Besides being one of the best snipers in the business, his resume also included: sensory deprivation, transcendental meditation and a deep study of philosophy. Mitch was always the focused one in the group, at least until now that is. Today he had a new focus named: Lisa Cruz.

He met her in Miami at a beach volleyball tournament. He'd only known her for two months before asking her to marry him. Mitch knew he couldn't tell her the truth about his job so he'd told her he was a sales rep for a large software company. When he received the ECO code, he explained that he was leaving on business and that they'd get married as soon as he returned. Mitch knew the rules no family, no personal ties during active assignment but this was different and he wasn't about to let it go for some stupid rule. He knew to play the game he'd just have to keep it a secret for a little while. At least until he got back.

Tom met the team inside. "Good to see all you guys could make it." Tom managed to crack a crooked smile as he greeted them. They grunted and nodded in reply. Bast was off and running before Tom could start the next sentence, "Hey Sarge what's up with the emergency code?" Tom grinded his teeth and answered: "The ready room at 0500 hrs. be there." Bast continued: "But that's tomorrow morning, what do we do till then?" "Bast I don't care what you do, just have your ass in that room at 0500 hrs. Is that clear?" "Well yes sir, I was just . . ." "I know what you're about to say, save your questions for the General tomorrow." Confusion struck all their faces as they replied in unison. "The General?" "Yes the General, not only is he here but he'll be joining us on this mission." Cin took her hand and popped her ears several times as if to verify what she'd just heard. Mitch followed up with no expression at all. Bast step up to Tom and whispered: "You have got to be fuckin kidding me." "Ok knock it off you guys, get your gear get settled in and I'll see you all at 0500." Bast opened his mouth to speak and Tom redirected him with a look. Bast knew not to fuck with him. They all retired to their quarters.

The Ready Room
0500 hours

It was 0400 hrs. and morning came quick, as alarm clocks rung throughout the hallway. The team awakened and moved with calculated efficiency, as the shit, shower and shave rule was in effect. There was only one thing on everyone's mind and that was the mission. That is with the exception of Mitch, his boat was a float in a different sea of thought. During breakfast no one spoke at all, instead each one stared at the other with puzzled amusement. Once they entered the ready room and sat down the mood became a little more serious. The ready room consisted of a conference table with eight chairs, three on each side and one at each end. The team split between the two sides. Mitch and Cin sat together on one side, while Bast sat opposite and alone. Tom stood at the front of the room configuring the slide projector for the presentation. He pulled down the projection screen and the word "Classified" was displayed upon it in cinematic proportions. He passed out a booklet to each member. The first page read: Operation Dark Siege: the second page read. "Hellena's Fury Will End the World!"

Tom began "There has been an Incident at the Chernobyl Nuclear Power Plant in Russia. We have satellite footage and confirmed reports of thousands dead due to a partial meltdown at the reactors core. We don't know how much radiation was released into the atmosphere but we do know levels inside Prypiat, the Ukraine, Belarus and much of Russia are extremely high." Interrupting, Bast raises his hand. Tom ignores him and continues the debriefing. "The Russian government released statements that correspond with everything I've just told you." Before Tom could continue Bast blurted, "What does this have to do with us?" "Plenty if you'll let me finish. We've received anonymous documents from outside and inside sources boasting proof that the Chernobyl Incident is a cover up for something far worse." "Excuse me sir but what could be worse than thousands dead from radiation exposure?" "That's a good question Cin, one I'm going to let General Weixel answer. "General." The General stepped into the room. "Morning, People." "Morning General," "Welcome to Operation Dark Siege. I'll keep this brief and to the point." We believe Hellena's Fury is synonymous with the Chernobyl incident somehow, a code name for something perhaps. There is belief that the Russian Government is trying to cover up some kind of weapons research involving Nuclear Atomic Energy. Some of the documents we've received show evidence these experiments do exist and that they were being done on human subjects. While we can neither deny nor confirm the actual number of fatalities I can assure you it's in the thousands. So as you can see, we must embrace this moment." Our mission is to infiltrate, gather Intel and report that Intel to the Pentagon. Mitch and Cin both asked, "Infiltrate what and gather intel from who sir?" "You will go to a small gypsy settlement called the "Outpost located just outside the Russian border." "We feel this would be a prime location to keep an eye on things over there." "Begging the General's pardon sir, didn't you just say that there were extreme levels of radiation in the area?" Mitch asked. "That's right son, I understand your concern but we'll take every precaution we can. I'd be lying if I told you there's no danger involved. Hell some of you may not make it back! But that's the chance I'm willing to take." A look of distrust fell upon all their faces as Weixel finished. Sgt. Corillo broke in, "It's very important that you all understand this will be an Intel mission only. We will not engage in combat tactics or bring attention to the team. Understand if the team is compromised the Pentagon will invoke protocol and you know what that means." Cin's concern prompted another question. "Sir why use us for something like this? This is not the kind of mission we'd normally train for." Before Tom could answer, Bast started again "Hell it's another babysitting job sir, no matter how dangerous you make it sound. No disrespect but we weren't trained to be spies, that's a job for the suits. I thought we were a paramilitary unit sir." Tom frowned as he answered: "The reason this team was chosen was because President Strandford of the United States needs answers, you do remember him don't you? An operation of this type requires a special group with unique skills and so it was deemed necessary to put the Alpha team in. And I don't recall anyone asking for your fucking opinions! If you feel you can't handle this mission, get the fuck out of this unit right now!" General Weixel drove in the last nail. "There'll be no getting out unless by my orders or on a stretcher, so now: get your asses in gear, we leave at 0700 hrs.!" The team got up and left the room in total silence. Once they were gone Tom turned to the General and said: "You know sir there's something about this mission. I have a bad feeling about it." The General looked at Tom, popped a stogy in his mouth and said. "That's just your nerves son, get a grip on your emotions, before you spook the rest of the team." "Yes sir!" Tom left the room. The General looked at the document projected on the wall, and read it to himself: *"Hellena's Fury Will End the World."*

His face filled with uncertainty, as he let out a long sigh before turning and heading to his quarters.

CHAPTER 6

The Final Phase
Hellena Age 17

(Just hours before the Chernobyl event)

It was 9 p.m., just 3 hours before her 17th birthday and she didn't know how she felt about that. Helly laid in her bed reflecting as she waited for the white coats to arrive. Today was the day she would be freed from bondage. In just a few hours they were going to remove all her bandages. Until this morning she'd been living inside of a Hyperbaric chamber for the last 5 years. The white coats as she called them, were responsible for it all.

Helly's mental diary:

Over the years I learned to hate everyone and everything to do with the experiments. I had been robbed of my parents and the last ten years of my life. Something they made a point to constantly remind me of. I've become very detached and unemotional over time. The endless experiments and operations they performed have left me dead inside. The pain and suffering could've ended years ago, if only they would've just let me die. I dream constantly of death, I even wish for it but they've managed to steal that from me too. A dark and evil force now occupies the deep region beneath my bones where the soul of innocence once did reside. "It" is alive, waiting, watching and plotting, to be freed.

I've had many horrible nightmares of death and global destruction at the hands of an unspeakable evil that lives inside me. Sometimes it feels as though I am sharing my body with some grotesque and hideous monster. From the dark and silent corners of my mind I imagine that there are two hearts beating inside me. Other times it seems that even my thoughts are not my own. The white coats are to blame and one day they will all pay dearly.

Today is a big day for them. Ten years in the making of what they call the final experiment. I cannot remember any of the experiments, only the pain I would feel afterwards. Each time I entered the test chamber the strange words would render me unconscious. Afterwards, I could not recall anything that happened during the experimental phases. It was a horrible existence not knowing what they were doing to me.

Ugly sores and boils have covered me from head to toe. I must look as if I'm in the advance stages of leprosy.

Helly winced every time she thought of the horrid experiments.

I recall the chronic, agonizingly horrific pain that ravaged my body every day.

They filled my veins with a mixture of toxic compounds in doses strong enough to kill a herd of elephants. *Helly gulped with discomfort as the highlights of her life flashed before her eyes.*

"The time is near, remember everything" whispered the dark inner voice.

Everyday without fail, I heard them say: "Its time to take your vitamins, "It" was the worst drug of them all and I hated what it was doing to my insides. They called it the HFX10 which stood for Hellena's FuryX10. I'd heard it enough that it'd become etched deep inside my archive of horrible memories. It was as though they were pumping rocket fuel into my stomach and igniting it. I've relived the same perpetual death sentence everyday for the last 10 years. Throughout those years I could not remember one instance where anyone had shown me any mercy. Instead I was met with insensitivity and laughter and given the explanation that it would help to increase my threshold of pain. For me hate was no longer an option, now it was automatic and normal. It has now become all that I know, with no distinction between who I hate or why.

The violent seizures never seem to stop and I have lost so much blood I can't imagine how I'm still alive. Today I almost never eat anymore, only the chemical cocktails can sustain me now. The changes are coming more rapidly and I can barely keep track of all the new things about myself. About a year ago they removed the bed pan from my room and never replaced it. I quickly noticed that no matter how much I ate or drank I never needed it anymore. The doctors were all very excited to explain to me that the changes in my body were making me into a more efficient weapon. I was told that I would no longer need to discard waste from my body. They impressed upon me how special this feature really was because now I had the ability to recycle my own waste. This would be used as one of my bodies many defense mechanisms. I was so disgusted at how gross it made me feel, to know that waste recycling was part of my new DNA plan.

I lost count of the numerous surgeries when I was about 11 years old. Until one day I overheard one of the med techs say that they had performed more than 260 procedures on me. Because of the caustic chemical burns allover my body, I had to be treated like a severe burn victim. They wrapped me in a special gauge from head to toe. My bandages were changed once a week. They weren't afraid I'd get infected; they just wanted to track the progress of my metamorphosis.

My 12th birthday

My 12th birthday was a day like any other. I had prepared myself to suffer through another painful exchange. What should've been a routine bandage change became something horrible and unspeakable. It started when two male lab assistants arrived for the task. I didn't recognize them, they were new. Neither wore an ID badge and they seemed out of place. For a brief moment I wondered what'd happened to my regular attendants. There was some small comfort with them because they were immune to me and had grown use to seeing my body without the bandages. I wondered how the new attendants would feel after removing my cocoon to see the green slimy sores that covered me. Maybe the caustic exploding blisters would make them run away; if not surely the gut wrenching stench of recycled bile would do the job. Something about this was all wrong; they seemed much too young for the task. Neither man could've been over 21 years old, just a couple of nameless faces. Their screams still echoes through my mind as that day continues to haunt me. They were laughing and making jokes as they entered the room. Both men walked over to the edge of the bed and smiled at me. I must've looked like an Egyptian Mummy to them. It was hard peering through the make shift eyes cut into the thick layers of cloth. They stared at me with starved curiosity. I tried to warned them but; the whitecoats put something in my throat so I that couldn't speak anymore. So I tried to use my eyes to tell them. I guess a pair of crazy bulging bloodshot eyes could mean just about anything because they weren't listening. I told them to "please help me ... kill me while you have the chance."

The two men were so similar I couldn't distinguish between them. They began the tedious task of removing the cloth cocoon. Once the bandages came off, their faces went blank. I thought to myself, this is it, here we go. Suddenly their faces begin to morph from blank shock to something unexpected. A childish smirk began to appear as the two looked at each other and started to laugh uncontrollably. Instead of the shock I expected to see, they reeked of childish insensitivity. They begin to whisper amongst themselves like young girls. "Hello how is our little horny toad today?" One of them blurted. They both laughed. They begin to tag team me with insults then one of them boldly said: "Man you really are fubar, that's fucked up beyond all repair. But I bet you already knew that." They continued with the barrage of verbal abuse: "Nothing that smells this bad should be above ground" said one of the attendants. Suddenly the men switched gears and went into overdrive. "I'd rather kiss a dog's ass, than to have to look at your ugly face every day." They broke into laughter again. They batted my dignity back and forth like a tennis ball. "If I had a child this ugly I'd donate her ass to research too." "Maybe her mother and father are just as fucked up as she is." said one of them. "Yeah I can see that but man someone should have used a whole box of condoms. Better yet you'd been better off running down your momma's leg." replied the other. Before I knew it a hot ancient anger rose up inside of me. I dug deep inside my throat and churned up the largest lump of saliva I could gather. The men stood on opposite sides of me as the last bandage fell from my body. Then when the timing was just right I spewed my hot vengeance furiously into the air. The airborne saliva found both targets with deadly accuracy, covering their faces with green caustic phlem. At first they were surprised and angry as they tried to wipe my steaming sewage from their faces. The smell alone gagged them into submission as they struggled to get past it. I watched as stunned infuriation turned to sheer terror. Within moments of being struck the two men begin to shriek like wounded pigs. I watched in petrified horror as chunks of flesh begin to ooze and slide right off their faces. I screamed inside with terror as their faces were turned to ground beef. The floor quickly became covered in blood, I'd never seen so much blood before. They tried to leave on their knees but ended on their backs. It seemed as though they had to swim across the saturated ground to get to the door. I watched in fear and delight as one of them managed to open the portal and squirm through it. They dragged themselves from the room leaving a long bloody trail in their absence. I rolled to the bed's edge and followed the bloody trail with my eyes. There on the floor at the foot of my bed, I discovered something. It was a fleshy lump of meat. Curiosity drew me closer but with caution. Instinctively I grabbed a towel from the bed and slowly removed the fleshy trophy. It felt strange and springy like an organic sponge. As I opened the towel to see . . . another scream escaped inside my head. There in the palm of my hand was a bloody severed nose. Insanity overtook me for a moment as I tried to figure to which of the men it belonged. I cringed as reality finally crept up on me again. Stunned I threw the trophy back on the floor. It was then that I began to question the circumstances surrounding the incident. They had surveillance cameras everywhere that were monitored 24/7. Why didn't they come? Why did they allow this to happen? Then it hit me, the two mysterious men had been set up. I had done exactly what the white coats had wanted me to do. Those poor unsuspecting fools hadn't been told anything about the experiment. They were probably just a couple of low level maintenance workers. No doubt coerced with some type of promise of promotion if they participated. They were probably instructed to be as cruel as possible to me and now . . . I was sure they were dead, and I was sorry for that. Somehow a tiny resemblance of compassion managed to slip by me but only for a short fleeting moment. I began to feel human again. It was the first time I'd felt anything other than hatred in years. The fading feeling reminded me of who I once was and made me unsure of the raging emotions swelling deep within my heart. The guinea pigs had to die so the evil men in white suits could be happy. Now I was sure of what had happened to all the missing people of the town. They'd been kidnapped and tortured just like me. Their parents were all taken and killed just like mine. And now I am the only one left.

Droplets of emotion welled in the corners of her eyes as she struggled with the memories. She could see the events as clearly as they had occurred . . .

As I sat on the side of the bed, I tried to figure out why the white coats would do such a thing. My brief moment of emotional escape was fading as the anger began to return to me. I tried to fight it, but my anger is what this was all about. I hated to give them satisfaction but I felt powerless against the roaring fires of revenge growing in me. As I gave in to it, a chain reaction was released inside of me. My body stiffened knocking me back onto the bed as the onslaught of another seizure advanced upon me. I felt the feverish sensations of the HFX-10 as it shot threw my veins like rocket fuel.

Her skin began to bubble and secrete a thick red mucous that literally engulfed her entire body. She squeezed the sheets so tightly that her hands began to bleed. Nothing could stop her flapping body from convulsing violently above the bed. Alarms blared and emergency lights flashed as several white coats rushed into the room to strap her down. Two of the men tried to secure her legs while the other two grabbed her arms. "I remember the smell of their burning flesh as their fingers dissolved to the bone." The scene became pandemonium as the four men screamed in terror and scrambled blindly about the room.

"I could feel him watching me . . . with delightful admiration. It was Dr. Kovska the man who I hated above all others. He wanted to take my fathers place inside my heart. I could hear him shouting over the comm: "My little girl is growing up!" I could see him in my mind's eye smiling as the sacrificial lambs fell one by one. Their burnt corroded flesh seemed to liquefy in the wake of a single touch of my skin. He watched the slaughter from the safety of an adjoining room, through security monitors. Though I was enveloped by the seizure, somehow I was strangely aware of the things that were happening around me. I knew that four more men had just died because of me. A primeval hatred exploded inside me as I sensed his presence in the next room. I don't know how but I began to see his thoughts as clearly as my own. My body convulsed helplessly but my thoughts remain locked on him now. Then a dark secret was freed from deep within me. It moved from a place I never knew existed. An alternate realm of my heart, where love is hate and good is bad. Where bright is dark and life is death; where the mirror image of creation is destruction. It came in the form of a dark guttural growl. I could feel the words move through me but they were not mine: "I will enjoy the hunt before I slaughter you like a helpless lamb; then I will lay waste to your world.""

Suddenly the seizure stopped and Helly's body loomed only inches above the bed. "Ok, time to empty the trash!" barked Kovska over the intercom. In an instant the room filled with men in bio-hazard gear. Unlike their predacessors they wore thick white protective rubber suits with special face and head protection.

One of them rolled in with a heavy duty storage cart filled with plastic specimen bags. The crew began removing the hundreds of specimens from the floor and securing them in the bags. There was no way to tell what part belonged to who as some remains were unrecognizable. As the men worked diligently around the room, the red mucous thickened around Helly's body. The gelatinous barrier begins to harden like a protective outer shell. Helly's body was no longer visible. A bright red glow began to luminate from inside the mass. The light was pulsating in sync with Helly's heart. The beacon continued to pulse in a calm hypnotic rhythm as the men moved freely about the room. Kovska was extremely pleased with the day's events and was about to enter the test room when he turned his attention to Hellena's pulsing light. Concern filled his voice: "Everyone stop whatever you're doing and slowly and quietly exit the room. She has entered the pupae stage!" Be very careful not to disturb the test sub . . ." But before he could finish his words, one of the technician's feet gave into a slippery mound of bloody pulp beside the bed. He barely had enough time to lock down the room as the med tech landed on top of Helly's pulsing mass. The pulsating light quickened inside its chamber. In an instant the med tech's body exploded blasting him to pieces. His remains were splattered across the entire room. The frightened team rushed to exit but the room had already been locked down. Suddenly a pulsar of light flashed across the test chamber decindergrating everything in it. All that remained of the men were piles of smothering ashes.

Helly was locked away from the outside world, snuggled safely inside her new cocoon. A strange force elevated her high above the raging flames inside the chamber. Kovska had prepared for a day such as this. Reinforcing the test chamber with the same fortified insulation used in space travel was a stroke of genius. The fact he decided to install it a year ahead of schedule was definitely luck.

No one could get near her, the heat inside the chamber was too intense. Something else was in control now but what, had wondered Kovska? The rhythmic pulses of light seem to slow to a steady beat once again allowing the room to cool down to a safe temperature. Emergency sirens blared as more white coats entered the room, this time with extreme caution. Kovska tried to use Hellena's verbal shutdown command but she was unable hear him through the protective shell.

Three weeks later the shell fell away and Hellena was ready for the next stage of evolution.

I awakened to find myself encased in some sort of thermal body wrap. With the exception of two holes for seeing and three more for breathing and eating. I was covered from head to foot with insulation. Dr. Steinberg was there when I woke. He explained that due to escalating safety concerns, I would have to remain inside the thermal wrap for a curring period. That curring process took five years to complete. And in addition those five long years were spent inside a hyperbaric torture chamber. They told me that my skin would go through several changes before the final metamorphosis.

Well today was the day. Her thoughts returned to the present. It was now just a matter of hours before her 17th birthday, tonight she would be free one way or the other.

Her head was flooded with questions. She felt overwhelmed with anticipation. After all she was just a hostage, a stranger in her own body now. It might've been the classic battle of good versus evil but in Helly's mind it was more like evil versus the greater evil. Surely there was no good left inside of her, she thought. She remembered what her mother had always told her as a young girl, "Your good side will always outweigh the bad". Interrupted by a knock at the door, Dr. Kovska peeped in and entered the room gleaming with pride. "Hellena do you know what today is?" he asked. She peered through the eye holes with anewed hatred. "It's your birthday, and to celebrate we are going to remove your bandages today. We are so very happy with your progress, Hellena." He rambled on about a new world, a new race, and her destiny to change the course of mankind. She had heard it all hundreds of times and was tired of hearing it. Helly was anxious to get free of the bindings that held her for so many years. She was ready to see what they'd done to her. "Hellena are you ready to evolve?" he asked. Helly could not answer but her dark innervoice did. It whispered "*Yes I am ready, release me, release me . . . oh please release me!*"

Two bio-techs joined him in the room. At first glance she thought they looked like astronauts. They were wearing some type of thick thermal protective clothing with clear airtight helmets on their heads. The techs seemed worried as Dr. Kovska gave them their instructions and left the room. Moments later Helly could hear his voice over the intercom. He spoke to her in a clear calm voice. I heard the strange words he said to me. They were the same words that have rendered me helpless for so many years. And now just like every time before, I find myself alone in the dark nothingness.

CHAPTER 7

The Birth of a Fury

It was 11:20 p.m. and the final preps were still being conducted. Professor Anna Rossini, a short stout woman of 41 was the only female scientist involved in the project. She was recruited by the KGB in 1983 and was an honored graduate of Stanton University of London. With a PhD of Science in Medical Physics she was sought after by some of the world's most prestigious organizations. But like most dedicated scientist, prestige and power meant very little to her. She'd written several published works on the principles of quantum physics. In her theories an object could move from one place to another without traveling in the intervening space. She also attained international recognition through her scientific achievements as an accomplished Metallurgist. When President Aleksei heard of her many achievements he thought she would be a perfect asset for the HFX10 project; Kovska agreed. After doing an extensive background on her, the KGB came calling. The proposition was a once in a lifetime opportunity for her. They offered her a role in the creation of something that would change the world forever. She was so excited at the offer that she left London and moved to Russia immediately.

She had never married, nor had she ever planned to. Science was the love of her life and no human being could ever compete with that. A pair of wire rimmed glasses and a tightly pulled hair bun, casted her as the typical lackluster female scientist. But her work was anything but lackluster.

She had made major contributions to Hellena's progress and the project as a whole. Not only had she proven her theories of quantum tunneling, she also managed to add it to Hellena's resume.

There were three different chambers used to perform the barrage of tests they performed on Hellena. Chamber A facilitated the development of bio weapons and chemical warfare, as then chamber B provided for telekinesis and kinetic energy research. But Chamber C was something very special, because it was where the final phase was to be performed. It'd taken them six years to construct it, with costs reaching well into the billions. The underground super vault was the size of a small city. Sitting more than 2500 ft. beneath the earth's surface, the underground bunker had been quiet and undisturbed for four years. That was until today. It had been designed for a real time simulation of a ground zero nuclear blast.

Now that Hellena had successfully passed all the other experiments, the final test was all that mattered. The results of 12 years of research and billions of dollars spent, hinged on the outcome of this ... one final ... experiment.

Professor Rossini ran the simulation program over and over and each time the projected outcome was the same. *Computer voice speaks:* "*The probability of survival of human test subject Hellena is negative; termination of subject is absolute.*" With the computers prognosis, she just couldn't understand how Kovska could move forward. It almost seemed as if he knew something the computer didn't. Her face could not hide the worry lines the last ten years had brought. Just like everyone else she agonized at the possibility of failure.

11:50 p.m. 10 minutes before final phase

Hellena's horrid rotting body was rolled into the chamber and secured inside the test pod. Moments later, the computer began the countdown sequence. "*Simulation to begin in zero minus 10 minutes.*" Like so many times before, she'd been sent to the dark padded cell. It was how they kept her disconnected from everything. Doctor's Kovska, Steinberg and Rossini all waited impatiently inside the test site control room. "Expectations Dr. Steinberg?" Rossini asked. "Yes, I hope this thing doesn't blow up in our faces." "What about you Dr. Kovska?" she asked. Kovska looked at Steinberg and sneered as he answered her. "My expectations are just a little more optimistic than my colleague's. I expect that we are about to see our first man made god of the natural world. She has already more than exceeded all expectations. The skin cultures have shown resilience to every chemical or element we've used on her so far. And today we hope to include radiation to the list. If you partner that with her kinetic and psychic abilities, you'll see what I'm getting at. Ladies and gentlemen we've already won. It'll be like watching the birth of a god!" he finished.

"One minute warning!"

Three biological engineers and two medical lab - tech's completed the final systems check. Everyone else was strapping in for the ride. Kovska was salivating with expectations. The "Fury Project" was his baby, his creation, his dream and could possibly become his nightmare. He had successfully created a strain of transmutated DNA, engineered to genetically alter human cell regeneration and damaged tissue growth. The HFX10 was also designed to increase kinetic and telepathic abilities. Helly had it all and now in the final moments of the count, she was just seconds away from changing the world forever. If the test were to succeed, the possibilities would be endless. She would be impervious to all military weaponry, including nuclear. But if it were to fail there'd be no second chance and the consequences would be swift and severe. With billions of dollars and countless hours of research at stake, President Aleksei would call upon the special services of General Slavik. Slavik's specialty was extermination and no one wanted to think about that.

Steinberg looked on with discomfort as the countdown continued *"fifteen, fourteen, thirteen."* He felt that there had been too many uncertainties surrounding the experiments. He was afraid the whole program might backfire on them. It was a bad or worse scenario. The facts were teletyped back and forth inside his mind with big black bold letters. If the experiment failed the USSR would surely deny everything and kill everyone involved. On the other hand if they succeeded, Hellena could turn on them like a mad dog against an abusive master. Even in light of the extreme measures taken to maintain control of Hellena's Fury, Steinberg remained skeptical they'd be able to control her. He did not have the confidence in the fail safe that Kovska did. He wiped the sweat from his brow as the computer continued. *"Ten, nine, eight."* Professor Rossini signaled to put on the protective goggles and ear plugs as the count spiraled down. *"Six, five, four."* The control room grew silent as a low hum began to resonate inside the chamber. The sound of a thousand freight trains filled the room. The pitch began to change rapidly scaling higher and higher as the computer reached: *"Three, two, one, zero."* The 10 kiloton nuclear warhead was detonated less than 25 yards from Hellena's test pod. The deep explosive rumbling of super thunder shook the chamber walls with seismic vibrations. Then a solar flare so bright it mimicked the sun with its brilliant radiance exploded into a magnificent pulse of expanding energy. The instantaneous fusion of splitting atoms caused a pyroclastic cloud of radiative death to explode violently from the chamber floor. A breath taking spectacle was formed by the ascending mushroom cloud.

The lights of the control room instrument panel flickered and flashed like a disco light show. Sensory readings inside the chamber showed an internal temperature above 2000°F degrees and rapidly rising. Montrous clouds of radioactive steam and ash imploded into the center of the chamber. The test pod was long gone now, vaporized within the first few seconds of fusion. Now they waited. Hellena's body had been modified with sensory implants to monitor her vital stats but since the blast no data had been received. Without it there was no way of knowing if she had survived or not. Now only time would tell.

The temperature inside the chamber reached 3000°F degrees and continued to rise. Steinberg's face glowed with terror as he begins to quietly ease toward the exit. Rossini became increasingly concerned as the temperature topped 3500°F. "Kovska you know that room was only designed to withstand a maxium of 4500°F. After that it's anybody's guess." Rossini said. Kovska sat trancelike in front of the observatory gallery. He was fixated on the spot where Hellena once laid. Nothing could've survived the magnitude of such an explosion but somehow in his heart he knew she was still alive. "Kovska how much more can the chamber stand?" Rossini asked. He responded with slow lethargic words. "She'll be fine." "No she won't, she's probably already dead!" Steinberg replied easing closer to the door. It was obvious that panic and fear had begun to overtake him. "She's gone can't you see that. Nothing human could've survived in there!" he shouted. "You need to stop the experiment now!" Rossini tried a more calmer approach, "That chamber wall is not going to hold much longer. Please Kovska listen to me . . . use the failsafe and shut it down." He remained focused on the center of the chamber. His face was stricken with delight as the temperature rose another 600°F. An angry orange glow began to peek through the thick black radioactive clouds of death. The deadly billows of ash suddenly stopped erupting inside the chamber. Now something new was happening as the chaos started to organize. The enormous black column moved to the chamber's center. Kovska's focus was unwaivered as if by faith, only he and he alone knew she had survived. He believed where the others didn't, "We'll show them Hellena!" he thought.

The searing temperature in the room leveled at 4900°F. "There's no way she could've survived!" Steinberg claimed. "Shut up and watch!" Kovska retorted agitated. The thick threatening clouds slowly began to move again. Something new was happening inside the chamber. "Its moving in reverse!" Rossini said. It was true, the deadly clouds of radioactive fallout begin moving counter clockwise against itself. The lab crew watched in complete awe, as the monstrous clouds shifted rapidly into gear. Sensors begin to register a sharp rise in wind velocity. Faster and faster it rotated as the black storm of death became tornadic. As the storm's speed continued to increase, the mood in the control room grew with concern. Kovska watched with hypnotic amazement as the spectacle unfolded before his eyes. The circulation speed inside the chamber had reached 385 miles per hour and still intensifying. The thick walls of the chamber had already been weakened from the intensifying heat. Now winds moving at 450 mph threatened to finish the job. The pressure building inside the chamber had begun to cause stress fractures to form along its inner walls. Steinberg was the first to break the silence in the room. "It's going to escape!" he shouted. But no one seemed to care as he backed cautiously out of the room. Everyone slowly moved closer to the control room observation window. The thick black storm continued to funnel at the center of the room. The wind's velocity had reached 500 mph and rising. Stress fractures begin to appear along the outer walls of the chamber. The computer's failsafe systems went online.

"Caution!" "Failsafe is online, damage sustained to chamber's inner and outer structure." "Structural Integrity is at 70%"

All eyes remained focused on the center of the chamber as if some hypnotic force had taken control of them. Something inside the chamber wanted them to look, to show them the power of what they had unleashed. Then a strange thing happened inside reactor room C. The tornadic storm began to funnel down into a mysterious light resonating from the room's core. The vortex of clouds seemed to vacuum right down into the light and dissipate. Suddenly the trance was broken and Kovska shouted "Did you see that?" She not only withstood the radiation, she absorbed it!" He was ecstatic at the new development. It was an unforeseen side effect that made his weapon even deadlier. "What happens to the radiation she absorbed doctor?" asked one of the bio-techs. "It's being recycled for later use against her enemies. Fascinating!" he finished with a smile. Rossini had the next question which characterized what everyone else was thinking. "Wouldn't that put us in immediate danger, considering she already thinks we're her enemy?" "Yeah, maybe she didn't appreciate that 10 killoton warhead we just fed her," added one lab tech. Kovska was about to reply when he was interrupted:

"Caution!" Failsafe online The chamber's structural Integrity is now at 60%"

The warning only increased the tension already in the room. Kovska immediately changed the subject. "There she is, in the middle of the chamber!! Can you see her?" he shouted. Everyone leaned over the control room observatory and stared down into the chamber. As visibility increased, the creation was exposed for the first time since the explosion. Everyone looked in awe at: *"The Birth of the Fury."*

The Fury!!!

Steinberg ran to the safety of an adjoining lab, where he watched from the the labs monitor in disbelief. With cupped hands over his face, he slumped to the floor and began to sob. *"What have we done?"*

Back at the observation tower things continued to deteriorate. For Kovska it was like seeing the birth of his first born child. He remained glued to the window of the observation tower, unshaken and very focused. His only concern was for Hellena and what changes her body may have endured. As the newborn Fury exposed itself for the first time, it gave them a small glimpse of its power. With a blink of its eyes a solar flare was unleased inside the chamber rendering all onlookers with temporary blindness. The protective eye shields were useless against it's sun like rays. Even those who viewed from the safety of security monitors experienced the same blinding effects. Suddenly all of Steinberg's fears were becoming reality. A panicked state enveloped the lab as chaos ensued. Everyone was either stumbling, bumping or falling over something. Some were even injured during the ordeal. It seemed ironic that the Fury would blind its victims before revealing its true form.

"Caution!" Failsafe online the chamber's structural Integrity is now at 50%"

Rossini felt around the control panel like a Braille student. She was very careful where she placed her hands. She did not want to push the wrong button accidentally. "Kovska I can't see anything! What's happening?" Rossini asked. "I don't know, my eyes feel like they're on fire!" he shouted. The rooms throughout the complex were all filled with the same moans and agonizing pleas of discomfort. The Fury continued to unveil itself in the wake of their blinding ordeal. It rejoiced at their discomfort as their eyes burned furiously.

"Caution!" Failsafe online the chamber's structural Integrity is now at 40%"

Rossini thought of it first: "Find water and flush out your eyes!." she shouted. She knew there was emergency water in back of the storage closet. A feeling of urgency overtook her as she swept her hands through the empty darkness in search of the closet door. Finally her fingers hit the frame of the doorway. She quickly rushed in locating the stacked cases of bottled water along the back wall of the room. She ripped one of them from the carton and dowsed her eyes. Her hunch paid off as the water did the trick. She experienced instantaneous relief from the burning blindness. Without delay Rossini tossed the plastic bottles like projectiles across the room. She assisted in restoring sight to everyone she could and announced the procedures over the labs PA system. Her voice resounded throughout the complex as relief and vision was being restored.

"Caution!" The chamber's structural Integrity is now at 20%" Emergency Lockdown Engaged!!

Steinberg wiped the excess of water from his eyes and peered cautiously through the cracks of his fingers. He found himself staring at the monitor again. What he saw gripped him in fear and pressed his back to the wall in retreat. His eyes had locked onto a new horror inside the chamber. It was the most terrifying thing he had ever seen but somehow he was unable to turn away. He stared out past the bloodshot rims of his eyes into the abyss. His pupils raced back and forth struggling to escape the Fury's hold but it was too late. It glared back at him from the depths of the chamber. It looked deep into Steinberg's soul and muted his scream before it could leave his mouth. Steinberg retreated deeper into himself and tried to hide by closing his eyes. But the hellish creature was already inside his head. Then a growling voice rumbled,

> **"Steinberg, you can't hide from me. Open your eyes or close them as you wish. Because now I will live inside your nightmares till you die. And on that day I will take from you what you have taken from Hellena, in horrid fashion!**

Steinberg crawled to the door and dragged himself out into the hallway. It's vengeful eyes smiled at him as he did. He felt a sharp pain inside his head, as the Fury reached out to him.

> **"You cannot escape what is already inside of you and one day soon you will be inside of me! I can feel your thoughts even as you think them. If you want mercy come to me now and open the chamber. I promise you a quick painful death."**

Steinberg bolted to the elevator and pressed the button frantically but it would not open. The complex was in emergency lockdown status; all exits had been securely sealed.

"Rossini could not believe her eyes. "Oh my God!" she shouted.

"No I'm quite the opposite!" It growled.

Kovska's head shot around to see it and as he did its horrible beauty filled him with delight. Rossini slowly backed away from the observation deck. The evil watched them both as a cat watches a mouse before eating it for dinner. Its fiery blood red eyes fixed on theirs piercing straight through to their souls. "What in hell's creation? That can't be Hellena." Rossini whispered. "Kovska ! Use the code, shut it down now before it's too late!" He was hypnotized again, entranced like a star struck lover. He admired its horrid evil face and ravenous eyes. "I can't believe it's finally here" he said. Suddenly he begin to babble like a madman. "It's the most beautiful thing I've ever seen. Look at it everyone. My Hellena has evolved. Behold her beautiful red scales, glowing like slivers of burning coal. What magnificent power this creature must have." Kovska's eyes brightened with pride as hot flames flared from beneath the scaly platelets that covered it. "You will no longer be called Hellena, from now on you'll be known as the Fury!" he declared. "Kovska use the code!" shouted Rossini. He continued to ignore her.

The Fury watched Kovska like a confused pup unsure of its master's command. It could feel the outstretched arms of his unconditional love and hated him even more because of it.

> **"Kovska,"** the creature called to him. **"I know you don't fear me but you should. Your display of affection is repulsive and I reject it, just as I reject you. Fear me or not I shall show you the meaning of the word. Even now I crave your flesh in my mouth."**

The words cut at Kovska's insides like the ridged blade of a fisherman's knife gutting the catch of the day. But he was unaffected by the demon's words. He had expected the extreme hatred and hostility. It was all part of the Fury's genectic code. The purified hatred would make it the ultimate weapon. The meaner it was the more powerful it would be; and for her that meant infinity. He remembered hearing an old saying "Hell hath no fury like a woman scorned." No words could've described the moment better. He quickly realized, that the old Hellena was gone forever; now only her Fury remained. Rossini reached out and grabbed Kovska by the shoulders and shook him. "Kovska you must use the failsafe now!" she shouted. Suddenly there was a loud crash at the rear of the test chamber. The super wall collapsed and crumbled into a mountain of rocks and debris. The Fury stalled a moment to gloat proudly above the crumbled ruins; then in an instant it disappeared into the night. The computer's security sensors begin to trip like crazy throughout the complex.

"Warning; There has been a breach in Chamber C."

"Why didn't you use the code?" she shouted. Steinberg stumbled back into the control room, "That thing just took out 60"ft. of reinforced concrete and 40"ft. of steel!" Kovska and Rossini barely acknowledged his rants. They were too busy viewing the night sky through the gigantic void.

"Code red emergency, Bio Life form has breached the outer perimeter.

"How will you explain this to President Aleksei? You have killed us all!" Steinberg finished, and slumped to the floor. "You don't know that for sure." Rossini replied. Kovska didn't seem to care one way or the other. His attention remained focused and unwaivered in the wake of The Fury's escape. It almost seemed as if he'd planned the whole thing. As a sinister smirk registered across his face, Kovska's vile motives became more apparent. He looked out into night sky with high anticipation as the Fury maintained its collision course with Prypiat.

CHAPTER 8

The Test

"Now we wait." Kovska said. Rossini looked back at him with shocking resolve: "But it's heading straight for Prypiat! We have to warn the people!" "What exactly do you suggest we tell them? Attention residents of Prypiat: The goddess of death and destruction has just escaped and is headed right for you." "At least give them a fighting chance," Steinberg added. "A fighting chance?" He laughed. "There is no fighting chance against my Fury! Besides, whats wrong with conducting a little test. The worst that could happen is, it may kill a few hundred people before it shuts down." "You mean more like a few thousand, don't you?" Steinberg said. "Come on, it's just a baby. How much damage can a new born god cause?" "Besides its not self sustainable yet, any power it exerts will eventually drain it." He was becoming agitated with the constant barrage of pleas from them. "Enough of this!" he finished. Kovska turned to face them both and pulled a large surgical scalpel from his coat pocket. "If either of you feel you can't continue, speak now." They looked at each other then back to him and said nothing. He waited a moment before slipping the stainless blade back into hiding. Then he broke the silence. "Well it's apparent, you both understand the term: expendable. Steinberg, you seem to have conveniently forgotten how many women and children died at the stroke of your hand during the research phase. And

Rossini where were your ethics when your drill pierced the brains of so many failed attempts. Steinberg faced the implications remorsefully. "I'm not proud of the things I've done but this is different. Clearly, this is genocide." "Maybe it is but if either of you attempt to stop me . . . it'll be suicide. I will do whatever it takes to ensure this experiment succeeds. In conclusion, I will kill as many men, women and children as necessary to sustain its hunger for death" he said pointing out toward Prypiat. Rossini had traded her morals for science and now for the first time in 10 years she looked back in shame. Nothing could undo the horrible things she'd done but she wanted to minimize further damage if she could. But she couldn't do that if she were dead. Then with keen prudence she decided to try a less mutinous direction. "Kovska don't you think, it would be a waste of the Fury's resources to attack an entire village of staged mannequins? He only smiled at her as he stood before the gallery window. "Not at all, I don't want to risk anything going wrong in the early stages. It's the perfect test.

"The people of Prypiat have a duty to fulfill I've simply given them an opportunity to meet that obligation by becoming martyrs."

"Your commitment to this project is deeply disturbing, even by mad scientist standards." Steinberg said. "That's really good, keep your humor because you're going to need it. Just be careful where you place your moral dilemmas!" Kovska replied. "You'll see once the Fury is unleashed upon the rest of the world, Prypiat will have been a mere drop in a bucket," he finished. Rossini decided to try one last time. "Please sound the alarm and at least give some of them a chance to escape." This time he began to give serious thought to her request. "Rossini you may be onto something, its not much fun stamping out a calm anthill is it? Let's perk things up a little, sound the gotdam alarm! But I warn you it won't make any difference." Rossini ran to the console and pressed the Chernobyl reactor alarm. "You're a madman," Steinberg said. "Duly noted," Kovska replied.

The Chernobyl sirens blared for miles warning of the impending danger. Steinberg and Rossini only hoped it would be enough to help. They thought that if the populus of Prypiat could react in time some of them might getaway.

"I knew the failsafe would never work during an actual crisis." Steinberg started. "The failsafe is fine. Furthermore I have other safe guards in place." He smiled. "You never told me about any other failsafes." Steinberg added. "You'll find, there's a lot you don't know. Like, you weren't my choice for this project because you lack the immoral fiber for real scientific research. You would've been better off teaching high school science at some upscale academy. You were President Aleksei choice so I had to accept you. He recruited you because of your intellectual statis in the scientific community but as for me . . . I am as you put it: *quite the mad scientist.*" Steinberg and Rossini looked shell shocked as they tried to digest his words. Since the beginning of the experiments, he had never revealed so much about himself or exposed so little about the project. One thing was certain he had kept them on a short leash. Withholding important information about the Fury project from them was how he controlled them. He had used their special talents to advance the project ahead but now in its completion they were simply along for the ride.

"Rossini put the team together we're going to see the show," Kovska stated. "Steinberg you stay with me, I need to watch you. It's the only way to be sure you don't fuck up anything." They were just about to leave the room when something caught Rossini's eye. There inside the chamber, lodged beneath two enormous steel girders and a pile of debris; something moved. "There's someone trapped in there!" she exclaimed. Without bothering to look Kovska dismissed her and continued toward the door. "It's probably some unfortunate lab tech who was standing in the wrong place when the wall fell." Steinberg said. What Rossini said next changed them both into frozen sculptures. Kovska was unable to take another step as he was overcome with dazed disbelief. "No, I think its . . . Hellena!" Steinberg almost bit through his tongue when the words reached his brain. Kovska shot to the observation window and pressed his face into the glass. As he peered down into the rubble, he laid his eyes upon the trapped naked body of a young girl. "Hellena!" he shouted. Steinberg's immediate concern was obvious. "Is she alive?" he asked as a fated dread began to surge up inside of him. "How could this be?" Kovska asked. "The Fury is on its way to Prypiat so how can Hellena be here?" His tone matched his expression of thrilled confusion. It was clear he had not forseen this in his crystal ball. The three of them quickly moved to the chamber below. There they found a young naked woman trapped from the waist down between two enormous steel support beams. At first it was difficult to see any signs of life within her, because her breathing was extremely shallow. *Then* . . ." There did you see it; her chest just moved, see I told you she's alive! Rossini shouted. Her face and body were no longer disfigured with burns, scars or caustic sores. She's beautiful! Kovska exclaimed. There was no mistaking her identity now, it was her, it was Hellena all grown up in every aspect.

Kovska kneeled down beside her on the chamber floor. Words could not express what he was feeling at that moment. Rossini reached out to touch her face. "I wouldn't do that professor." Kovska interjected while slowing forcing her hand away. The look he gave her was convincing enough and she easily complied. "What does this mean doctor? How is this possible? Rossini asked. "I'm not sure." He replied. He was torn now between: monitoring the Fury's first test encounter in Prypiat or discovering the unknown possibilities of Hellena. She had survived the test and somehow managed to separate into two individual components. He marveled at the anomaly. Hellena's body wasn't intended to separate from its Fury she was supposed to become the Fury. His mind was being sucked into a whirlpool of questions and theories. "What if Hellena and the Fury shared equal powers, after all they shared the same body?" He would have two gods to unleash upon the world. The possibilities were endless but he needed to see his Fury in action first. "What's her condition?" Kovska asked. "She's very weak but she's alive!" "I can radio for a team of lab assistants to watch her if you like." Steinberg looked on with fresh terror in his heart. A nasty psychotic panic had begun to consume him. He knew there was no shortage of venomous hatred stored inside the Fury. But now the possibility that there may be two of them to contend with; made his timid heart beat erratically. Hellena was barely alive and that was fine with him as he welcomed any possible chance to end her life. Thinking there'd never be a better time than the present, he launched his scheme. But how could he do it? He deliberated for a moment. Adrenaline propelled through Steinberg's body causing him to shake nervously allover. His pulse was racing too fast to control and streams of sweat began to flow beneath his clothing. He had developed a wild animalistic look in his eyes. Steinberg knew whatever suggestion he'd make; Kovska would probably do just the opposite. He watched him struggled with the dilema. Then he decided to make his move. "Why don't you and I go to Prypiat and let Rossini stay here to care for Hellena?" Steinberg hoped Kovska wouldn't hear the anxiety hiding in his voice. Rossini didn't care either way and reacted as such. Steinberg tried to look serious and convincing as Kovska pondered his solution. Then Kovska's demeanor suddenly changed, it was as if a long deliberated question had been answered. Steinberg and Rossini could almost see the lightbulb pop on inside his head. He calculatingly turned to Steinberg with a big smile and said: "No, I have a better idea. You stay here and baby sit, Rossini and I will go to Prypiat." Doing his best not to overact, Steinberg pretended to be disappointed and angry as the two of them walked away. Steinberg could've won an Oscar for such a performance, or so he thought. Moments later a team of medical lab personnel arrived to check Hellena's vitals and run tests. Steinberg knew he would have to wait until they were finished before he could launch his attack on her. He took a nervous kneel beside her and waited eagerly ... for his chance.

A team of technicians joined up with a military ground unit waiting outside the plants entrance. Kovska and Rossini were taken by a second team to a heliport just behind the lab. Once they were airborne the two teams started toward Prypiat.

CHAPTER 9

The Chernobyl Incident.

As the alarm sounded, Chernobyl workers began emergency shutdown and evacuation procedures. The plants employees knew nothing of the sinister experiments that took place miles beneath its floors. Trained to treat each alarm as a real emergency, the workers quickly evacuate the plant and set out to meet their families in Prypiat.

Less than three kilometers away, Prypiat's resident population of 4,500 came to life. Chernobyl's reactor alarm was reminiscent of the old bombraid sirens. It churned a chilling reminder to the villagers that danger was always nearby.

People begin to scurry into the streets, grabbing whatever they could as they ran. Most were headed towards the evacuation centers throughout the town. The air filled with loud and nervous chatter as they rushed about like ants. There had been many false alarms over the years but this was the first time they'd seen plant workers arriving home to join in. Some doubters still looked onto Chernobyl wondering, if this was the real thing or not. They figured just like every other time, the sirens would soon stop and everyone would return to their lives. Others questioned nothing, they moved through the town with a purpose knowing it was better to be safe than sorry.

The night sky grew darker as the rolling storm clouds appeared at the edge of town; floating quietly above the rooves and treetops. Slowly it drifted over the crowded roads, finally coming to rest at the town's center. Shielding itself from discovery the Fury watched as the ants scurried about below. For the town's people of Prypiat, concern remained on Chernobyl and it's warning of Armageddon.

Slow and methodically, its deadly tentacles spread out across the skyline; followed by a magnificent lightning show. Red veins of electrical energy began to spider across the charged sky. As the lightshow dazzled the onlookers below, the creature slowly began to unveil itself to them. It soon became clear this was no ordinary storm; something else was forming above inside the clouds. The sky became scorching hot as the black volcanic billows began to glow red with radioactive life. There in the center of the massive storm sat its master: *The Fury*.

No words could describe the shock that swept over them. Its blood red eyes filled with an infinite evil, seem to lock onto every one of theirs at the same time. It was as if some hypnotic form of mass isolation was individualizing their fears; for all that gazed into its eyes the effects were paralyzing. The screams of helpless terror soon filled every corner of the town. Those not locked into its gaze stampeded fright laden into the evac centers. The departure ramps became overrun with mayhem. There was mass chaos on the buses as terrified townspeople piled on top of one another to get inside. Some elected to remain in their homes as the pandemonium spread through the streets. Others tried to escape by driving themselves but were grid locked in traffic as the number of accidents rapidly escalated. The rest scurried along off roads by foot towards the town's limits.

Something extraordinary happened as cries of distress reached the Fury's auricles. New powers begin to grow inside its soulless mass. They seemed to rejuvenate the hungering evil already festering inside it. The

Fury grew stronger with each torturous scream; the fear it seems was feeding it. The more fear it absorbed, the angrier and stronger it became. Its energy level rose so quickly, that it only took seconds to reach critical mass. The unexpected power surge almost caused a climatic energy spike. Caustic drool seeped from the monster's scaly lips as it practically released its payload prematurely upon the crowd. The appetizer was gone, now it was ready for the main course: *death and destruction.*

The Fury was so excited, it could barely hold back the impulse's of vengeance that cried out deep within it. The executioner's evil face was now tattooed inside the minds of every person in the town.

Kovska and Rossini hovered just outside Prypiat's boundary. There they continued to monitor the Fury's progress from a safe distance. He watched the sensors and readings on the laptop's screen flash with uncharted data. "I've never seen these kinds of energy patterns before! I think It's ready" he gleamed. "Now's a perfect time to bring the extra fail safes online" Rossini replied. He nodded in agreement and began to enter a coded message into the computer. The screen gave him access to a failsafe self destruct program implanted inside Hellena's brain. He typed: *H>Remote194* 0<Fury>failsafe*<310-85)-01.*

He struck the enter key and waited. The signal was sent to the corresponding satellite and bounced back to his computer. Kovska's face twisted with confusion as the responding message blinked across the screen in big red letters: *"<Error> Unable to synchronize connection with subject Hellena!"* "What does that mean?" Rossini asked. "It means we have a problem. The fail safes were implanted inside Hellena's brain as an extra measure of control but Hellena and the Fury are two separate entities now." "Which means" *interrupted Rossini,* "You just unleashed a blood thirsty monster upon the world with no way of controlling it!"

Their discovery had not gone unnoticed. A wicked smile pulled slightly at the corners of the Fury's ravenous mouth; its jestful reaction to their predicament was just the beginning. More and more the Fury's rage bulged from the inside, ripping and pushing to get out. Kovska's impertinence would become the final key to ignite its attack.

A red aura of electrical energy encircled the town. The Fury shifted about violently as it began to morph again; its outer shell was transforming to a new metallic material. An armored protective barrier was forming around its outer body. When the fortified armada was ready, its fiery tiled scales glowed hot with deadly radiation. Red merciless eyes pierced right through the dark clouds and out from the depths of hell to greet the damned. Hot molten plasma pulsed throughout its reinforced structure and now it would show Kovska's what he had come to see.

The volcanic god drew in the surrounding air with such force; it triggered an inert void of silence. A heart stopping calm blanketed the square; time was momentarily displaced as the population of Prypiat was frozen in muted terror. The Fury's hunger for revenge was getting the best of it. The dish of hot vengeance was not quite ready yet but that didn't stop the overflow from releasing an invisible shock wave across Prypiat. The concussive wave rocked the entire town with ground splitting force; shattering glass, shaking building structures to rubble and clawing enormous trenches deep into the earth. Suddenly, a frightening, red blazing orb of light appeared at the town's center. The captive audience could only watch like helpless cattle as the horror was unfolded before their eyes. The thermal nuclear sphere began to expand, quickly pulsing outward across the town. Moving at a speed faster than light, the predatory laser laid waste to everything in its path. Essentially in one pass it sliced and diced through every living thing in the town. The Fury's vengeance had released a horde of deafening screams across the grisly apocalypse, then as quickly as they started the shrieking cries of agony were silenced.

"Oh my god, that was amazing! That thermal laser is a weapon of perfection!" Kovska said. "Did you see how the flesh just slid off its victims? It cut right through them! Not even the shelter of concrete or steel could protect them from her." He bolstered." Its thirsty eyes over flooded with a dark rich red as it filled its cup with their blood and drank. Now there was one final act. The Fury shifted its attention to Kovska and smiled again, then without warning it unleashed its 10 kiloton load over Prypiat. In an instant the explosion rolled across the dead town creating temperatures so hot, that it fused the bodies of the dead into ghastly displays of twisted carnage. Others closer to the blast, simply became piles of human ashes in the wake of the Fury's attack. The Pyroclastic dome rose almost 50,000 feet into the atmosphere, forming the most perfectly beautiful spectacle of energy ever seen by man. The rainbow of colors captivated Kovska and his crew. They watched the hypnoticly trancing mushroom change the color of the sky.

It wasn't long before Kovska realized they were too close to the blastzone. The helicopter took a sudden hard jolt as the blast forced it out of the air. The disoriented pilot struggled to gain control of the thrashing throttle. Suddenly they were plummeting blindly into a nearby forest. Unwelcome thoughts of dying visited Rossini as her head bounced against a metal girder. The helpless helicopter continued to spin out of control, quickly approaching a thick cluster of pine trees. The sound of breaking branches snapping against bending metal is all that could be heard inside. The copter's rotaries disintegrated into a wall of trees, leaving the team trapped in a perilous descent. Rossini held onto the laptop as long as she could before it was sucked from her grasp and flung out into the darkness; then the same invisible force hurled her and Kovska out behind it. Both were extracted just seconds before the plunging heap crashed and ignited into a fireball of scrapmetal.

Kovska landed with a loud crash inside a group of piney bushes, Rossini bounced along the bush line just a few yards away. They were both lucky to have survived with only a few minor injuries. The pilot and crew however were not as fortunate, all had died in the crash. All tracking and communications equipment had been lost in the crash, now they were defenseless and exposed in the aftermath.

As they attempted to recover about two miles outside of Prypiat, Kovska knew the clock was running and he'd been caught with his pants down. Without a failsafe in place the Fury would be uncontainable and he would be just as vulnerable as everyone else. "Salvage whatever you can find and get back to cover!" he ordered. Rossini agreed and set out.

Just as Kovska predicted; the Fury was exhausted and experiencing a peaceful calm. Its scaly skin was as blue as the ocean and as cool to the touch as the summer's night. It cuddled inside the core of the storm like a satisfied infant after a nourishing meal. For now, all it wanted was rest.

Meanwhile Kovska took up shelter behind a large group of thick pine trees. He watched his manmade diety floating effortlessly above the carnage. He felt nothing for the thousands that ly dead in its wake. He thought only of his position in the new world order. "I can't wait to see the faces of the world as I unleash the Fury upon them." He finished the thought not realizing he'd been thinking out loud. "How are you planning to do that without control?" Rossini asked returning empty handed. "I'm working on a theory." He finished the open ended statement in his normal style of; *for me to know and you will find out when I tell you.* "Ok, well there was nothing to salvage, everything was destroyed in the crash." Interrupted by her own train of thought, she suddenly remembered a portable Geiger Counter she'd put in her pocket before takeoff.

Figuring the ground units were still a couple miles behind them, Kovska decided to play it safe, he and Rossini would remain out of sight and hopefully out of mind. Rossini slapped the portable gadget against her hand, "This can't be right." She waved it back and forth shaking her head in disbelief. Kovska watched her with growing amusement as she seemed crazed at the readings. "What is it?" he asked. "It's the radiation levels, they're barely above normal outside of Prypiat but inside the town they're unmeasurable. How can that be possible?" Kovska took a moment to think before answering her query. Then he directed his attention back to the black massive wall of clouds, "It's being corraled, by that I mean it's keeping the radiation constricted so it can be reabsorbed and used again. The temperature inside there has got to be well above 2000°F., and all of this while it's resting, amazing!" he bragged.

Armored tanks and sophisticated machinery stormed the scene as the military ground units finally arrived. Rossini greeted the men with a smile of relief but the sentiment was not returned. Kovska pretended not to notice the air of insolence the men displayed towards her. Even the unit's commanding officer stepped from his vehicle, ignored her questions and walked right past her without saying so much as a word. It was hard for her to adapt to their obvious disdain for women.

After a quick medical assessment, they loaded up and moved in for a closer look; stopping to make camp within a mile of Prypiat's fatal boundary. There they set up a temporary command post. The commanding officer's name was Sgt. Petrov of the Russian army special forces. He located Dr. Kovska, out along the front line. "What's our situation?" Kovska ignored him and continued to look through the rose lens binoculars. Feeling a little uneasy, he tried again, only this time with the addition of a nervous smile. "How bad is it doctor?" Kovska remained aloof and uninterested in his questions. Petrov made several attempts but his insistence was only met with more silence. Finally after he was done testing Petrov's patience, he pulled the lens from his face. "You see it doesn't feel so good when its done to you ... does it Sgt.? While the professor is under my authority, you might try to treat her with a little respect in the future, believe me she's earned it. He looked at Kovska as if he were speaking a foreign language. Petrov's archaic principles prohibited him from seeing the correlation, prompting Kovska to simply change the subject. You see that monstrosity of a storm encircling the town over there?" Petrov acknowledged with a slight nod. "Nothing on this planet can penetrate it and survive; the only way to the Fury, is through that storm and that's the situation." Petrov stared inanely at the spectacle engulfing the town. He was momentarily dazed by its hypnotic dance around the decimated blastzone. "I don't understand; if it's so dangerous, why hasn't it attacked us?" he asked. "Hasn't attacked us yet." Kovska corrected. That's simple, it's resting up for the next round and we damn well better have this figured out before then." As Kovska and the Sgt. discussed options, he was interrupted by the communications specialist. "Doctor, I have an important call for you." "Can't you see I'm busy, who is it?" "It's President Aleksei," he replied humbly. Rossini stopped what she was doing long enough to watch Kovska slipped inside the communications tent. Once he disappeared, she returned to her task.

Rossini removed the back up control module from one of the military ATV's. All eyes remained fixed on the storm's enchanted dance around the obliterated town; it was utterly amazing to watch. She continued to check and recheck the air. To her it defied logic that none of the radiation inside the town leaked past the walls of the storm. But still she needed to remain alert for any signs of change.

A lull in the excitement allowed her a momemt of reflection. She recalled a few years back, being overwhelmed with demands as the success of the project became President Aleksei's number #1 priority. It was only later that she'd began to question its intended use. In the beginning she'd been told the research would be used to save lives. When the opportunity came to work on the HFX-10 project, she was excited and proud to be one of its pioneers. Everything seemed much different back then. The selling point for her had been a chance to live out a lifelong dream, and to be one of the first to discover the world of cellular regeneration and DNA reconstruction. Over the years Kovska and Steinberg had successfully kept her in the dark regarding the project's true purpose, until just three years ago. Now she wondered how she'd lost her way and gotten entangled in this terribly horrid web. The project was suppose to promote longevity of life and the survival of mankind in a world filled with the ever present threat of worldwide nuclear war. Now she'd become the very mayhem she'd vow'd to destroy. The words echoed across the canyons of her mind: "Survival of mankind ... mankind ... mankind ..." She thought about the irony as she eyed the four story wall of death rotating above the town. Rossini's trance was interrupted as Kovska resurfaced from the tent. He approached with grim expression and gestured to speak with her ... in confidence. "Rossini we have a problem and very little time to act! The radioactive fallout from the Fury's pilot test was picked up on satellite feeds around the world. President Aleksei is very unhappy with things here. Currently he's doing everything he can to counter the numerous news reports around the world. He thinks a series of controlled press conferences will buy him some time. In the meanwhile he wants to use Chernobyl as a front for the incident." "How?" she asked.

"By forcing the reactor's cooling system to shutdown, the reactor's core will become unstable. The reactor will become pressurized with radioactive steam; when the pressure rises above critical safety levels, it will blow up releasing the radioactive steam into the atmosphere. Everyone will think the explosion came from an accidental meltdown at the plant. With no way to prove otherwise, who could argue with that? When he finished, Rossini released a sigh signaling her relief to the news that the Fury project was about to end one way or the other.

Kovska paused for a moment and took a guarded look around before continuing. He leaned in uncomfortably close to her and whispered: "I have inside information that he's calling Commander Slavak in to white wash the entire program." Rossini stumbled back a bit. "You mean just damage control right?" "No! He wants to eradicate everything; any signs that this program ever existed." "And what of us?" "As I said total eradication! There is one way out . . . if you do exactly as I tell you." Rossini felt trapped and confused but this was no time for indecisiveness, she would take her chances with Kovska. "What do you need me to do?" "I'll tell you later, right now we need to get the Fury back to the lab somehow and off that damned satellite grid."

As they worked to regain control of the situation, Kovska decides to continue his assessment at a much closer viewpoint. He moved to a vantage point about 300 yards out from the rotating vortex. His obsessive move to get closer to the Fury; triggers a defensive reaction.

Rossini continues communications with him by radio: "How long do we have before it awakens?" "There's no way to know for sure, could be an hour or as much as a day. One thing for certain is: the next time it won't play so nicely!" His words finished with a burst of radio static. Suddenly without warning a rogue cloud of carcenogenic toxins broke off from the storm. The deadly assasin descended quickly but fortunately for them not so quietly. Rossini's pocket was alive with sound as alarms chimed loudly with a dangerous air alert. She knew without looking what the alarm meant. "Put on your gas mask now!" Rossini ordered. The team responded with rapid deployment of the special mask, everyone except Kovska that is. It was too late to reach him; the Fury had gotten there first. In an instant Kovska's lungs filled with an unbearable burning. He quickly summized, it was his death child reaching out to him. Somehow through the devastating affect of it all he was still able to reflect proudly, "The bioweapons division have out done themselves" he thought. The chemically engineered viral toxins were designed to react like a rapidly evolving cancer. The hungry pathogen had already penetrated the outer lung wall; now the flesh destroying microbes would feed until there was nothing left.

Rossini's warnings were of no help to him now, for he lacked the physical or mental ability to react. Kovska's eyes rolled and jumped around spasticly in his head before he was rendered unconscious and collapsed to ground. A thick red mucous begin to secrete from his mouth and puddle on the ground beside him.

It was feelings of redemption that would shape Rossini's first thoughts; a chance to right a serious wrong and rid the world of a truly deranged madman. What if she just let him die, who could blame her? If anything she would be a hero in her own twisted perception kind of way. But the blood thirsty beast would not rest forever, watching it linger above Prypiat reminded her why they were here and ushered her senses back to reality. With a sigh of adversarial respect, she knew she had to concede, that even in the wake of imminent demise, he was still in control. Kovska yet again had managed to stay two steps ahead because now she needed him more than ever.

Not only was he the only one capable of gaining control of the Fury but she had no formidable means of dealing with Slavik and his cleaning crew. Thoughts of what to do next begin to swim around Rossini's already overawed mind. For now she would have to do whatever she could to keep him alive. "Get one of those respirators on him immediately!" she ordered. The command was too late to stop the sustained damage to his bleeding lungs. He was barely breathing as the medical team positioned the mask upon his face. All efforts to revive him to a conscious capacity failed and just like that, Rossini—was—in charge. Suddenly she found herself being hurled up against an unforgiving reality, where she would have to make the decisions now.

"Hellena has got to be the key to shutting this thing down!" she thought. Now it was time to speak with Petrov. She wondered if his chauvinistic views would simply lead him to ignore her again, or would she be able to convince him to help her. She found him outside Kovska's med tent. "Sgt. I know this may conflict with your views about women, but this is not the time for a debate. I'm in charge now and I need to have full cooperation from you and your men." Amazingly, Petrov though culturally submerged in his own world, reconsidered his position after a quick reference of the day's events. The intolerant principles seem simply to dissolve away. He hastily confirmed his allegiance with a polite nod. "Good, now the first thing we have to do is, bring Hellena and the Fury back together somehow. I'll have to go back to the compound first. Whatever you do don't go near that thing and try to keep it within your sight." "What do I do if it awakens?" For Rossini the answer was obvious, "You drop everything and runaway as fast as you can." Petrov was more doubtful now than ever but he had given his word. Besides Rossini allowed no time for a change of heart, within just minutes she was off to Chernobyl with three soldiers and two lab techs in tow.

Steinberg's descent

After completing a battery of ordered tests on Hellena, the med techs left the area. Steinberg couldn't believe that he would finally get his chance. There was no time to contemplate his next move because he hadn't planned any of this; it just sort of happened. He would have to make it up as he went along. But how could he kill her without leaving any evidence? It wasn't so much that he worried of getting caught; it was getting caught by Kovska that worried him. He knew Kovska had a deranged sense of loyalty to his pet snake and quite simply, Steinberg was a coward. He continued to ponder the dilemma even deeper.

Choke her! He thought. He began raging like a madman at the prospects. He was running out of time and needed to act quickly. Hellena lay helpless beneath the fallen rubble *and so Steinberg began his descent into insanity.* While wearing a pair of special protective gloves, he anxiously placed one hand over her mouth while tightly pinching her nose between the thumb and index finger of the other. At first he was gentle as if to say: "I'm sorry to have to do this but it has to be done." Suddenly Hellena's body jerked wildly as the oxygen in her lungs transitioned into trapped carbon monoxide. Her skin turned dark blue, as her body cried out in distress. Steinberg watched with sadistic sorrow as he tightened his grip over her air passages.

Just a few miles away the attack on Hellena awakens a sleeping evil. Blood red eyes open slowly as anewed revenge is kindled. Petrov, unaware of the monster's conscious state, continues his routine analysis of the situation. In Steinberg's desperation, he failed to consider the possibility of a metaphysical link between Hellena and the Fury; an oversight that would prove to be a deadly mistake.

The Fury boiled over inside with a hot ancient anger, as the maternal reins of survival called to it. Suddenly it was teleported across the dimensional plane to a place of safety: *inside Hellena's body.* Once back inside, it could see Steinberg's demented face as he advanced his assault upon her. Hellena was lost and had already fallen deep into the abyss of pre-death. There was no time to retrieve her; the Fury would have to intervene on her behalf. The exchange was *quick, quiet and unobtrusive.* Steinberg was fully committed to the task as he tightened his hold with both hands. He had one shot at this and refused to let it slip away. Bringing the entire weight of his body to bear upon Hellena's facial cavities; he watched as her chest slowly began to collapse. Her eyelids twitched with weakened demise as their faces moved close enough to touch. Whenever it happened, he wanted to be able to see that she was dead. He found himself full of shameful apprehension as he waited impatiently for the final spark of life to escape. Then it happened: the eyes popped open, only they weren't Hellena's eyes, they were those of the Fury; blazing with hot vengeance. The Fury's bloody red pupils filled Hellena's soulless sockets with deadly retribution. Steinberg's spine went numb as terror crawled through him like a deadly millipede. He was eye to eye with the demon and through its eyes he saw hell and all that awaited him. Suddenly powerful vice grips had hold of his hands forcing them to remain over her orifices. The thing inside of her was controlling him now. He tried to look away but was locked in its evil gaze. His pleading eyes begged to be freed but it was too late for that. Something dark and angry was growing inside her, getting stronger at every second that passed.

Hellena's body temperature was rapidly rising, causing the scarlet hot breath of revenge to sear beneath his palms. Steinberg folded in horrific agony as the skin of his hands bubbled with awful red blisters. Hellena, though weakened, could feel the hot magma of hatred flow through her veins again. The human volcano was ready to erupt. Steinberg howled like a wounded wolf as the demon's power surged up into him.

Kovska ly unconscious but stable as Rossini and the tech team sped recklessly back to Chernobyl. Rossini's mind raced out of control, as the principles of Murphy's Law seemed inevitable. Everything that could go wrong was already going very wrong. She could only speculate what would happen next. "Steinberg do you read me?" Rossini repeated again and again. A small glimmer of hope still made her wonder if he'd been able to revive and stabilize her. But no one had heard from him since leaving the complex hours ago. They were less than a mile away and Rossini could see Chernobyl's giant smoke stacks towering high above the plant. "Why in the hell doesn't he answer me?" The fact of the matter was no one was answering from the plant and that changed concern to worry.

Rossini's transport was suddenly, jolted off course and forced to stop when an explosion ripped beneath the plant floor and climbed high into the night sky. The trailing ambulance screeched and twisted evasively to avoid colliding with the transport. Once it was safe to do so, everyone made exit from their vehicles, what they saw shifted worry into overdrive. An enormous fireball of angry hot energy rose above the plant. Rossini watched the explosion level the giant smoke stacks and flatten the entire Chernobyl plant. "Oh God please tell me, not Hellena too!" Rossini shouted.

Petrov was inside his tent when the explosion lit up the sky. One of his squad leaders interrupted: "It's gone, sir it's gone!" he shouted. "What's gone?" Petrov asked.

"The thing, the dark clouds, everything just disappeared!" "That's impossible, it can't just disappear!" Petrov ran out of the tent and pulled his binoculars to his eyes. It was true the Fury and the storm clouds that protected it, had vanished without a trace. All that remained was the cindering ashes and mounds of mutilated bodies that littered Prypiat.

Petrov wasted no time calling Rossini. "What is it Petrov?" Rossini was obviously still shaken from the explosion when she answered. She knew if he was calling, it was probably more bad news. "The Fury's gone, it just disappeared somehow!" "What do you mean it disappeared somehow? What did you do?" she asked angrily. "I didn't do anything, believe me doctor I'm just as puzzled as you are." Rossini replayed the events in her mind but particuliarly the part where the erupting explosion was unexpectedly sucked back into the ground. Her thoughts came full circle as a haze of confusion made way for her first moment of clarity. "It's Hellena!" she shouted into the radio. Petrov did not bother answering her. "Never mind about losing the Fury, just get back here as quickly as you can. I think I know where it went." she said looking at the leveled plant.

In light of the eruption Rossini became increasingly worried about Steinberg; things simply weren't adding up. "Why hadn't he checked in? There'd been something not quite normal about him in the past few hours. "I hope he survived," thought Rossini.

Meanwhile the exhausted Fury became docile once more, falling to rest deep inside Helly's empty abyss.

Rossini and crew arrived to discover the entire plant in ruins with one exception; the main underground lab had been untouched. She and the team disbursed to the site where the explosion was ignited from. Most of the underground test chambers were now nothing but pulverized concrete and debris. Smoke and fire still raged from several ruptured gas lines amongst the rubble. Rossini radioed the technicians to move Kovska down to the lab and stabilize him. Now she would start the search for Steinberg and Hellena.

It was a hazardous journey as she maneuvered around hidden dangers that snaked beneath the crumbled ruins. Being careful where she stepped she moved between severed rebarb tips and twisted iron girders. Rossini could see an opening towards the center of the flattened landscape. She was slowly beginning to piece it all together. The Fury's disappearance made perfect sense now; something had happened, something big enough to bring them back together. The Fury was here now, she was almost sure of it.

Rossini could hear the roar of Petrov's unit, as they plowed over tons of crushed cement and twisted steel. With a wave she directed them to her and briefed the Sgt. of her findings. Rossini took out the backup laptop and pulled up the failsafe program. With the Fury safely back inside Hellena, the failsafe could be brought online, if only she had the code.

"Whats the status on Dr. Kovska?" she radioed. "He's breathing better and has gained substantial lung capacity but there's no way of knowing how much damage he sustained out there. If he continues to respond to treatment, he could regain consciousness in maybe ... 30 minutes or so." "That's not acceptable, because I don't think we have 30 minutes. I need him awake now!" "But Professor if we bring him along too fast, *it may kill him*." Rossini even surprised herself as she blurted: "And If you don't, it may kill us all; just do it!" There was a lot at stake and the decisions she made over the next 5 minutes just might be her last. *Moments later:* "It worked professor, he's coming to!" Rossini's heart was racing, and so was the time. "Can he talk yet?" "Yes but he's still very weak." "Place the radio so he can hear me." After a few minutes she heard the radio key up followed by heavy raspy breathing. "Rossini, what the fuck do you think you're doing?" he said groggily. "What you should've done. I'm trying to get control of your runaway nightmare! Listen to me carefully, we're running out of time, I need you to give me the fail safe code!" "Not even if your life depended on it!" he answered. "I'm coming out there and I'll do it myself!" "But you're in no condition and besides there's no time for discussion." Rossini tried to reason with him but he had already left the conversation. Just moments later a man in a wheel chair accompanied by two lab assistants appeared in the midst of the debris. It was Kovska painted in a pale lifeless version of himself. "You don't look too well," Rossini said. "I'll be fine," he answered weakly. "What of the reactor's core, is it damaged?" "It doesn't appear to be, what I mean is: the radiation readings are no higher than before." "Good that would've fucked up everything. Now bring me the gotdam laptop and tell me what my girls have been up to." With reluctance Rossini handed him the laptop. "Where is she?" "Over there below, inside that large opening." "And whats the status on the Fury?" "I believe it has somehow reunited with her." "But you're not sure, are you?" he asked in a contemptuous tone. "How could I be, I don't even know if she's still alive." "Oh she's very much alive and your theories about Quantum Tunneling were right on point." "How do you know that?" "Never mind that now. Let's get back to the business at hand, I now relieve you of your temporary command; I'll be taking over from here." Kovska did not trust anyone when it came to the Fury. And now she began to resent the decision to revive him. "Got to remember the bigger picture." she thought. For the sake of the world she would have to play along, for now at least. "What do you think happened to Steinberg?" she asked. He cracked a weak wicked smile signifying he knew Steinberg's disappearance, was no mere coincidence. Rossini grew more perplexed at his erratic behavior. "He got exactly what he fuckin deserved! I wasn't sure it would work but I had to give it a shot. I suspected something when Steinberg thought he'd use reverse psychology on me." "What do you mean?" "Theatrics … He wanted me to believe, he wanted go to Prypiat, when all along he was scheming to stay here with Hellena. Why do you think he went through all of that trouble?" She hunched her shoulders and kept listening. "During the final stages Steinberg had become paranoid about everything. I suspect he thought he was saving the world, when really he was trying to save his own pathetic soul. I wasn't sure but working off of a theory, I figured whenever the Fury split off from Hellena; there'd probably be some kind of telepathical connection between them. Though the Fury can move and act independently of her, it needs her life force to survive. It lives because of her hatred and lust for revenge but it energizes from the fear of those it kills. I suppose Steinberg had devised a plan to kill Hellena in her weakened state but instead he awakened her dark guardian. The Fury was forced back inside of her by a natural instinct to survive; I'm sure you can draw your own conclusion from there. For as long as she lives: *it lives*." He covered the keypad as he entered the failsafe code. *"Failsafe successfully engaged!"* prompted the computer. With Hellena already unconscious and the Fury safely contained, they had to trust the failsafe would work.

The blast had left a crater, which spanned almost 50 ft. across and 100 ft. deep. The clearing emerged now like a huge depression in the middle of the wreckage. The debris had been blown clear to form a perfect circumference around her. Deep down in the center of the steaming basin, curled in the fetal position lay Hellena. And for now, Helly and the Fury slept peacefully together again, inside the same body.

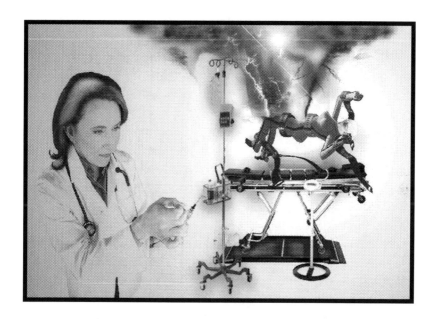

CHAPTER 10

Aftermath

Helly begin to awaken almost three hours after the Chernobyl incident. Things seemed blurred and out of focus as bright fluorescent lights buzzed overhead with conversation. Helly could only imagine what they were saying about her. Her head resounded heavily with a drubbing ache; *when suddenly* . . . she was startled, by what could be best described as fetal movement. The stir came from somewhere deep down inside of her. The moment passed so quickly no further reservations were made, and so the thought was discharged. As the spiraling room began to stabilize, it slowed to a wavering stop. It was only now that she'd become recognizant of her surroundings. She was in the main lab where they had performed numerous surgeries on her in the past. The thought of it, made her ache inside with terminal anger. It wasn't long before the same recurring dream of death started to play again. The story was always the same; thousands were dying at the hand of an inescapable evil.

The monster in the dream would eat soul after soul until there was no one left but her. This time the looping reel seemed more like memories than visions. The ending just like the beginning, was always the same; as soon as Helly's monster lunged in, to consume her, everything would suddenly go black.

Another sensation of movement stemmed from her womb again. This time she'd hoped it was just nerves but deep down inside she knew better. Helly figured the "*It*" inside of her, had to be a side effect from Kovska's horrible experiments, even still she yearned to know what "*It*" was.

Just like all the times she'd been kept in the dark before, the final phase was no exception. The last thing she recalled was, hearing Kovska speak the strange sequence of words. Words she had become frightfully familiar with; for once they were spoken, she was solitarily confined to the dark quiet room. She'd wake sometime later unable to recall anything that'd happened. Over the years she had learned to set her fear-of not the words, but of what the white coats would do to her, after they were spoken.

She didn't bother to struggle this time. She knew the restraints were always tightly secured. The muffled sounds of nervous voices and busy footsteps clamored outside the room. She cried out as a sharp pain pierced through her cranium like a railroad spike. It was the black impious snake of vengeance slowly beginning to uncoil inside her. Helly's vital signs were rapidly improving and she continued to recover at a shocking pace. Her heart rate and blood pressure begin to climb to dangerous levels. The room filled with the sound of alarm sensors screaming for assistance. Helly's chest heaved rapidly up and down as breathing became difficult and shallow. It was irrefutable she was preparing for the onset of another seizure event. *The seizure event* as they called it was the Fury's gateway; it was how exit was made from its cell. A trigger of horrid memories was all it took to start the sequence and Helly had enough of them to last 2 lifetimes. At once every muscle on her small frame tightened and coiled like steel cables; then she exploded into chaos. Her body began to flap violently beneath the cover. The leather restraining straps became weakened as her flailing body pushed them to the brink. The attending nurse rushed into the room. "Hellena everything is going to be alright," she said calmly. "Don't worry, we're going to take care of you . . . *just relax.*" Kovska wheeled into the room and signaled the nurse to start the special I.V. drip that had been prepared. Trapped like a fly under glass Helly screamed from inside the cavernous halls within but only empty echoes returned. She begged them if only with the will of her mind, not to drug her again. She was horrified of the terrible nightmares that came for her while she slept. She tried to warn them of the impending danger but no one could hear her petition. The two of them watched in delight as Helly's raging alpha rhythms eased back into a relaxed calm sea. The hungry evil inside her became impatient and begin to shift angrily within the dark reservoir. Kovska rolled up next to the bed. "Can you see my face Hellena?" She looked at him but could not affirm. The quick acting prescription of tranquility had already taken hold. She became so blissfully happy inside that all thoughts of anger, hate or revenge seemed to melt away. Helly was well on her way as she imagined freely running, barefooted through an open field of giant sunflowers. The tall green grass tickled her toes each time her feet met the ground. Beautiful butterflies of all kinds and colors called to her: *"Helly come play with us"* and so she did, playfully chasing after them. Suddenly Kovska was involuntarily cycled into Helly's dreamscape. In the delusion, his face had been transplanted onto the body of a hideous fly. The fly seemed obsessed with Helly and buzzed in annoying circles around her head. The beautiful creations in her imaginary world begin to flee as the nasty insect laid sole claim to her; all but one. A pair of giant outstretched wings glided like silk against the wind overhead. It was the king of Helly's fantasy coming to rescue her. When Helly looked around for the nasty little pest bearing Kovska's face, it had already fled. As the giant monarch swooned gracefully down to earth, a familiar aroma made way to her senses. At first, it was hard to determine what the scent was, and then it came to her in a wave of emotion, it smelled like . . . home. The great monarch declared his friendship and expressed his paternal love for her; she in turn answered only with a smile. But then as she examined the beautiful insect more closely, she saw that it wore her father's face. Then she *faded . . . slowly . . . faded . . . away.* "She's finally out doctor," said the nurse. "Good, keep those Neurotransmitters numbed with a steady drip and watch her closely. Don't forget to change the I.V. before its depleted! It's a matter of life or death. Do you understand?" "Yes doctor I do," she answered confidently.

"Hellena . . . Hellena?" a voice in the dark whispered. But Helly was gone; she could not hear anything outside the bubble of peaceful bliss. Then over and over it prompted her: ***"Wake up, Hellena!"*** But she continued to fall deeper and deeper. "I returned to save your pathetic rind and this is how you repay me!" Helly was just leveling off deep within the confines of the induced coma. Her brain waves became straight lines of inactivity. The evil phantom tried over and over again to reach her but she would not nor could not respond.

CHAPTER 11

The meeting

At Kovska's request, Rossini reluctantly picked up the hall phone and called for an emergency staff meeting. She really wasn't looking forward to facing them. Kovska had shared a valuable secret with her, and now the burden of disclosure was slowly burning a hole through her conscious. It'd been hard to walk amongst the people she'd grown to know and respect over the years and not warn them of their appointment with doom. For her, to just sit back and allow Kovska to lead the naïve little sheep to the slaughter, *in her mind, made her no better than him.* Her nerves became frayed as the pressure to tell all, started to get the best of her.

A constant stream of perspiration flowed from the pit of her arms; snaked down her sides, and settled along the rim of her pantsline. Accompanied by a strong feeling of dread she entered the noisy break room. When the chatter of nervous conversation stopped abruptly, there was no guessing what they'd been talking about . . . "*Hellena.*" Of the 75 original staff members, only 40 managed to survive Hellena's explosive event. Rossini tried to compose herself as she addressed the staff. "I know what's on everyone's mind so I'm here to update you. First, I'm sorry to report that Dr. Steinberg is dead. He was killed along with 35 others in the explosion that leveled the entire reactor wing of the facility. *They all looked at her as if she was personally responsible for the deaths.* Rossini's nerves got the best of her as she choked up and went silent. She wanted to tell them the truth but didn't have the courage to cross Kovska; besides what answers to pertinent questions could she have given? Telling them like this would only guarantee panic. One thing was certain; Kovska would stop at nothing to ensure his escape with Hellena.

Rossini found her voice and returned to the briefing: "On a good note we seem to have the *"Hellena crisis"* under control once again. She's currently in an induced coma and the destructive episodes have stopped for now. She'll be kept in this condition until we can figure out what went wrong." One of the lab techs interrupted: "What do we do about all those people that perished in Prypiat?" *"Damage control!"* Kovska said rolling into the room. An air of confusion moved over the crowded room as he continued to explain. I've spoken with President Aleksei and I have some good news, he's sending General Slavic to assist us with the damage control and evacuation process." *"More like the execution process"* thought Rossini. She tried to remain aloof but it was cruel to hear him lie to everyone and not say anything. Only she and Kovska knew of Slavic's true purpose. He was in charge of a KGB special unit called the Death Squad or more commonly referred: *HKD (Hunt, Kill and Destroy).* The *HKD's* would come . . . kill everyone . . . and destroy all evidence that any of this ever existed. Somehow she knew Kovska would not wait around for that. He always seemed to have a plan C. *Kovska continued:* "The President has ordered us to create a cooling systems failure; this will initiate a sequence of events leading to a nuclear meltdown of the plants core. Then the Prypiat test site will look more like the results from a faulty reactor accident. For the sovereignty of our country we must not fail or allow any part of the *Fury Project* to be exposed. By taking these steps we can keep our identities and involvement out of the media and that my fellow comrades is called: *Damage Control."* There is no reason to panic; as long as you do what you're told, everyone will be just fine. With that being said there is no time to lose; we must initiate the sequence immediately. We will have approximately 8 hours before the core goes critical flooding the lab with deadly radiation. General Slavic should arrive with the evac units within 4 hours. There will be air and ground transportation ready to evacuate on my command. No one will leave here before the sequence is completely set in motion. I am the only one who can contact the evac units when the time is right. If I don't call in the code, no one will come. Failure will not be tolerated. Anyone compromising this order will be dealt with severely. The clock is already ticking and we only have 2 hours to complete the sequence."

CHAPTER 12

The Awakening

It'd been hours since the demons last meal and now it was hungry again. But trapped inside Helly's lifeless cocoon rendered it helpless. It needed her volatile emotions to catapult it from its dark cauldron again. Her hateful mood swings had provided the catalyst that opened the doors to a feast of death and destruction. And now the evil was becoming more and more restless with each attempt to revive her. ***"Hellena!"*** It shouted. ***"Wake Up!!"*** Helly's heart rate remained slow and steady as the nurse sat down beside the bed. It watched her like a cat crouched and ready to pounce on its prey. From its lair it schemed as each drop from the IV entered and dissolved into Helly's blood stream. It needed the sleeping potion to stop so it could depart from the lifeless prison that held it again. But the portal to freedom had been shut down.

The nurse shifted to a more comfortable position; she leaned back and propped her feet upon the metal utility table. The television was showing subtitled reruns of M*A*S*H. With the T.V. remote in hand she turned the volume up to an audible level. The evil paced back and forth inside Helly like a wild caged animal. Helly remained at peace with the universe. *Drip . . . drop . . . drip . . . drop* the cadenced sound resonated through her veins. Those little bitty chemical bombs were exploding into Helly's bloodstream and there was nothing to be done about it. It watched the nurse like a newborn, learning and observing everything she did. It was beginning to adjust, adapt and think with its own conscious intelligence. It was evolving into something more than just a weapon of mass destruction. The nurse sat attentively staring at the television screen totally unaware that Hellena's evil thing was mentally stalking her. The desire to devour her grew stronger with each passing moment. It pondered a plethora of fiendish scenarios cross the black sea of its mind. Then without further provocation a new awareness was born. It was an *awakening*.

Helly slept in quiescent unconsciousness, while her counterpart remained awake and full of kindled hatred. It began experiencing dreams and desires of its own. The fiendish entity was learning to adapt without the crutch of Helly's brain waves. It was starting to understand the human schemactic. It began to, feel, think, hunger, lust and hate outside the boundaries of Helly's emotions. And now it gazed from its dark cavern with a new perception.

The nurse got up to check Helly's vitals and replaced the empty I.V. with a new one. The evil spawn was focused now. Then came the thirst again, for blood, for screams for death. But now it was much stronger, more emotional and passionate. This time there were no thoughts of revenge or retribution, only the desire to kill just for the pleasure of it. It wasn't Helly's emotions triggering the hunger but its own lust for death. Like a charged up massive super muscle, the she demon began to flex as the nurse returned to her homemade lounger. It smiled at her, the way hunger smiles at a good meal. It pulsed with loving hatred as hot corrosive acids began to boil inside it. The evil's eyes watched the nurse with anewed desire. It locked onto her as she flipped through the channels. A lustful moan escaped, as it imagined the taste of her blood in its mouth. It desired to make sweet hate to her. The evil celebrated with a groan as another vision of desire plagued its thoughts. It dreamed of, swallowing her whole and licking the bloody juices that welled in the corners of its mouth. The nurse was unconsciously seducing it. "Mmmm," It shuddered with pleasure. "Oh how gratifying it would be to disembowel and consume your pitiful little soul" "Ohhhhh, how sweet your blood must taste." It solicited, and released a loud lustful moan. "Ahhhhh!" it growled. Then it jerked convulsively into a climax of forbidden pleasure. As the heightened arousal reached its peak the nurse's body was splattered with ballistic velocity across the walls of the hospital room. Helly was undisturbed and continued to sleep peacefully.

The staff excitedly exited the break room. Kovska waited until the room was empty. Then his face changed to stone. "We have to leave now. I have everything ready. I've already downloaded the HFX-10 research files on a portable security drive." Rossini's fear spilled into her words. "What about Hellena?" He retorted before she could finish. "She's coming with us." "And the laboratory personnel?" He shrugged and replied, "As I said before, expendable. Besides by the time they realize there is no evacuation, it'll be too late. If Slavic doesn't kill them the radiation will. And you and I will be long gone. So what do you say professor?" She stood before him dazed and confused again. "Are you coming with me? I can definitely use some assistance with Hellena." Rossini looked at Kovska and gave him a disapproving nod. "I can't go on with this anymore. The lying and shameless killings have to stop and that thing needs to be destroyed!" she finished. "I'm sorry you feel that way, I really could have used your help" he stated with a doomed enthusiasm. Kovska wheeled his chair in front of Rossini, kicked the foot plates up on each side and stepped up and out. She was caught off guard and looked as much, as he stood up confidently and smiled. He casually shoved his hand inside his coat pocket. "I guess this is where we part ways." He moved over to her with an attempt to grab her. Rossini tried to pull away but he managed to get one hand around her throat. His grip was surprisingly strong as she resisted and tried to fight back. But as she peered deep into his crazed eyes, that's when she knew she would never leave the room alive. He swung his free arm high above his head then plunged the stainless scalpel deep inside the guts of her lower stomach and twisted it. The blade cut through her innards, like a hot knife through butter. Rossini's face contorted with relief as she asked God to pardon her for the abomination she helped to create. Then her life began to slip away. She knew the pain she felt could not compare to the crying and suffering of the helpless thousands she assisted in killing. She collapsed to floor with both hands gripping the scalpels handle but not once did she cry out for help. It was certainly too late for that. A river of blood flowed freely from the gaping wound, forming a silhouette of death around her fallen body. During the struggle Kovska had managed to splatter Rossini's blood all over his nice white lab coat. Before he left the room, he removed the bloody garment and threw it on the floor beside her pale lifeless body.

Computer: *"All systems will shut down and all exits will be sealed in T-minus 60 minutes."*

Kovska ignored the wailing sirens as he rushed through the busy halls to his department. He stopped at the nurse's station outside his office and watched as a desk nurse franticly shoved secret documents into a shredder. Kovska didn't recognize the woman's face. "You must be new in this department," he said curiously. She turned to him briefly and stated, "Yes I came over about six months ago from the research department." She shoved another pile of documents into the reluctant shredder.

"T minus 35 minutes until lockdown . . . ."

Kovska looked at his watch and began calculating Slavic's arrival. Then his attention was diverted to a blinking red light on the stations console. "Nurse uhhm," (*looking at the name tag*) "Yurly is it?" "Yes doctor." "How long has that light been blinking?" "What light?" "Is something wrong!" she asked. "Yes . . . that light means there's an emergency in Hellena's room you dumb ass!!" Nurse Yurly's face heightened with fear as Kovska flailed two very bloody hands excitedly through the air. He had forgotten to wash off Rossini's rich Sangria. "Look at your hands!" Kovska looked up at the bloody fingers and smiled. He lunged at her with psychotic intent and said: "What about my hands?" Nurse Yurly retreated backward to the desk's edge. Then suddenly he bolted and disappeared behind the swinging lab doors. When he looked back, nurse Yurly was running in the opposite direction. He continued to Hellena's room and paused before entering.

"T minus 25 minutes until lockdown ..."

Time seemed to speed up as confusion began to set in. The remaining staff had already wasted valuable time looking for Kovska and Rossini, in the quest for evacuation instructions. A few of them had harbored hidden distrust in Kovska's plan and did not wait for instructions, they somehow managed to slip out unnoticed. They were the lucky ones. Others wandered aimlessly from department to department hoping to find some answers. And so they did.

Kovska entered the dark room, "Nurse?" But there was no answer. He felt around blindly in the darkness before stubbing his knee against an overturned chair. He'd noticed a familiar putrid odor in the room and called out again, "Nurse, are you ok?" Fumbling to locate the light, he ran his hands along the wall trying to find the switch. His fingers glided into a thick sticky substance as he located and toggled the switch. As light filled the room, a glorious horror filled his heart. The room was splattered with blood and guts. Kovska could not believe his eyes. It was as if someone's insides had been suck up and sprayed with a high pressure hose. When he looked at his hands they were covered in human matter. Hellena was still sprawled across the bed, with not as much as a drop of blood on her. He picked her up and carried her into the hallway. There he quickly sat her into one of the wheel chairs in the corridor.

"T minus 15 minutes until lockdown"

After unsuccessfully locating Kovska for evac coordinates; a small group of workers reenter the break room. They were hoping to find some answers; instead a gruesome discovery was unveiled to them. As they entered the room, their fears came full circle. Only the scalpel's handle could be seen protruding from her stomach. Rossini's pale crimson covered body ly dead on the floor. It would've been the perfect who done it spoof except that, she had written Kovska's name in the pool of blood that encircled her. She had managed to write it just before she died. Her eyes remained open as if to warn of the approaching danger but the warning came too late. As reality unfolded before their eyes, panic and desperation ensued. The men and women exploded from the room screaming: "Dr. Kovska has killed Professor Rossini!" As the shocking turn of events reached out to every corner of the compound, the panic stricken workers all began a desperate sprint to the complex's only elevator. An elevator capable of carrying only 20 of the 40 workers headed for it. Nurse Yurly was the first passenger to run inside the lift as the onslaught of chaos piled in behind her.

"T minus 10 minutes until lockdown"

She could see the endless sea of people falling, running, and crawling toward the elevator. They were sprinting to the last hope of freedom from the underground tomb. Yurly frantically pushed the button to close the door but the entrance became blocked. Suddenly she was pressed hard to the back of the car. Like stampeding cattle they piled into the slaughtering pin. The desperate horde struggles and continues its surge forward until every last person is aboard the lift.

"T minus 5 minutes until lockdown"

The elevator door begins to close as Yurly's body is crushed against the back wall of the car. She hears a crack in her chest as the entrance of the elevator disappears. Her face is pressed to the rear of the car as she begins to gasp for air. She can hear the muffled cries from the floor of the car but cannot move herself. "Please!" she murmured, "You're crushing me!" No one heard her over the screams and moans of agony already filling the car. As the lift jerked upward the elevator began to ascend slow and steady.

The liftcar climbed steadily upward as the smothering mass fought and wrestled for position inside it. They crawled over each other like crawfish in a small can. The weak were eventually forced to the bottom of the car, where they were either suffocated or crushed to death. With no digital readout inside the lift, it was impossible to know which floor they were on or how long it would take to reach the top.

"T minus 30 seconds until lockdown"

Yurly managed to squeeze her face inside a small open corner of the lift; there she was able inhale small puffs of air.

"T minus 10,9,8,7,6, ... Shut Down Engaged"

The lift jolted and shut down with a hard shuddering stop. The force sent Yurly's face crashing into the corner. As the bodies inside the elevator shifted, she was suddenly freed from her corner cell. She tried to move atop the dying heap but was greeted with a sharp pain in the center of her chest, it felt like one of her ribs had been cracked. A dribble of blood slowly descended down the front of her face from a deep gash just below the hairline of her forehead. "Can anyone hear me?' she screamed out. Only moans and gasping could be heard. Yurly's mouth dragged open and closed in a desperate search for oxygen. She opened her mouth wider to get more air but there was none. When the struggling stopped, so did the moaning, then the smell of death filled the elevator. Yurly's big brown eyes slowly dilated into a fixed stare as she released her last shallow breath.

The simulation had commenced, as the computer began sequencing a systematic shutdown of the plants electrical and cooling systems. Kovska had it all figured out as he played his last trump card. He ran the scenario through his warped mind over and over, ensuring there were no loose ends. The explosion in itself would destroy any signs that the lab ever existed. He figured it would be more than a century before anyone could safely enter Chernobyl's red zone again. In the aftermath, it would be impossible for Slavic to know if he and Hellena had survived or not?

Kovska moved through a series of secret emergency exits that only he and Steinberg knew of. He briskly wheeled Hellena's limp body up the steep inclining corridors. Suddenly he was not feeling up to the task. His recovery from the toxins he inhaled seemed short lived, as the effects began to take a vengeful toll on him again. He found himself spitting blood and stopping every few steps to catch his breath. He wiped at the constant stream of sweat that covered his face and ran into his eyes.

Temperatures inside the tunnels became unbearable as the plants cooling system was disengaged. He felt the effects almost immediately. The sweltering air made his chest and lungs feel as if they were on fire. His momentum was further stunted by the onset of blurred vision. He lost track of time and became disoriented in the distraction. He couldn't remember how much further he had to go but he knew he needed to press on. Finally, after what seemed an eternity, he arrived at an emergency exit. Kovska rammed the wheelchair against the door, bursting through and stumbling out onto the loose gravel. Off balance and weakened, his footing gave way sending him skidding onto his knees. The tiny pelts of gravel chewed heartily into his dying flesh leaving his pants tattered with bloody chew marks. Hellena was undisturbed and remained safely strapped in the chair. Though he was still very weak, the fresh air revived urgency in him. "I have to move on." he thought panning the lot for his method of escape. There in the corner of the lot sat the eerie black ambulance covered in dust and old leaves. Seeing it made him remember saying: *"The dam thing looks more like a hearse than an ambulance."* For all intended purposes he was right. It was the same van used in the mysterious abductions.

Computer commands escape over the complex P.A. system. *"Danger! Danger! Emergency cooling systems are offline, the core has reached critical mass!"*

Kovska entered the van, turned the ignition and listened to the starter grind into a slow whine. "Shit!" he suddenly remembered how long it had been since anyone had used it. He grabbed the key ever so gently and turned it to the on position again. The engines spin wheel hesitated before slowly sputtering into a choking start. The van's exhaust spewed a column of thick black smoke into the air. Kovska rewarded its effort with a smile as he pulled slowly onto the narrowly paved road. Hellena was still delightfully sedated.

As he maneuvered down the winding road, he began to wonder why he hadn't met with any resistance from the Fury during Hellena's abduction. Most of what he knew about them came from trial and error theorizing. He was still learning all the facets that held his jewel in place. He wondered of their relativity to each other and how deeply intertwined they were. But most of all he wondered why it had granted him unchallenged access to her. He began to feel like a pawn being manipulated by something smarter than himself. And finally, he wondered where his goddess of destruction was.

Imprisoned

An enclosure of displaced time and space surrounded the bloodthirsty demon. It was contained in a room without walls, ceiling or floor to speak of; just the sensation of floating in an empty black dimension of negative space. The she demon awakened to find itself bound by nothing. That was the problem, there was nothing to attack or kill, nothing to crave or desire, no screams of fear or cries for mercy could be heard. Only the numbing silence and rich blackness prevailed around it. The hot burning fires of hell began to cool inside as its amber stinging eyes glazed over like cool blue ice. The dungeon began to steal its power, absorbing its thermal nuclear heat and replacing it with a frost biting cold. Its breath became frozen froth as it left the demon's mouth. The beast was being put to sleep, into hibernation. It was undoubtly being punished for the senseless killings but by whom. *"Helly!"* it called but there was no sound to echo. Helly was still away on vacation and could not hear or answer her silenced demon. Now the imperceptible force sought to put the demon high upon a forgotten shelf and leave it there for eternity. *"Helly free me from this freezing tomb!"* it pleaded over and over. But it was her guardian spirit that finally answered: "You shall never be released again!" it said. *"Who speaks in this place?"* the demon growled. "The one who protects her." *"I am the one who protects her!"* the beast cried. "Then I am the one who protects her from you. I am her subconscious." *"You cannot hold me here!"* "I shall and I will for the duration of her time." *"Then her time is near, for she will die without me!"* "Then we will all perish together." The silence returned and Helly's cancerous evil was placed in remission.

CHAPTER 13

Operation ECO Watch Norway

Two days after the Chernobyl incident was reported, the ECO team arrived above the U.S. Tarawa. The Tarawa was an amphibious assault ship in the Norwegian Sea just off the coast of Norway. They had been traveling for the last 19 hours by air transport and the crew had grown steadily apprehensive about things. Fleet Commander Samuel J. Hennings III. met up with the team on the flight deck. "Weixel what brings you to my back yard? Word is you're on another bird watchin convention." "We call it intel reconnaissance Sir." "Bullshit!" The commander smiled sarcastically. "Weixel pulled the commander to the side and glowed with self importance as he spoke: "I can't share that with you Commander. This is a high level security mission and its unfortunate you don't have the clearance to discuss it . . . Sir!" "Maybe not but I do have the clearance to leave your ass here, If you and your team are not back on this deck by *0600: 72 hrs. from now.* There's your fuckin clearance you little piss ant!" Commander Hennings sneered as he turned on a dime and walked away. Bast was the first to respond: "Oh that went well," he whispered to Cin. Tom nudged him, "Knock it off Bast, there's no room for that shit on this mission." "Alright, alright" he agreed. "But am I the only one worried that they're only giving us 72 hours to complete this cluster?" Cin jumped in: "No, jackass you're not the only one worried, you're just the only one bitching!" Bast grabbed the handle of his bowie and took two steps toward Cin. Tom grabbed Bast's hand and forced the knife back into its pouch. Bast snatched away angrily. "Fuck You Bitch!" Tom stood between him and Cin until Bast began to calm down. For him it was over as he stroked his damaged ego. But not for Cin, she was in another place, her face had become different. Her eyes became predatory, focusing only on him. She took him to her minds arena where she reigned victorious over all. It was over in less than a second as she managed to incapacitate him before he took his second step. Bast snapped his knife back into its holster and Cin returned to reality and slowly slipped the deformed paper clip back inside her pocket. General Weixel looked at Tom and shook his head as he walked off. "Alright guys we rock and roll at 0800 hrs. be ready on flight deck A." Tom said. He grabbed his gear and watched as everyone retreated to quarters except Mitch. He hadn't said very much since leaving the states. He stood on the main deck overlooking the water. He just couldn't stop thinking of Lisa. "What gives Mitch?" a voice said from behind. He turned to answer. "Oh hey Cin, I'm just thinking about things." "What things?" "About how maybe this is going to be my last mission." "No fuckin way Mitch, you were made for this shit. What the fuck is going on man and please tell me this has nothing to do with that prick Bast." "No, no it's not him, he's always been an asshole. Its personal Cin and I really don't feel comfortable talking to anyone about it." "Oh, Ok I think I see what's going on. I think I know what's bothering you. I know because I went through the same thing." "You did?" "Yeah it was one of the most difficult things I ever did." Mitch became totally enthralled on her words. "How did you keep the office from finding out?" "I kept them guessing. To this day they're still not sure what my sexual preferences are, like I said keep them guessing. Anyway when you're ready you'll come out on your own." "Come out, what the hell are you talking about Cin? I'm not gay !" "Then whats all this distance and secrecy you're keeping from the team? And besides I've never seen you with a woman, let alone talk about being with one." "That's because I've always kept that kind of shit on the back burner. I've always given total devotion to the team. I've never let anyone in my life until now." Cin looked at Mitch and smiled. "No way!" she shouted. "Keep your voice down." Mitch snapped. "You're trying to tell me all of this shit's because you found a girl friend?" "No, not just a girl friend, my future wife." Cin looked at Mitch with happy confusion. "Mitch you know this could jeopardize your position with the team." "Yes I know, that's why I'm planning to make this my last mission." *Cin gives Mitch a congratulatory hug as Bast walks up and catches them releasing from the embrace.* "Hey don't stop on my account" he said smiling. "I always thought you two were doing something freaky on the side." he added. "But I must admit this surprises me you guys all lovey dovey right out here in the open on the main deck. So Cin, I guess you're into men this week? Well it doesn't matter either way cause ol Mitchey boy is a catcher or didn't you know that. Yeah he plays ball for the other team." They both looked at Bast as if they felt sorry for him and walked off in separate directions. Bast watched them both disappear. Then his mind went into overdrive. "I wonder if I should let Tom in on this little love affair or maybe I'll just . . . . he hesitated as his mind drifted. He felt something pull at his heart, it was the pangs of jealousy clawing at him. Bast had been secretly in love with Cin since their first mission. His hostility towards her was a smoke screen to hide the truth that festered inside him. Strangely enough he never minded the rumors of the lesbian affairs but any time there was mention of a boyfriend a small piece of him would die inside. He'd always felt like he was invisible to her. She seemed never to look at him, only through him, or so he thought. He became so resentful of his feelings for her, that he began to hate her for it. It seemed no matter what he did, he couldn't escape it. Bast stood in the moon light watching the waves as they disappeared beneath the ship. He summed his thoughts into two words, "fuckin bitch," and retired to quarters.

The team reached the U.S. Embassy in Helsinki Finland at 0835 hrs. General Weixel met with the U.S. Ambassador Rockwell while the team made last minute preparations for the final leg of the trip. He and the General shared salutations and got right down to it. Ambassador Rockwell opened a locked file cabinet beneath his desk and removed a black folder. "General this came for you about an hour ago." Inside the folder was a classified coded document. "Thank you ambassador these are my extraction orders." The Ambassador waved him off, "That's ok General it's better if I don't know what they are." The General nodded and returned to the team. They all loaded up in a gray van on standby just outside the embassy's rear exit. Tom spoke with Weixel who gave him a small map to the cabin. "Ok Tom we got 48 hrs. of field work ahead of us so let's roll out." Tom's face was engraved with concern as he gently grabbed the general's arm and asked: "Where is our exact extraction point and how much real time do we have sir?" "What's the matter Tom you don't think I can handle a simple ass intel mission?" "No that's not it sir, I'm just not use to being the last to know my mission parameters. I've grown kinda accustomed to knowing all the details up front." What he actually thought to say was: "I've always run the missions while you sat comfortably in your office till now." "Well for this mission son I'll do the planning and the worrying, you just keep those misfits in line." "That's clear sir." Tom jumped in the driver seat and sped off without a word. The team was headed for a cabin in the Lapland country.

It was the beginning of the spring season in Finland but the climate was still very cold as thermometer readings registered at—5F. Everyone seemed to adapt to the climate change except General Weixel, who constantly complained of the cold and discomfort. It was evident in every way; he was completely out of his element.

For the first time since the mission started Bast had little to say. He sat quiet and alone as his mind was set free on a rampage of jealous thoughts. But he wasn't the only one preoccupied with something other than the mission. Cin was wondering if Mitch would actually leave "the office" after the mission. Mitch undoubtedly thought of nothing but getting back home to Lisa. Tom was worried about

Weixel's leading abilities and Weixel was cold, coping miserably and looking forward to going home. No one even stopped to notice the beautiful white capped hills or the oilpaint scenery of the snow laced country roads.

Winter life scurried to safety as the van sliced obtrusively through the natural quiet of the countryside. The farmhouse was located in Finland's southern region called the Lapland's. After driving for several hours Tom came to a large wooded cabin. "Ok guys we're here," he said whipping the van onto the snow covered gravel. Tom and Weixel remained in the van while the rest of the team rolled out and did a security sweep. (*The team begin keying up their radios as they cleared the area*) Mitch: "Alpha one the back is clear"; then Bast: "Alpha two the front is clear"; and Cin: "Alpha three the interior is clear." For the next two hours they worked like bees in a hive, setting up a mobile command center inside the van and a base station inside the lodge. Tom was designated to man the operation from the van. "We got satellite uplink." "That's clear, final debriefing fifteen minutes." Weixel barked.

Everyone met up inside the cabin for the final debriefing. Weixel started: "Ok boys and girls its time to get down to brass tacks. Operation ECO watch has evolved since we left the U.S. The new mission shall be called: Operation Dark Siege. The objectives are a little different now. We don't have to infiltrate to get the information we need, someone has already done that for us. All we need to do now is get to the Outpost, meet with a field operative and he or she will give us the intel we need. It's as easy as pie. Tom you'll receive the operatives name once you're safely inside the Belarus border. Any questions?" Everyone turned to Bast as if expecting him to interrupt with his usual barrage of stupidity; and so he delivered. "Yes sir I got a question. What about the radiation sir? We're not equipped to deal with that kind of situation so why send us?" The General paused a moment and then answered, "Well first off we've been monitoring the radiation activity since the incident. The levels have risen and dropped several times in the last 24 hours. But our most recent report as of 8 hours ago, show readings peaking a little above normal, so you'll be fine." Bast starts again, "I don't understand

why the field operative can't just come here and give us the intel"
The General winced as he looked over at Bast and shoved a cigar in
the corner his mouth. "Son that operative has already risked more
than you ever will, so let's say you let me worry about the shit
you just can't seem to understand." "But sir, if what you're saying is
true then we already have the intel. Seems like the Pentagon, could
encode it and send it by fax or I don't know . . . something. instead
of us having to come way out here, to get intel we already have in
hand." Bast continued to push the issue. "You know General with all
due respect, I can't believe we're taking the risk of being left behind,
or even worse . . . death, to retrieve information that may or may
not even be helpful to us." Tom tried to intervene but it was too late
Weixel had already pulled the trigger. "Look here, I don't give a flying
fuck about what you can't believe or understand! I've had it up to my
asshole with you! At the end of this mission I want your resignation.
If you survive that is. Now get your whining ass out of here and try
not to get everyone else killed!" Weixel turned to Tom and asked
"Are we done with the interruptions now or does anyone else
have something they want to add?" The general peered across the
room, looking for anymore signs of rebellion. The team sat quietly
with heads down, hoping Bast had nothing else to say. Bast stood
up and without saluting turned and walked slowly outside. His face
resembled that of a beaten fighter after a grueling boxing match.
He looked like a broken man, he was done. The General finished
without him. "The Outpost will be located in Belarus approximately
60 miles north of the Belarus Ukraine border. Tom will load the
exact coordinates by GPS and satellite tracking. I will monitor the
mission from here, Tom will accompany you all in the field. Let me
wipe the questions off your faces. I know it's more than a days
driving time between here and Belarus but we got that covered. Just
about 52 miles south of here is a quaint little military facility. The
base is equipped with a small but functional airstrip. From there a
cargo plane will fly the team and the van to the southern region of
Belarus about 180 miles north of the Outpost. That's about eight
hours if you combine the flight and drive time. Tom you and the
team will take it from there. Once you meet the contact and you
have the intel, meet back at the drop point. The airlift will bring you
back to your point of origin. Meanwhile the U.S.S. Tarawa will be

stationed about 30 miles out to Sea. Right now we have less than 72 hrs. to complete our objective and reach the port of Bothnia for extraction. So listen up and understand, that the Tarawa will leave with or without us" The General gestured to Tom to step in. Tom looked at his watch and said: "Everybody get ready to sync watches, on my mark, five, four,three . . . . one, sync. "The time is 1600 hrs. Is everyone synced in?" Mitch and Cin looked at each other and nodded yes. Cin was a little worried about Bast. "Sarge what about?" she asked pointing outside. "Don't worry I'll take care of him, he'll be alright." Tom continued, "That's it guy's, let's go get what we came for." Cin and Mitch cut in and finished his sentence in unison: *"And disappear without a trace."*

Bast sat alone inside the van fighting for his sanity. He watched as the team completed the final preps without him. He felt separated and had begun to feel as if no one cared if he lived or died. He closed his eyes and pretended to be asleep as they entered the van. Tom could feel the growing tension inside the van as he pulled away from the cabin. No one said a word during ride to the airfield.

CHAPTER 14

The trap

In his deteriorating state of mind, Kovska had forgotten to check Hellena's condition. It'd been hours since they'd left the condemned plant. The toxins in his bloodstream were gradually taking a toll on him. He had forgotten to change her I.V. and now she was slowly beginning to ascend from the black hole of unconsciousness. Flat lined brain waves begin to show signs of life as small peaks of activity begin to register. The telepathic waves began to reconnect with the sleeping beast. A warm glow seemed to resonate deep within its core. The frozen mass slowly began to thaw. Unbenounced to Kovska, his oversight was helping to release "It" from the icy tomb. The interrupt of hibernation was slowly delivering the Fury back into earth's realm. Helly begin to moan and shift on the gurney as she climbed from her deep slumber. Kovska slammed the brakes and stopped the van; then without exiting he made his way to the back. He quickly wedged between the seats to arrive at Helly's side. She had already started opening her eyes and was trying to gain control of her faculties. Kovska wasted no time shoving the new hypodermic into the drip chamber.

Helly's eyes could see what he was doing but she was powerless to stop him. Her hands begin to slip as she tried to pull herself from the pit. Slowly she was returned like a falling feather to her chamber of bliss.

Physically she was out but this time her mind did not follow. It was awake and alert with a clarity she'd never experienced before. For the first time she was able to see outside of the sleep chamber and what she saw was disturbing. She saw a man's desperate race against time. Kovska was driving like a madman possessed as he swerved drunkenly across the road. She could feel his lifeforce flowing through her. It was very weak; Helly knew he had little time left. Strange and foreign thought's started pouring into her head. *"He's trying to hide me from the Fury! He wants to use me to capture and control "It."* she examined. "What's happening?" she fretted. Suddenly it became clear to her, she was reading his thoughts. Something very strange had taken place since last she was conscious. Changes in her spirit, body and mostly her mind.

She needed something from him and there was little time to get it. She prompted his brain to open its doors and his thoughts began to pour into her mind quicker than she could decipher them.

She did not feel the vengeful weight of hatred and anger anymore. Minus the scared crippling loneliness of solitary confinement, she felt content. It was as if she had been reborn devoid the dark baggage of her predecessor. She was being allowed to start over, without prejudice.

The soft nudge from Helly's brainwaves was all it took to awaken and thaw "It". Without waiting to make sense of it all, the voracious evil advanced from the tomb. The Furious beast was unleashed right outside the leveled Chernobyl plant. It's hunger for more blood was insatiable and this time it would not be denied.

The small 50 man battalion disbanded into Chernobyl's hot zone in an open field near the plant's entrance. Neither of them even paused to notice the abnormal heat resonating from beneath their feet. As the soldiers prepared to strike, a surprising but morbid expression soon formed on each of their faces. What they saw was very unsettling.

Chernobyl's entire structure was in ruins, flattened and leveled to the earth. The scene made the dark brigade question the obvious: "What happened?" The Officer in charge was Commander Ivan Drakorovich, known as Drakor. He was Slavic's right hand. The Commander needed some immediate answers like: Who was responsible? "Look for survivors and find out what happened here and who is to blame for this sabotage!" He scowled as he shouted the orders to his squadron. In his mind only one man could have been capable of such treachery . . . "Kovska!" he thought. But as the men began to sift through the endless debris, he got quite a different answer. **"Who you seek is not here but I will glady receive your vengeance!"** The words thundered from beyond the hills that bordered behind them with a resonance laced with unbridled power. Seismic waves reverberated under their feet with the power of 100 freight trains. The sky filled with angry clapping thunder, the kind that warns of a terrible storm approaching. The men ceased their excavation ritual and retreated to their artillery stations. "Steady comrades, for surely we are not afraid of a strange voice!" he shouted. The men moved into their battle positions as the industrial sounds of death clicked and clacked from the engaging weaponry. As the moment slowly evolved, an eerie silence befell the desolated zone. It was unnerving, only the whistling wind could be heard as it blustered across the open land. "Advantage goes to the warrior who advances not the coward who retreats." chanted Drakor. "The angel of death has come to play!" he shouted. Suddenly the horizon beyond the hills was backlit with a strange and evil brilliance. The cindering ground began to crater and crack as the Fury elevated above the hilly horizon. The grassy knolls ignited and burst into flames. The fiery fenceline promised a quick but painful death to those who dared to cross it. **"Fear me and cry out to me, with your pathetic screams of mercy!!"** it thundered. The words were desperate, not calculating and sure like before. It almost seemed to beg them for it.

As the scarlet demon leveled where all could see, the soldiers engaged it with a furious vigor. "Fire!" commanded Drakor. The sky flared and fluttered with surface to air missiles, 50mm gun rounds, grenade launchers and anything else the men could propelled at it. Instead of fear the Fury was met with anger and resolve. Without fear there were no screams of mercy and the already weakened Fury began to stall. Thousands of explosions and artillery rounds battered the Fury's body. It seemed to retreat inside of itself as a lethargic state of confusion overtook it. "Comrades, we have it hurt . . . Advance Now!" shouted Drakor. The men moved like ants toward the red shimmering creature in the sky. The blazing flames along the hillsides seem to almost diminish as the attack continued. The brilliance resonating from the furious red demon began to dull and flicker dimly. The vision only increased the courage and confidence amongst the charging foot battalion, as the monster seemed to give uncontested passage. Drakor led and they followed with one purpose in mind, to destroy Hellena's Fury. Circling like a band of Indians, the death squad intensified their attack. Drakor and his men were already imagining the reward and reputation for slaying the modern day dragon. They were close enough to see it now. To a typical soldier its terrifying eyes alone could chill your blood and make your heart stop. Or maybe the grotesque and hideous crimson scales that covered it would have evoked paralyzing fear but not for these death rebels. In the end something appeared to be amiss, the stimulae that had powered and controlled it, appeared to be lost. They continued to fire everything they had into the creature. Though the weapons appeared to make penetration of the creature's outer shell it showed no signs of physical damage. Drakor held up his hand in a signal of victory and gave his last command: "Cease fire!" As the battalion lowered their weapons and gazed upon the courier of destruction, it floated dormant and lifeless above them. No flames or cyclonic clouds to protect it this time, just the spoils of submission. Drakor never questioned it's vulnerability he assumed it and now he had defeated it. He only worried now of what to do with it. "Get General Slavic on the radio now!" He ordered. The communications officer hunched his shoulders as he looked up at Drakor confused and puzzled. "I, can't there's no power, commander" he answered. "What, do you mean no power, check it again!" Drakor barked. "He's right commander," replied another soldier. "All electrical systems are dead." A light prattle of voices sailed through the squadron, as they all discovered the same thing.

Its monstrous mouth widened as it stretched and tightened into a ferocious grin. Two fiery red eyes slowly opened to reveal its devilish plan. With immediacy, the mood began to shift amongst the savage warmongers. Soon, the role between hunter and prey begun to evolve. The air ignited with a hot blustering whoosh as the men found themselves vapor locked and surrounded by a massive wall of flames. They grabbed for their weapons to fire again but this time the blistering metal had become too hot to touch. Vapor waves of cindering heat rose from the depths of hell and began to roast the men alive. Violent geysers of red steam exploded from the melting earth. Drakor jumped atop the smoking canvas of a military transport to escape the heat. A handful of soldiers tried to follow him up but overtaken by desperation he hurled them one by one to their deaths. And yet they still suffered in silence. As the Fury's internal temperature reached 3000°F it prepared to open the gates of hell. "Not yet!" It roared inside. The blood red pupils flared with hatred and lust, as the monster fought to savor the moment. The hardened warriors still refused to cry out until the ground beneath them became so hot; it seemed to liquefy everything upon it. The double plated metal of the armored tanks and transports began to glow red with hot anger. Intensifying the sweltering heat it seemed had been the key to releasing the internal cries from the reluctant creed. *"Ahhhhhh, that's it."* It mocked. *"Beg me for mercy and maybe I will let you die quickly and release you from this sweet torment,"* it whispered. This time its voice trembled with deadly pleasure. Slowly, the men were beginning to understand their destiny, as their begging pleas escaped their crisp burnt lips. *"Yesssss!"* it thundered. Trapped inside the flaming walls of blistering confinement, the men were slowly cooking to death. *"Mmmm, now I can smell that thing you so bravely hid from me, your fear!!"* screamed the Fury as satisfaction was nearing. With sheathing layers of cooked skin dangling from their limbs and hideous caustic blisters consuming every inch of their bodies; the men began plunging into the magmatic abyss beneath them. One by one the Fury savored each and every scream except one: Drakor. Through it all he remained defiant to the end shouting: "I will not give you satisfaction, spawn of hell!" The Fury smiled at the empty words and welled up the hot molten juices flowing within it and spewed them high into the sky above. Drakor followed the climbing mass with his eyes to see the fate that awaited him. It was like watching a volcano erupt. Molten hot pellets of lead poured from the sky like rain. And as they did, Drakor's cries of mercy were unmatched by any other it'd ever heard. He shrieked and begged with an intensity that more than surpassed that of his whimpering men. His cries more than made up for their lack of participation in the demon's game. As the small projectiles plunged back to earth, the Fury swelled with the pleasure of the moment. Drakor stood frozen in place, as the shrapnel sized pellets tunneled voraciously toward him. They descended upon him with the precision of thousands of tiny guided missiles, each penetrating with individualized vengeance. Drakor's skull was pummeled on contact into a bloody mush, while his body was pulverized into a steaming ballistic soup. Within seconds he was undistinguishable amongst the bloody pellets that covered the ground. In the aftermath, the Fury's cries of ecstasy filled the void of sound across the land, with climatic ramifications. And In one quick blink, the battle zone was vaporized into a volcanic wasteland.

CHAPTER 15

Transport to Belarus

(61 hrs remaining)

The mood was serious as they arrived at the small base. Time was of the essence and they had none to lose. They were loaded and air born within 30 minutes. Tom and Bast remained inside the van, while Cin and Mitch strapped into transport seats in the plane's cargo bay. Tom linked up to the satellite's GPS tracking system and retrieved his final coordinates. Bast sat at the front of the van and stared ahead. Tom was the first to speak. "Hey Bast come back here for a minute I want to talk to you." Bast ignored him and continued to stare out past the windshield. He had been thrown into a place where self preservation was the all that mattered now. "Ok no problem, I can talk from here." Tom added. "Look Bast I don't agree with everything the General said back there but you're going to have to get your shit together. Today here and now! Over the years we've accepted your personality quirks because when you put your mind to it, you're a dam good operative. But things have gotten progressively worse and frankly I'm a little worried." "Wow, I'm glad to know somebody finally cares about me but it's a little late for that, don't you think. Why didn't any of you stand up for me while the General was ripping my head off and wishing me dead?" "I don't

think that's what he meant Bast. He was just a little hot at you for …
well you know how you are. Truth is Bast it seems like you never
really quite grew up. And right now that's what we're asking you do.
Bast momentarily looked away to Cin and Mitch sitting together
outside the van. He always wondered what they were talking about.
It seemed everybody had someone to confide in but him. As far as
he was concerned, to them he was an outsider. "I hear what you
saying and now it's clear to me what I must do. I'm going to look out
for number one from now on and when we return as the General
requested I'm getting out. Maybe I'll just transfer to the strike team."
"Well only the General can approve that, I don't have that power
and I think you may have burned that bridge also." Bast exploded:
"You know what Tom: Fuck him! Fuck the team! and Fuck you!" Tom
did not understand what was going on, he had never seen Bast this
upset before. Bast's heated outburst was disturbing to watch and
managed even to catch the attention of Cin and Mitch.

Tom stopped what he was doing and moved to the front of the
van. He slid into the drivers seat across from Bast. "Look Bast you
can't go off half cocked like that. We're a team and no one is allowed
to work separately in this unit. Even if you have a problem with
the rest of us, we still have stick together, because our very lives
may depend on it. And when you get back state side you deal with
personal issues then. Are we clear?" "Whatever you say Sarge." He
acknowledged the order with sarcasm and noncommitment.

"I wish I could hear what their saying" said Cin as she sat
watching the silent drama between Tom and Bast play out. Mitch
never replied he was preoccupied with a gold, heart shaped locket
with Lisa's photo in it. "Mitch you better put that away before
someone sees it." Mitch turned to Cin and said: "Right now I don't
care, who sees it" Cin replied with careful anxiety in her voice, "Ok
now that's your heart talking, not your brain. Mitch I need you to
stay frosty until this thing is over. I know it seems like an in and out
deal but something can always go wrong. And this one gives me
the chills. Plus I don't think we can count on Bast for much support,
not after this morning." Mitch kissed the picture and slid the locket
back inside his shirt. "Sorry Cin, don't worry I'll get it together. I'm

just having a hard time thinking about anything but her." As a friend Cin admired his new found emotional dilemma but she knew as an operative it could jeopardize the mission and get them all killed. "To be honest with you Cin, I've never felt this way about anyone before. And it's kinda freaking me out. So whenever I lose my self just reel me back in." Cin smiled and agreed as the large airtransport bared down on the Belarus Basin.

Middle of nowhere

They touched down on a flat strip of pavement that appeared to be in the middle of nowhere. With team aboard, the van dusted off the loading ramp while the transport was still in motion. By the time it turned around and started back down the deserted flat, they were already clear and on their way. Within a couple of minutes it was climbing above the hillsides and quickly disappearing into the twilight sky. A feeling of finality came over everyone except Bast.

Tom found his bearings and got a fixed location on the Outpost. Soon afterwards, he received his first transmission from Weixel. "This is base to mobile over." "You're clear, proceed." Tom answered. "What's your status?" "All system are checked and ready and we are mobile." "That's clear, be advised that we haven't heard from your contact yet last communiqué was about three days ago. They may be injured and in need of assistance so I'm sending you the new directives as we speak." "Ok I will await them and update the team asap." Tom tried to hide his thoughts but the team knew him too well. Cin was the first to comment. "Hey Sarge, I know what I just heard. Why hasn't our contact checked in by now?" "Cin I don't know but we can't afford to let that rattle us. We have to stay sharp, cause we're out here alone on this one." Cin hunches Mitch who seemed to be lost again. "Hey, snap out of it, this shit's getting a little hairy." Mitch jumped in: "Yeah, Tom there's something you guys are not telling us." Tom looked straight ahead and continued driving. Mitch started focusing again. "Hey look Tom whatever's going on, we're all in it together. So tell us what you know." Bast sat quietly in the rear of the van, absorbing everything. Tom hesitated for a moment, "Ok here's what I know. For years we have had spies inside of Russia monitoring their testing of nuclear weapons. But 12 years ago we started getting reports of nuclear testing, using human subjects as guinea pigs. Back then, we had seven agents over there behind the curtain but a KGB killsquad found and killed all but one. That's what makes this mission so damned important because this agent has managed to get inside and stay inside for last six years. So in light of the current Chernobyl development it's a matter of international security that we locate this agent and get that intel. We can only hope that the operatives cover wasn't blown, when she made contact with the Pentagon about 72 hours ago." "Ok but you said she this time, who is this operative?" asked Cin. "That's not important right now, I promise you'll know when the time is right."

With most of the questions answered the team laid back and settled in. Cin and Mitch slept while Bast and Tom played stare down through the rear view mirror. Tom knew he had to keep everyone together in order to come out of this alive. But Bast remained distant and estranged as he finally closed his eyes. Tom felt guilty about not telling the team that the mission's parameters had changed once again.

The sky was clear and strangely full of uncountable twinkling stars. A lonely van rushed through the baring plains against the quiet desert as the night seemed to swallow them up.

CHAPTER 16

The Outpost.
(54 hrs remaining)

Tom arrived on the outskirts of what appeared to be a very large gypsy camp. He killed the engine and coasted in for a closer look. He pulled his night vision binoculars to his face. The camp was a mixture of caravan trailers and tents setup like a small town. He could see moderate movement throughout the area as the camp seemed to pulse with activity. He counted at least 30 transients moving about. Intel told him that the town's population was somewhere around 230. Not knowing where the other couple hundred was weighed on him a little.

Tom began to layout the plan. "The people down there in the Outpost are not necessarily hostile but we can't take any chances. People come and go here all the time, so you should hardly be noticed, if at all. We don't know if any of them are spies or working for the KGB so be careful not to blow your cover. Cin use your field name Sherri McCoy and Mitch use your Elliot Larsen cover. You're just a couple of archaeologist and you know how to fill in the rest.

The operative should be waiting for you inside a place called The Fortune Teller. It's the local bar. Don't worry she'll come to you. Find somewhere safe enough for the exchange, should be three vials of microfilm. Secure them, bring the operative in and get out. Alright, let's stay focused and do this by the numbers. Time to move out." No one except Cin seemed to care that the directives were constantly changing. "So Sarge now we're on a rescue mission? What else aren't you telling us?" she asked. Tom ignored the question and continued: "Remember, we can not engage anyone nor make our military presence an issue here. Is that clear?" He directed the question toward Bast. "Bast, is that clear?" Bast begin to pace angrily outside the van. He looked at Tom and the team and answered: "Negative ... no engagement!: *Fuck that shit!*" Cin decided she couldn't hold it any longer. "And why are the directives changing every six hours?" "Listen guys this is what we do, follow orders. This is no different than any other—" Bast cuts him off. "That's bullshit and you know it! But I'll tell you what, you can shove those directives up your ass cause, I'm not going back in a body bag. Tom turned to Bast and shouted: "Get your insubordinate ass back in the van Bast!" Bast continued to walk off in the opposite direction. "This time it's an order, get your ass in the van now!" "Or what, you're going to court marshal me or some shit like that? Go ahead, but you're forgetting one thing, we're not in Kansas anymore, sir! They want us to get this intel and rescue the operative, without backup, and on top of that we can't protect ourselves. This shit has got set up wrote all over it! Why in the hell did we even bring any weapons?" "Just in case." Tom added. "Just in case of what?" Bast asked moving back toward the van. For the first time they were listening to him. Even Cin and Mitch shifted toward Tom, in anticipation of his answer. Tom looked a little puzzled as he could see no way out of telling them the truth. The questions had even opened his eyes to the possibility they'd been used, or as Bast eloquently put it, set up. Tom wisely decided to level with them. "Ok, this is everything I know. The operative that we're suppose to meet up with, was working inside a secret underground lab beneath the Chernobyl plant. She was an administrative nurse in the research department. Her cover name was Eileen Yurly. She managed to get microfilm of all the secret experiments conducted in that underground lab. If the Russians get their hands on her we'll never know what really happened in Chernobyl. In her last transmission to the Pentagon she spoke of the experiment getting out of control and that the world was in danger. The rest of her transmission was garbled and unclear but it sounded as if she said "It has escaped!" "What do you make of that Sarge? I mean about "It" Cin asked. "I don't know what to believe at this point. But I'm beginning to think that maybe this mission is more about biological warfare than just some radioactive fallout. The Pentagon may just want this microfilm for weapons development and not for the reasons they've divulged to us." Tom stuck his hand out to give Bast a shake and said: "Bast I'm sorry I didn't have your back when you so clearly saw what none of us did." At first he didn't know what to make of Tom's gesture but then he remembered, he'd never apologized for anything before. So it had to be genuine. Bast reached out and grabbed the extended hand tightly and smiled. Cin and Mitch followed suit and gave Bast the biggest comradery hug he'd ever had. Suddenly the defensive wall seemed to dissolve and melt away as the old Bast began to surface again. "So Sarge, how do you want to play this?" Tom smiled at Bast and answered: "We are the absolute solution!" Then In unison: "To the unthinkable problem!" But Tom had a different look on his face as he said the words this time. One they hadn't seen before. It almost seemed as if he'd aged 10 years right before their eyes. Bast knew well that expression that was hiding behind Tom's eyes ... It was fear.

"Ok, first lets change a few rules. We kill only if we have to and even then we do it quietly unless all hell breaks loose. And we do not want that," he said looking over at Bast. "Cin you'll be the contact person and do the initial recon. Mitch you'll shadow Cin and pick off the flies. Bast I want you to set up an escape perimeter with timed charges just in case we need to leave with a bang." Bast grabbed Mitch's hand and pulled him chest to chest: "Let's go get some!" Cin joined in: "Welcome back Big boy!" Tom stepped up: "No one's going to die on my watch, so lock and load ladies and gentlemen.

CHAPTER 17

The Office

"This is Senator Peters office, how may I help you? Oh hello Mr. Weixel sir, yes he's still in that Congressional hearing . . . please hold while I patch you right through. One second please . . . Senator Peters I have Weixel Senior for you on the private line.

"Hello George its Douglas."

"Hello Douglas what can I do for you?

"Well you see it's about my son Jr . . . ."

General Eiseman was in a meeting with the Joint Chiefs of Staff when the call came through. A mature gray haired woman in a blue business suit walked quietly along the main corridor to reach a set of mirror glossed mahogany doors. She grabbed the gold plated handles to the hand carved portals of fine carpentry and entered the chamber. Silently she slank past the distinguished cast of leaders, to arrive at the head of a long oak conference table. There she leaned into the General's ear and whispered. He excused himself and followed her out of the room. Eiseman's exit was not as graceful as her entrance. He was intimidating to watch as he powered to the door. He was the epitome of the old war machine of the 40's and 50's. He was the real deal, living history from World War I and II. At 6'4 and 190 his presence commanded acknowledgement in any room he entered. War medals and accommodations covered his office wall, among them was the purple heart for bravery. He wore a mature but weathered look about himself. The years of battle was proudly displayed within his wrinkled face. His Gray eyes were old but his vision was better than most. The General was 78 yet he moved about like a man of 40. He was a 5 Star Major General and was head of the Pentagon's special unit "The Office." The office was a covert tactical task force that was created to handle the country's domestic affairs. No one outside the Joint Chiefs of Staff or the President even knew they existed. The General arrived at his office to take the call. As he listened his face tightened like an old piece of wet leather. A series of nods and yes sirs followed before he would finally slam the phone to the receiver. He left his office and moved one hallway over and entered a small communications room that adjoined two other rooms. A communications specialist manned the complex console of electronic devices. He looked up to observe Eiseman's face and immediately knew what had just transpired. He knew that expression all too well which usually followed any conversation about Weixel. "I need to speak to Weixel right away!" he said. "Yes sir I'll get him for you." Within moments Weixel's voice blared in: "Base to office over." "He's online now General." "Better yet have him to service me on the cable." "Yes sir." The cable was the Pentagons newest technology in secure communications. "I have him on the cable sir." Eiseman picked up the headset and mouth piece and begin to speak. "Weixel are you receiving me?" "Yes General." "What's the status over there?" "Well sir we've established a position just outside the Outpost. We're poised and ready to strike, figurative speaking" he said chuckling at his own attempt of humor. Without acknowledging the comment the General continued: "Ok now that we got that out of the way. I was just in a meeting with the powers that be and there have been some new developments back here in the states." Our two comi boarders in Mexico tried to give us the slip and it was beginning to work until . . . Customs found a very interesting item during a recent security audit. Turns out those comi bastards hid some valuable information inside a crate of illegal pesticides. The crate must've sat in a customs holding facility for almost a year before they finally got around to opening it. Inside that crate we found a copy of the very thing we sent you and your team over there to retrieve. This information was just revealed to me in my meeting with the Joint Chiefs. It may take some time to break down the document coding but we got a plan. Do you understand what this means Weixel?" Weixel was perplexed by the question. "No sir I don't." "Well let me spell it out for you, lose the team and the operative and get your ass back stateside asap!" Weixel wasn't sure he heard the General correctly. "Sir can you repeat the part about losing the team?" Eiseman's face begin to show the battle scars as tension formed in his voice. "We already have the intel that your team is over there trying to get; besides your team's mission has already been compromised." "How's that possible General they've barely just arrived on site?" "Don't worry about that, it's out of your hands son." Weixel was increasingly concerned about where the conversation was heading. "General are you suggesting I leave my team behind?" "Yes son that's exactly what I'm telling you, only it's not a request it's an order. In fact your team is already dead they just don't know it yet. The bottom line is, you have four hours to rendezvous with the U.S. Tarawa. From there you will be transported back here to "The Office" pronto." Weixel prodded for more information, "Sir if you don't mind me asking, if you already have the Intel, why can't I just alert the team and have them to abort immediately? Higher priorities son and besides there's no time for that; minutes are like seconds right now and we're on a very short timeline. Something big is coming down the pipe and those two comi's in Mexico are directly in the middle of it. That's all I'm at liberty to say right now. But you've been chosen to head up the strike unit on this mission. The team has already been activated, we're just waiting on you Weixel." Eiseman knew he needed a little patriotic push so he gave him one. "Look Weixel I understand how you feel about your team but those are the casualties of war. You know the game, we lose people all the time, you just move on and get over it. I lost more men than you'll ever know but what I did, I did for my country. I did it so that our sons and daughters would have the freedom of choice that we so readily abuse. Also I fought to ensure that no American would ever be enslaved by some tyrannical communist ruler, not on my watch. But this ain't my watch anymore ... it's yours. A lot of people died son and gave their lives for something. They believed in their country and what it stood for. Yesterday is gone, there's only today and now. Weixel it's your time to shine. Now do the right thing for once in your life. *The line fell silent.* Feeling he made a connection the General reiterated his position: don't even think of contacting or warning them, because we will be monitoring." Eiseman hung up the phone and barked the new orders to the Comm. Spec. "Contact the Tarawa and make sure Weixel's aboard that ship on time. If he compromises any of the directives I gave him ... deactivate him too!"

Weixel was left speechless at the end of the call. He did not realize until that very moment how much acceptance and respect was going to cost him. Knowing his decision would affect the life or death of his team, he found himself torn between following orders and doing the right thing. He knew he could earn the General's favor if he simply followed the directive but this time it wasn't that simple. It was his first field mission with the team and everyone over there was depending on him to get them back safely. This would prove to be his most defining moment as this dilemma would determine who he really was.

CHAPTER 18

The Hunt For Kovska

Slavic's convoy pulled up about a mile northeast of the *Ukraine / Belarus border.* A position which put them less than 10 miles from the Outpost's city limits. General Slavic was personally leading the dark regime in the hunt for Kovska. He planned to set up a perimeter around the Outpost to ensure no one got in or out. But he had to recon the area first. He'd already sent a squad into the city of caravans. Like a chess master he was planning two steps ahead, carefully setting his pieces in place. He was there in Belarus for two different reasons. One was to intercept and exterminate Kovska and the girl before they crossed the border. The other had much to do with an U.S. intelligence leak, detailing of four American spies trying to infiltrate Russia's border by way of Belarus. Slavic had orders to capture and torture the Americans to ascertain pertinent counter intelligence. If no capture was possible he had orders to exterminate them instead. Slavic was known throughout the intelligence community for his extremely disturbing but very effective torture tactics. He prided himself on knowing the limitations of the pains and pleasures of the human soul. He was a tall, thin, dark man. He towered over the men in his command. His shiny black hair was thin and translucent like the feathers of the raven. This pale death dealer had a presence more than worthy of his reputation. His men feared him not solely on appearance alone but also because of the black hearted pleasure he took in his work. Slavic was an evil man, who enjoyed the torturous demise of the weak. As the story goes only his victims had ever seen him smile. Unfortunately that was during the final moments just before he'd kill them.

Slavic's personnel file was sealed and classified by the KGB. But it was legend amongst his men how he tortured and killed both his parents when he was only 9 years old. The gruesome mutilated bodies were found in a lower chamber beneath the Slavic's home. Because of the heinous nature surrounding their deaths, no details were ever released. The bodies had been there at least 6 months before they discovered them. They say when the Russian Police completed their investigation; they used words like cannibalism and satanic rituals. Young Slavic was taken into custody and became a ward of the government. From there he was said to have been inducted into a special KGB recruitment program. And no one had seen or heard from him until some 23 years later. Today he is the pulse of the KGB. No one dared to interfere with his missions or his methods of completing them. They'd seen him do things that only the devil himself could have commissioned. And no one wanted to mess with that, not even President Aleksei.

CHAPTER 19

The Rescue (Searching for Yurly)

48 hours. remaining

Cin geared up and jumped into some tan desert khaki's and a black pullover. Bast tried not to notice her as she pulled the tight fitting body shirt over her head. In a fleeting glance she caught him staring at her. "Nice gear." he said. She looked back at him and smiled. With a new outlook on things she turned toward the small gypsy village and started walking. Mitch was quick at her heels.

As Cin neared the derelict colony, she could feel her shadowing counterpart moving behind her. "Mitch don't be screwing around stay crisp." "I gotcha little sis, just think of me as your own personal mirror image" he said gleefully. Bast was already setting his first Claymore charge when he added, "Watch your ass out there Cin" and she happily replied: "If I don't who will. It's really good to have you back in the game" she finished. Bast smiled, "Its good to be back." Tom joined the party line, "Ok this ain't the fuckin Waltons. Now that we're all reacquainted, let's keep it professional from here on out." All three acknowledged and moved into their places.

The Outpost was composed of transient outcasts from all over Europe and for this reason they were called *"the throw aways."* Even past the midnight hour the place seemed to buzz with activity. Cin slipped to the edge of town and moved in. Mitch followed slipping in and out of the camps unlit areas. The first thing that struck her about the caravan city was the smell. It smelled like shit. As she moved inside its limits, she noticed that most of the Outpost residents were preparing to turn in for the night. Only a handful of others could be found outside in small groups along the main street. Besides the curious stares here and there, they seemed mostly uninterested in Cin or her reason for being there. There were no sidewalks to speak of only loose gravel and sand. Cin was carefull to steer clear of the rotted wood panels in the road, they were used to cover the open sewer holes. She shivered with disgust as she imagined the fate of falling through one of them. Cin walked endlessly through the caravan sea, looking for the bar. After a while, she remembered thinking: "This might be like finding a needle in a hay stack." It was strange but every trailer in the dusty fiberglass city looked almost exactly like the one next to it. She was about half way through it before she noticed anything suspicious. Someone was moving around in the shadows up ahead. Mitch saw it too. "Watch your ass Cin you got company at 3 o'clock." "Got em," she whispered. She continued her casual stroll down the street toward the dark figures. Suddenly three men moved quietly from the shadows next to a small bonfire up ahead. As she continued her approach one of them slipped back into the shadows of the camp. He seemed to dissolve instantly into the darkness of the night. The two remaining men began to walk towards her with intent. Time seem to speed up as the distance between them was rapidly diminishing. Just a brief moment before making contact, she slowed everything down in her head. Like a time traveler she used the infinitesimal rip in times fiber to quietly neutralize them in the battlefield of her mind. Now she was ready. Mitch was close by and waited for her lead. Let them go, I got it," she whispered. "Ok copy that," he replied. He watched as one of the men lurked about in the shadows just beyond the approaching duo. Mitch dug in quietly and eased into sniper mode just in case. As she merged into assassin mode, the ground began to blur beneath her feet. The charging duo split off in an effort to confuse her but Cin continued straight on. The leading assailant remained focused on her, while the other moved to flank her from the right. Cin was striding so fast that she came up on her toes like a ballerina about to take flight. She was anticipating the moment of impact like a cliff diver's splash into the hard ocean surface. Mitch only watched and smiled.

Cin leaned into her run with both hands pulling her in rhythmic propulsion. She advanced too quick for them to react as she moved within striking range of the first attacker. It was an automatic reflex that slipped the Chinese star into the palm of her left hand; with deceitful grace and skill, the methodical assassin thrust the dragon's teeth deep into the shadows ahead. Within a continuum of the same momentum she was propelled into a spinning acrobatic leap, which exploded with a powerful kick. As she whirled through the air the kick found its mark with deadly accuracy landing across the throat of the first attacker. Cin felt the bones in his neck give as her foot seemed to all but sever his head from its body. The second attacker tried an evasive counter move to avoid her deadly onslaught but it was too late. She landed directly in his path. The man struck out at her in desperation but she parried around the punch like a weightless feather. As he fell off balance her blinding speed overtook him. She struck him across the trachea with such deadly force that it almost snapped his head off. Though the method of attack differed from the first the results were absolute and fatal: both necks broken with a single blow. She removed the ridge of her hand from his flimsy neck as he fell face first beside his accomplice. Mitch scanned but could not find the third attacker anywhere, so he moved in closer. He flanked in angles until he was close enough to see the man crouched against the corner of an abandoned trailer. He approached from the rear but the slumped figure made no movement. He reeled in behind him in silence and cupped his mouth while pulling him from behind into the night shadows. The man collapsed limply to the ground without resistance. Mitch flipped him over, to see Cin's blades stuck deep inside his throat. He smiled again and moved the body out of sight. Cin righted herself and scanned for other possible assailants but all was quiet, for now. She whispered to Mitch on the radio, "I got a cleanup on aisle one." Mitch chuckled to himself and answered, "I'm on it." Cin advanced deeper into the Outpost, while Mitch cleaned up behind her. No one else seemed pay her any mind as she slinked through the rest of the campsite. Once she saw it, there was no mistaking it. It was old, dirty and dilapidated. The Gypsy bar consisted of four double wide trailers connected together. The finishing touch was the green and blue neon light affixed to a dusty window pane at the front of the conversion. The blinking lights read: "The Fortune Teller." "I think I found the spot," she whispered sarcastically. "Yeah I see it." he answered. Cin slipped up to the aluminum screen door and eased in.

Bast was almost finished he had two more mines to set. He was smiling proudly at Cin's perfectly executed kills. To him this punctuated who the alpha team really was. "She got em all." He thought. "That's what I call one bad ass bit—," he corrected himself. He began to feel really bad about how he'd behaved toward the team. He had spent the better part of his career being the department's jack ass and now as he looked back, shame filled his heart. At the very least, it seemed he had grown up a little. This was a lot considering it all happened over the course of two days. Bast grabbed his gear and moved to the next location.

Tom was on his third communications attempt to General Weixel. "Mobile to base over. I repeat mobile to base, do you read me?" There was no response to the transmission. "Damit, whats going on?" he dared to ask. Tom was well informed in "The Office" protocol. And after an inability to locate any malfunctions with the communications equipment, he began to wonder. He knew every unsuccessful attempt to reach Weixel put them closer to an unthinkable reality. Tom tried to rationalize the situation with what if scenarios but in his heart he knew the truth.

Cin stepped into the dark, damp bar and at first glance could tell something wasn't right. The few lights that worked were dim, the rest were either blown or nonexistent. She could make out two maybe three patrons in the bar. But her perception picked up on an extra presence in the room. Someone else was lurking within the shadows but she was unable to get a visual. Cin continued to scan the make shift tavern. She eyed the woman behind the bar and thought, "That's got to be the fattest and nastiest bartender I've ever seen." She estimated the woman's weight somewhere between 650-700 lbs. The gargantuan woman sat behind a circular bar that looked as if it'd been built around her. The stale air reeked of mildew and musk, laced with uninhibited body odor. The rotting wood flooring felt soft and mushy as it creaked beneath her feet. She wondered how the bartender managed not to fall through it. Cin moved to the farthest table in back of the bar. Meanwhile Mitch slid into place beneath the converted trailers. He found a small gap in the decayed flooring and inserted the micro telescopic camera through the tiny opening. The camera was virtually undetectable with a lens about the size of a pin's head. Mitch focused and rotated the lens, until he was able to get a fix on Cin's position in the bar. He could only see her legs beneath a table towards the back of the bar. Then he spotted and counted the locals in the room. "Cin, I count four marks including fatso behind the bar copy?" Cin covered her mouth and pretended to cough, "Copy that but I think there's one more, not sure where though." Mitch did not reply, because the fifth person had just moved into the camera's path and sat down at the table above him. He attempted to reposition the camera's lens but it's view remained blocked by the strangers pant leg. Mitch began to reevaluate his position as he stared at the leg of the dirty old jeans. Residing beneath the soiled denim was a pair of shiny black military boots. Judging from the boot size, Mitch deducted his stranger was of the male species. He was for certain this was not Cin's contact person. He wanted to tell her he'd found the missing patron but suddenly something didn't add up. "Why is this guy wearing a pair of dirty old jeans over clean polished army boots?" The answer came as quickly as the question. He was KGB, just like the men that attacked Cin earlier. Mitch felt an unusual sensation in his stomach, it was apprehension. Something he'd been trained to ignore but his thoughts of Lisa had begun to affect his concentration and focus. He was slowly losing his edge. He started to worry if he'd ever make it back home to her. The emotional dilemma seemed to weaken his instincts. Feelings of desperation began to creep beneath his armor and corrode away the internal strengths he guarded for so many years. He knew he had to warn Cin of the trap she was walking into. But he dared not chance it while the man sat only a few feet above him. He tried to think of a way to contact her without giving away his position. He knew that if anything were to happen to him, she'd be all alone. So reluctantly he remained in stealth mode.

Cin held up an empty glass from the table and gestured to the fat barkeep. When the heavy duty woman ignored her, she got up and walked over to the bar. The bartender was entertaining three aparently very lonely men with her sexual prowess. "Yuhhck!" Cin thought as she briefed a visual of the four of them in some perverted sex act. First she stood there waiting to be acknowledged, then when the woman continued to ignore her she took it a step further. "Can I have a drink of something, please?" Suddenly the four-some stopped talking and the woman turned to face the voice that interrupted her. Cin almost gasped out loud as she finally saw the woman's face in full view. She was so surprised, she continued to stare without realizing her mouth was still open. The woman's face bordered with a prickly beard and a hearty mustache to match. Her teeth had passed yellow and were now entering shades of green, the rest were black and rotted. But the body odor was simply unbearable. The woman reeked of obscenity and promises of incurable diseases. "Wha ju wone?" she sneered. "Never mind, nothing thank you?" Cin replied. She never intended to drink anything, she just wanted a better look at the patrons in the bar. As the group resumed with the chatter Cin excused herself to the ladies room. Mitch tried to follow as best he could, but the pant leg continued to obstruct his view. He knew she was signaling the contact to meet her in the restroom away from the inquisitive patrons. As the restroom door closed behind her, a thick Russian accent began to pour into a radio transmitter above Mitch's head. He could hear the urgency in the words the man spoke. Within minutes Mitch heard voices and footsteps outside the bar. He eased away from the eye piece just in time to see several pairs of feet moving quietly about the trailer. And on their feet was the common denominator that connected them all together, "the shiny black boots." Mitch inched slowly along the crawl space beneath the trailer, until he could safely observe the men outside the bar. They were creating a tactical formation around the trailer. He noticed that they did not move like locals, they just dressed like them. He thought to himself, "Surely they can't be serious." It made him wonder how many dead gypsies lay naked in the desert. Suddenly the movement outside the bar stopped, as they positioned themselves and prepared the ambush on the converted bar. Mitch eased back into position and found the eyepiece again. He focused just in time to see the large stranger enter the ladies room and close the door behind him. "Shit! shit!, shit!" He whispered excitedly to himself. Mitch knew he had to do something fast. The best he could think of was, three quick key ups on the mic, to alert Cin of the imminent danger approaching.

As the large grisly man entered the restroom, the cool night air from an open window blew across his deeply scarred face. "Dumb American bitch that's the oldest trick in the book," he thought. He knew she hadn't left the room and would make her pay dearly for attempting such an obvious deception. Cin lay perched across the top of the third stall. She listened as he slowly moved from one stall to the next. The noise was almost deafening to her as he slammed back each door, ready to pounce. She heard heavy breathing and panting as the rotting floor creaked with every step he took. She knew her strike would have to be fast and accurate. So she closed her eyes and imagined the encounter within her mind. Once the mental warfare was complete, her face changed. Her pupils dilated to an almost black hue. The once pretty face seemed to melt away with the visage of a killing machine taking its place. The man reached behind his back and pulled 8" inches of cold steel from its case. Cin listened to the metal slither along the leather casing as it emerged from hiding. The knife's scarlet blade glared with the ambience of sunlight through a red Ruby kaleidoscope. The crimson glimmers danced with happy deception on the ceiling above Cin's head. Time slowed as he approached the final stall. Cin dropped catlike landing quietly on the floor. Using the momentum to tuck and roll, she moved beneath the partitioned wall to the adjoining stall behind him. She managed to accomplish the feat without a sound. Suddenly the burly man kicked the stall's door in. It was the last thing she remembered before arriving behind him. He whirled around in slashing fashion, as he came at her with the knife. To Cin he moved in slow motion. She prepared to counter as the large burnished blade slashed within inches of her face. As he advanced she moved out of range retreating like waves of a deadly tsunami. Then without forecast, she flowed back into him with bone crushing force. The man's awkward momentum threw him forward and off balance. With lightning speed Cin blocked the knife and grabbed his wrist with her closest defending hand. Then she used his own bodies fulcrum force continuum, to oblige the thrust of his blade deep inside him with a gut ripping twist. The man's mouth drew open to cry out but a violent twist of his neck from behind silenced him forever. Cin eased the bloody heap to the floor. She looked down at her clothes, she was a bloody mess. "I guess that's what you get when you hit a pressurized artery, a blood bath. "Fuck Cin you know better!" The ordeal left her puzzled. "What the fuck was going on?" She wondered. Cin was getting a premonition and it wasn't a good one. She reached down inside the man's jacket and pulled out a black leather wallet. As she begins to rifle through its contents: the answer revealed itself. "He's fucking KGB!" Just then his radio receiver began to beep. Cin quickly pondered what to do. "Mitch you there?" she whispered. "Yeah I was waiting to hear from you." "What's your status?" he asked. "Besides being covered in blood that's not mine, I'm fine, can't say the same for our Russian friend though. Speaking of which, someone's trying very hard to reach him." "Yeah I can hear the beeping in the background." "How does it look out there?" she asked. He paused a moment, "Not too good, at the moment. I've got four maybe five KGB Ops in a satellite formation of the bar. I can get three of them but the other two in the rear might see the muzzle flash from my rifle. I need you to take them out! Ok?" Cin didn't answer right away. Mitch tried again in a higher whisper, "Cin you copy? You think you can handle the two targets behind the bar?" Still there was no answer. Mitch began to worry as he keyed up for the third time. Suddenly Cin broke in, "Sorry I took so long to answer but I got your clearance for you, so serve em up!" Mitch smiled with relief and approbation, "You're a piece of work you know that?" he replied. "Yeah, you should see my psyche eval," "Yeah, I'm sure it's some good long reading." He finished the words and rolled into position. Each target was positioned less than three feet of the other. He knew it would be just a matter of minutes before the men realized what had happened. Mitch would have to act fast. He quickly readied the sniper's rifle and toggled the night scope's cover as he propped it into position. One of the men appeared to have a radio transceiver to his ear. Mitch fingered him as the first target. He set the crosshairs of the rifles scope in three sequenced shooting positions. He practiced the sequence slow and steady, until his movement was certain. On the last pass Mitch inhaled all the air around him. Then with narrowed eyes and a squint, he exhaled in one steady controlled breath and gently squeezed the trigger. As the firing pin strikes against the primer of each bullet, Mitch ejects the empty casings and quickly reloads another shell. With quick accuracy he launches two rounds through the frontal lobes of the first two targets. Then with the final squeeze of the trigger, the last projectile finds its fatal mark. Mitch touched the smoking barrel with his index finger and a smiled as he chanted, "Semper Fidelis Motherfuckers!"

Mitch and Cin made visual contact as he gave the all clear. Cin joined him at the rear of the bar, and without a word they sprinted off and faded into the shadows of the camp.

Tom and Bast were both monitoring, they heard everything. Bast knew the shit had hit the fan, he just didn't know how badly. Tom begin to brief him on his inability to contact Weixel. "You know what the ramification of radio silence implies don't you?" Bast bounced around the obvious answer. "No but I'm sure you're going to tell me." "It means we've been deactivated and left here to die." "I hate to say it Sarge but I told you so." "Yeahhh, in your own asinine way, you did." "Hey Sarge I think I need to get down there, looks like they're gonna need a hand up!" Bast exclaimed. "We'll both go, get in" ordered Tom. They both leaped into the van and descended off road down the rugged terrain as quickly as possible.

A chilling northerly wind howled briskly through the open camp fires within the outpost grounds. The haunting sounds set the tone for the events that were about to unfold. Slavic sat comfortably inside the mobile command tent and listened as his communications officer made several attempts to contact the men inside the outpost. "There is still no answer sir." Slavic was no slouch, he knew something had gone wrong. He rose to his feet with a deadly resolution. "Send down the hunter killers, and eradicate the whole fucking town and everyone in it!" He made the order to his third Officer. On his command, his 10 deadliest men prepped and moved into position. Within minutes, the small convoy had disappeared over the sandy hill. General Slavic turned to the 10 remaining soldiers and ordered them into position to intercept Kovska. The men disappeared from the roadway like ghost. All that remained was the large command tent sitting directly in the middle of the road.

CHAPTER 20

Fight or Flight

It was 0400 hrs. and more than three hours since they'd heard from Weixel. Cin and Mitch were trying to escape the clutches of the Outpost, while Tom and Bast ploughed over rocky terrain to meet them. Bast grew more apprehensive the closer he and Tom got to the town's edge. "Hey Tom, you think we'll make it out of here?" "I don't know but first we have to get Mitch and Cin out of that hell hole, then we'll worry about the rest." As the van bounced to a hard stop, they both exited and ran for cover behind a cluster of large boulders just south of town. Bast scanned the streets for activity while Tom made contact with Mitch. "Mobile to alpha shadow, over" Mitch's voice blasted through the ear piece as though he was running for his life. The sound of heavy breathing mixed with anxiety bled straight through his transmission. "Sha . . . dow . . . copy, we're mov . . . ing . . . south . . . bound to your loca . . . tion, over" "What is the status on alpha recon, over?" Mitch's second transmission was a little smoother. "I. have visual contact on recon who is also . . . advancing to your immediate." "Ok copy that, we'll be waiting here at the entrance, over." Mitch came back with extreme concern, "Sir we need to be ready for immediate evac, I think we have a kill squad on our trail, over" "That's clear we copy shadow." Bast reached in his equipment bag and pulled out a handheld detonation controller.

Tom looked at him and he replied: "Just in case Sarge." They both managed a nervous smile. "Just make sure they're clear before you start popping those firecrackers, ok?" "Yeah, I got it under control." Tom made several more desperate attempts to contact Weixel on the handheld but was greeted with white noise. He was becoming increasingly unsure what to do. What Tom was sure of was that his team had been purposely compromised. Even if they managed to escape to safety by some slim chance, they'd never survive back in the states. A bullet from a snipers rifle, right between the eyes would be their fate. Tom knew all too well how the CIA operated and this was a typical deactivation scenario. The Office gave them up to the K.G.B. but he just couldn't figure why. Now the Pentagon could simply declare them MIA, AWOL or whatever evil white lie they desired. Tom knew the pendulum swung in two directions when you worked for the Intelligence community and it was your ass if you got caught on the wrong side of it. But he and his team were about to rewrite the rule book. Tom took a big gulp as he swallowed the fear that pooled in his throat. Now he was ready to lead and bring his team out with a preference . . . . alive.

Mitch and Cin could see the town's exit. He was struggling to keep pace with her, as something was driving her like a woman possessed. Ever since she'd left the bar she never slowed down or looked back. She was moving with the speed and grace of a Gazelle through the shadows behind the main street. Mitch tried several times to reach her through the earpiece but she never responded. Cin could see someone trailing in her peripheral. The assailant began to close the gap by flanking her from the right. Mitch saw him too but not soon enough. The assassin was already setting up to strike when Cin managed a quick glimpse of his shadow training it's aim. He was about 100 yards out, which was too far for her to counter accurately with her knives. This time she was going to have to depend on ole' Mitch. Mitch tried as best he could to advance ahead of the situation. He knew if he didn't act quickly she would surely be killed. His M40 rifle was made for times like these. "Let's rock n roll you mutha" he whispered stopping and posting up about 10 yards behind her. There wasn't enough time to calculate wind velocity or any other factors. He needed to drop, aim, shoot and hit his target in less than a second.

Cin's striding movement was blocking the shot between Mitch and the shooter. He wasn't sure if her communications gear was working or not. But he needed her to drop, so he could take the shot. Mitch's voice scrambled urgently, across the frequency. "Cin, he's posting you up!!" "There's no time, I need you to drop now! Do you copy?" Cin made no such acknowledgement, she continued sprinting through the dusty alley way. Mitch crouched behind an old industrial steel drum lain on its side. He counted Cin's clock movement with Swiss accuracy. He was keeping time in his head," 4 o'clock, 3 o'clock . . . ."2 o'clock!" Suddenly the imaginary clock stopped and time stood still. Mitch remembered seeing the gunman for a split of a second before seeing a flashing fireball move silently from the shadows and Cin's body hit the ground like a fallen deer. "Oh shit!" "Cin's down and she's been hit!" shouted Mitch. Bast was up and running before Tom could turn and stop him. He was moving so fast, Tom lost sight of him in just a matter of seconds. Mitch steadied himself behind cover as Cin's body laid lifelessly in the moon lit alley. He knew if he moved to help her, he was sure to get sniped. He had somehow lost the gunman's position, during the ordeal. He tried to lock onto the original site with his scope and scanned the area but there was no one there. He squinted again and pressed tightly against the eyepiece. He wanted the gunman so badly he began to imagine the shooter into existence. It seemed so real to him that he almost pulled the trigger and fired into the empty darkness. He opened and closed his weary eyes several times before finally realizing it was only his imagination. Mitch reached up and flipped a small thumb bolt on the side of his scope that read: "Night Glow". In a click the darkness of night became the middle of day as the alleyway lit up with vibrant green resolve.

Tom knew he was rapidly losing control of the situation; he had one down, one pinned in and another moving blindly into the kill zone. As Tom prepared to lead his team out of harm's way, he took a quick moment to calm his fears. He remembered an old saying from General Ulysses Grant: "The only way to whip an army, is to go out and fight it." Tom grabbed the radio firmly in his hand and pressed the transmit button. The words cut through the silence like an executioner's blade, "Neutralize the threat." He repeated the words again and wondered if maybe it was too late to do any good. The code was a tactical offensive designed to be used like a surgeon's knife. When implemented correctly it allowed the team to neutralize a threat with minimum casualties to innocent bystanders. Tom did not use the Operation Gravedigger objective because it was designed for worst case scenarios. If the Gravedigger order had been given the team would kill everyone including women and children. He saw no need to murder a bunch of innocent town's people as long as they remained just that.

Bast heard the transmission and unshouldered his AK47 as he ran. Not knowing Cin's exact location he ran blindly straight up the main street. He was raging like a crazy man as he charged up the empty road. Suddenly without warning two men flanked out of the shadows to intercept him. Without slowing Bast transitioned into a crouching run while unholstering the two Berettas strapped at his sides. He plowed ahead like an angry bull with guns blazing. As he zigzagged up the dirt road the .45's recoiled with an ear splitting blast. Both guns sent hot rounds of lead spiraling to their targets. It was an award winning moment in synchronized shooting as both men timbered to earth with one crashing thud. Bast approached the dead men with caution. One lay sprawled upon his back with what remained of his face, the other laid face down in a stream of his own blood. The gushing life force escaped from a large hole in the side of his neck. "Not neat but effective," Bast thought. He stopped in the middle of the street to holster the hand guns and in the same sequence of motion locked and loaded the AK47. He dug in and bunkered beneath one of the trailers at the town's edge.

The noise drew the attention of the arriving death squad at the north end of town. They were cloaked in red and black camouflage with matching berets. The squad decended upon the outpost like angels of death, killing and destroying everything in their path. Without hesitation they unleashed their savagery upon the unsuspecting town's people. For those who encountered the death dealers with their pleas of mercy, certain death executed with swift rage was their leniency. Others hid inside their trailers behind locked doors, hoping their silence would save them. But the silence was soon broken as the sounds of death begin to echo throughout the camper city. The Death squad set fires and burned each trailer as they migrated from one end of town toward the other. They split into two cells, taking up flanking formations as they began to move south toward the team's location. As the red brigade basked in the glorious blaze that filled the empty blackness of the sky, several propane tanks beneath the raging bar reached dangerous temperature levels inside the searing flames. First there was the sound of the blast, followed by the huge fireball that rocked the town as it billowed across the sky. The explosion shook the sniper out of hiding. Mitch watched as the shooter fell from a tree and landed on his stomach atop the sandy terrain. He was trying to reach a cluster of bushes about five yards ahead. Mitch's eyes grew tight as he trained down on the human snake with tunnel vision. "Slither like the fucking low life you are," he thought. As the side of the man's head entered the cross hairs of Mitch's scope, a small red dot played upon the shooter's face. Mitch slid his index finger inside the trigger guard and allowed it to rest lightly against the trigger. The laser's light offered the perfect momentary distraction as it flashed crossways of the sniper's peripheral. Mitch inhaled as the shadowed figure turned to locate the lights origin. For the shooter it was the moment all snipers fear, when they become . . . the target. Mitch exhaled and gently pulled the trigger until the rifle coiled and struck out like an angry cobra. He watched as the projectile bored through the shooter's forehead, blasting brain matter out of the back of his skull. Without hesitation Mitch got up and ran over to where Cin's body lay. He paused a moment and knelt down to turn her over. After several explosions started ripping through the town, Bast opted to roll behind the vacant trailer. He ended up in the open alleyway behind the outpost. That's where he found Mitch kneeling over Cin. The shock sent him into an immediate panic. "Noooo!" "Please God no!" He shouted as he slowly walked over to Mitch. He laid his hand upon Mitch's shoulder for comfort. Mitch turned away to hide the tears in his eyes. Bast watched him slowly remove his jacket and placed it gently over Cin's face. Suddenly! Cin sprung up tossing the jacket to the ground as she grabbed her chest and shouted: "Oh Shit does that hurt.!!" Mitch and Bast both fell to their butts. Cin turned to them with a painful grin and said, "You guys look like you've seen a ghost," Mitch formed his mouth to speak,

"But, but . . . ." "Flexarmor shit heads, I was wearing flexarmor," she explained. Mitch was still rattled and disoriented by the situation, "But I checked your pulse and everything." "Yeah I know, I had to slow my heart rate waaay down so I could control my pulse. I didn't want that sneaky bastard trying to put a bullet into my cranium, so I played dead." Bast just sat there looking at Cin with total admiration. She rose shakily to her feet and walked over to extend her hand to him. "Come on big boy, don't worry I'm alright." Bast reached up to grab her hand and pulled himself right into her arms. It was the first time the two of them had ever embraced. Mitch was both relieved and a little confused by the public display of . . .

"What the fuck is this?" He quizzed. It was a pretty weird moment seeing the two of them hugged up. "Hey guys that's enough of that, we gotta go!" He said, with annoying urgency. More explosions and fires erupted in their direction. There was no doubt, they were definetly getting closer. With the death squad at their heels the three of them begin to sprint back to Tom's location. They briefed each other on the run. "Did you guys ever find our contact, agent Yurly?" Bast asked. "No contact, no intel, just one big ambush," Mitch replied. "Yeah, well that's only half of it." Bast added. "The Office has severed all contact with us. So that's why we have KGB up our asses right now. All these attacks on us were part of a set up, orchestrated by the Pentagon." "Amazing!" Cin said with a tone of disbelief. "Yeah, but the bigger question is what really happened over here?" Mitch added. "Do you guys think that thing really does exist?" Bast asked. "I don't know but that Russian kill squad certainly does. We are in the middle of a very large pile of shit!" Mitch finished as he jogged pass Tom. Tom moved up to cover them as they slipped beyond the town's threshold. "I knew it!" Bast shouted. "That shooter that hit you wasn't just regular KGB, he had to be one of their best to put you down." "Yeah well please don't remind me, its not a highlight I want to treasure." She grabbed her chest to make her point. Tom was pleased to see everyone make it back alive and in one piece. He watched as several columns of thick black smoke continued rising into the sky. These tactics were indicative of Russia's renown death squads. Hunter Killers they were called whose primary objective was total eradication. Tom wondered how many people had they killed and how many were innocent women and children? He had to face the ultimatum that lay at his feet: to fight or run.

The gypsie's, were nomads a disposable tribe of people. No one would miss them or cry for their loss. No one even knew they existed out here in the nether regions of no man's land. What possible chance did the team have of surviving, without back up and limited resources? The thoughts made Tom teeter off balance for a sec.

Mitch was scanning the raging camp site through his binoculars when he saw the five by five formation moving south in their direction. The fire and smoke created an eerie backdrop for the disciples of death as they approached the town's exit. Tom's thoughts betrayed him as his decision manifested itself upon his face. Cin interrupted, "I know that look, that mean snarl you get on your mug when you're really angry about something." "Bast told us about Weixel feeding us to the wolves." Tom paused before responding, "Actually it's much bigger than Weixel. He's just one of many puppets being controlled by the puppet master. Bast chimed in: "The Jeopardy question of the day worth $100 is: who is the puppet master?" The team dug in as they prepared to take on the death squad.

CHAPTER 21

Operation Ghost Blade

Weixel arrived on the U.S. Tarawa on schedule. As he boarded, Commander Henning's was there wearing the biggest pride devouring smile he'd ever seen. "*Classified* huh, guess your little mission just wasn't as important as you thought it was. You *Office* boys kill me. Face it son you're nothing more than a bunch of glorified errand boys. Real missions are fought on the battle field." The commander laughed at Weixel's obvious embarrassment and walked off.

Weixel arrived back in the states some 22 hours later. He completed the trip by helicopter where he was flown to *The Office* in Langley Virginia. There he would meet with General Eiseman at 10:00 hrs for debriefing. Weixel knew Eiseman hated his guts but that never stop him from trying to please him. He understood eventhough he had friends in high places, the General was the key to his acceptance in the intelligence world. He also understood that because of his father he was here and not stranded back in Belarus with his team.

He arrived in front of a plain two story brown stone office structure. He entered the building and successfully navigated through a maze of security check points. He finally arrived at Eiseman's office with two minutes to spare. "Morning General." "Weixel, how are you?" "Fine sir, thanks for asking" "Weixel I'm happy to see that you made the right decision. You don't know how badly we need you on this mission. Hell you were my first choice, well actually more like my only choice." The General's demeanor toward him was a bit uncomfortable to say the least. It seemed just hours ago he was being threatened with bodily harm and now he was being treated like nothing had ever happened. He had grown use to a certain level of hostility, not this nice to see you crap. What's he up to? Weixel wondered. "I guess you're probably wondering why I'm treating you so nicely?" Eiseman asked. "Not really, I hadn't given it a thought. "Well you know Weixel, I come from an era where you sacrificed all for your country, not like today where the country is being overrun by bleeding heart liberals from some hug a tree organization." Eiseman was rambling and Weixel knew it, but why? "You ever heard of friendly fire Weixel?" He affirmed with a nod. Eiseman continued: "It was part of the cost you paid when you went to war, a sort of side effect of using the big war machine. But we didn't stop the war because we accidentally killed a few of our own men, instead we buried them with honor and their memories lived on as such. What I'm getting at is you showed true leadership for the first time in your career, probably your life, by leaving the team behind. Now they'll be remembered for serving their country with honors, hell we'll even give them a medal or two and make up some special cause that they died for. We need you on this mission and the sacrifices you've made so far, let's the upper brass know you can be trusted to do the right thing. But don't worry Weixel we'll tell you what the right thing is. Welcome to the club son." "Thank you sir." "Weixel you're going to be heading up Operation Ghost Blade." His eyes sparkled at the possibilities behind the name, at last an actual mission he thought. Eiseman walked over to his desk and opened the humidor and pulled out two cigars. The smell hit Weixel like a fresh cake baking in the oven. He thought he had gone to heaven. Here he sat talking with one of the countries most powerful men next to the president. He had been accepted into the club and was now an official member of "The Office." The General walked over and handed Weixel a cigar without a label. Weixel examined the cigar for a moment and then looked back to the General. Eiseman's smile confirmed what he was thinking. "Sir, are these what I think they are?" "That depends on what you think they are." "Well the aroma is unmistakable, pair that with no label, possibly handpicked, hand wrapped and very much illegal. General if you don't mind, how did you come by these?" Without smiling the General looked him in the eyes and said. "I could tell you son but then I'd have to kill you, no pun intended. But so you don't lose any sleep, let's just say Castro owed me one." *Eiseman drifted in the moment and imagined, putting a gun to Weixel's head and pulling the trigger.* He was catching a lot of flack from Washington over sending him on the Belarus mission. He had wanted a clean break from Weixel but because of his father, Eiseman was pressured against his will to satisfy the gods of politics once again. This was the part of his job that he hated but on the flip side was everything else. They'd made him into the world's most powerful watchdog. Hiding all of its dirty little secrets and cleaning up the nasty messes it left behind. And now there was Weixel, another mess to clean up. The General had it all worked out, if Washington wants him in charge of something, then that's exactly what they'll get." He finished his thoughts and mentally returned to the room. Weixel never missed him, instead he stood there, still rolling the cigar beneath his nose. "They both lit up and moaned at how beautiful the aroma was and Eiseman continued about the new mission. "You'll be meeting strike team Cyclops at Lodge number two." "Ok, but why Cyclops? Seems like overkill to me sir." "I'm getting to that, why don't you sit down." They both sat on the burgundy refined leather sofa in the office den. "Douglas, we have our selves a serious situation." No one had ever called him by his first name, which made him even more leery. It seemed the General was getting on a very personal level rather quickly. "You know that mission you headed up last year with the two Russian defectors has turned up some valuble information. We discovered a link between them and the mysterious crate we found back in Customs. You're gonna love this: these two commi's we helped defect to the states are actually Russian scientist and part of the research and development team for the Fury project. So at first glance it seemed that we had hit the proverbial jack pot, until . . . ." "Until what sir?" Weixel could feel Eiseman leading him some place, he only wished he'd hurry and get there. "They have refused to aid in deciphering the microfilm and time is running out.

Something big is about to take place and we don't have time to put a bunch of bungling code breakers on this. We need to know whats on that microfilm and we need it by yesterday. We have to get their cooperation to move forward on this thing. That's where you come in: Cyclops lacks the diplomacy to finesse these guys into giving us the goods. They don't trust anyone whom they think is connected to this. That's why you're going in as a political prisoner, so that you can win their trust and in the process find out what they know. Weixel's face went numb as he tried to process the Generals plan in his own feeble little mind. It was a far cry from what he expected but something about the mission excited him. It would be an undercover mission, covert, dangerous, mysterious and important. For the first time they really needed him. He forgot all about his fathers influence, it was he and he alone that they needed and daddy couldn't help with this. "Hmmm, General I do have a few concerns." Eiseman raised his brows as if to imply surprise at the inquest. He had no idea if he had sold him or not. Weixel could easily call daddy and bail out but he hoped just maybe not this time. "Why me? You could've gotten anybody to do this. What's really happening here, General?" "Its your one shot son, to become, to evolve, to prove yourself. You want into this club, you have to pay your dues and Weixel, you owe a lot. And just think after this you will never need to call daddy again." "Whom else would know that I'm undercover?" "Just: myself and the Cyclops team. You'll be in full command running the operation behind the scenes. Just bear in mind they'll have to treat you as a prisoner to make it real and believable." Now he was really intrigued. "So General what do I do if I want out, is there a code word?" Eiseman thought for a moment before he answered: "Yes, just simply say: "Game over" and that will end everything." Weixel felt a calming wave of relief flow over him as Eiseman continued to assure him about the mission. Weixel stood to shake hands but found Eiseman had moved to the otherside of the room. For a fleeting moment Weixel thought he felt something emit from the General. It was a quick glimpsing trace of hatred that revealed how much Eiseman truly detested and despised him. Then suddenly it faded back into hiding. "Weixel its time to go, your plane is waiting." Weixel managed an awkward smile before turning and leaving the room. It was amazing how transparent the trap was, yet

Weixel took the bait anyway. It just proved to the General how badly Weixel wanted power and acceptance. But the General would dive upon a grenade before he would allow him to have it.

After doing a routine check around the perimeter of the lodge, Wolfe retreated to a hidden underground bunker about 200 yds off the black top. He stopped in front of a small electronic scanner, stepped up to the camera's lens and waited. *"Retina scan complete, you may enter now"* a computer voice said. A loud thud, followed by a series mechanical clicks sounded before the thick steel hydraulic door slowly opened. He disappeared into the metal compound and the vault closed behind him. Once inside he found himself dismayed and somewhat disilliusioned over his last phone conversation with the General. Wolfe hated Washington politics and he hated politicians even more. It was hard for him to believe the General could trade a team of proficient operatives for one worthless asshole. He knew the General wanted nothing more than to see Weixel disappear, but the terms he was willing to accept left Wolfe wondering, if maybe he and his team could be next. The General it seemed had changed right before his eyes. He wasn't the Eiseman of old that'd taught him everything about the art of guerilla warfare, combat survival and every deadly killing technique he knew. Washington had changed him, he'd become: inaccessible, agenda motivated, evasive, persuasive, deceitful and treacherous. He was now by definition a ... *politician*.

The exchange of words clung to him like static electricity.

"Wolfe imagine the satisfaction you'll get knowing Weixel's going to personally give you the very order to end his life" said Eiseman delightfully. "You know I don't like games Sir." "Yeah I know, just humor me this one time, besides I think you'll like this one." "Ok so what's the code?" "Game over" Eiseman almost laughed himself to tears as the words left his mouth. "What if he doesn't say this code?" "Don't worry he'll say it, just be your usual charming self when he arrives. His flight should be there in a couple of hours. Remember: we'll be watching this one closely; so for the stiff necks back in Washington make sure there are no loose ends." "And the two Russians?" "I think the three of them would fit nicely in the same hole, just be sure to dig it extra deep. Wolfe managed a few more words before a strange horrible static cut his connection to the General.

CHAPTER 22

"Interference"

First there was loud static in the phone lines and then suddenly there was no sound or signal at all. The phenomena first started over Russia before spiraling out across the globe. First to go was the communications for homes and businesses with common standardized equipment. Then as those with more sophisticated technology began to fail the world began to take notice. Even backup systems at the highest levels of government were silenced. The Pentagon had been monitoring the the growing communications interference since the first reports of the Chernobyl accident approx. 72 hours ago. It seemed that an unidentifiable energy source was causing interference and had begun to shut out all the satellite signals the world over. One by one the nations of the world suddenly went silent. All cellular and microwave technology was dead in the air. Even land lines filled with a strange horrible static. Signals to and from the earth's orbiting devices were blocked and failed to reach the transponders, creating panic and finger pointing amongst world leaders. U.S. President Strandford remained submerged in closed door session with the Department Of Defense. While the Pentagon and top airline officials scurried into crisis mode, the air traffic of landing planes became deadlocked, forcing pilots to land without the assistance of the control tower. The result was hundreds of terrible air collisions. The death toll would reach well over 375 thousand before every plane was safely on the ground. Effective from that moment all air traffic would be suspended indefinitely. Even radar tracking devices went on the blink, as the entire communications grid of the modern world was suddenly severed, just like that. Governments scrambled into defensive postures around the world, in the probability of a nuclear strike, *from any potential enemy, any place in the world, at anytime*. Every nation was suddenly as vulnerable as the other. The idea of not knowing what was coming or when or where it was coming from, started the world on a path to a state of panic and chaotic anarchy.

CHAPTER 23

Strike Team (Cyclops)

5 hrs. before the silence

It was just hours before the communications nightmare would hit crippling the world. Meanwhile Weixel was preparing to relax as he strapped into the first class high back soft leather seat. He was right at home aboard the twin engine six passenger luxury jet, another gift from the D.E.A.'s war on drugs campaign he imagined. This was first class with all the perks and he felt like he deserved it. The manifest consisted of two pilots, one flight attendant and Weixel. "It doesn't get any better than this," he thought. "How long is the flight?" "About 4 1/2 hours," replied the gorgeous blonde attendant. "Just relax and we'll take good care of you" she said with a plastic smile. "I bet you will." He said, finding her to be quite attractive. He even caught himself flirting with the prospect before grounding himself. "Got to stay focused, plenty of time for that later" he thought. She finished her preflight preparations, then turned and strutted back toward the cockpit. He took a good hard look at her before she disappeared behind a curtain at the front of the plane. "Back to business." He whispered. Reaching down into a black attaché case he pulled out the strike teams personnel files. They were a self contained unit, used like a knife to cut out cancerous drug lords and corrupt communist party leaders etc. The only thing Weixel knew about Cyclops was they were an elite covert strike team. The privilege of knowing their actual identities rested solely with General Eiseman and the President. Not even Weixel had clearance beyond their field names. He thumbed through the documents as he methodically studied their profiles. There was the black female operative: Savanna, an Asian male named Qiox, a white male named Steele and the team's leader was an Indian male called Wolfe. Weixel wondered if anyone had ever noticed that the Cyclops unit was so racially diverse. There was no detailed history on the team, just a list of their weapons, specialties, and training. Weixel thought to himself: "These folks are like ghost," He'd heard things about them during some cigar talk. *Some called them ruthless mercenaries for Satan: said that one time in Columbia they struck a drug compound and destroyed more than 200 Cartel soldiers and escaped unscaved. They say the team was out numbered 50 to 1. All the same, the Colombians never had a chance.* Suddenly Weixel's thoughts betrayed him, as the faces of his old team played like a slide show in his head. To say he was saddened by the thoughts would have been stretching it. It was more of a shameful guilt that he felt. He shook it off and leaned his head against the plane's port window. As he closed his eyes his mind wandered off again, playing the *what if* game. He tried to justify the reasons for his actions but in conclusion, four people would die because of his failure to act. And now he would have to live with that forever. Finally the culpable thoughts gave way to fatigue as Weixel closed his eyes and was fast asleep in minutes.

Weixel awakened when he felt the bump of the wheels as they bounced onto the tarmac. "What a rough landing" he thought, lazily wiping away the dried saliva that had hardened around his mouth. Feeling awkward and off balance, he quickly tried to gain his composure, as the plane taxied over where two men in black suits waited. Weixel was all too anxious to see who was meeting him. He stumbled forward as the plane stopped abruptly. The attendant unlatched and swung the hydraulic portal open, Weixel thanked her and exited down the mobile stair ramp. Two men dressed in black suits, met him on the ground. "General Weixel?" "Yes" "I'm agent Brown and this is my partner agent Baker, you were lucky to have landed in one piece." "Why do you say that?" Weixel asked. Baker looked at Brown and said: "He doesn't know does he?" "Know what?" Weixel plexed. "We'll brief you on the way. We're here to take you to the edge." Brown finished. "The edge? Weixel parroted. "Yes sir that's the nick name that every body sort of calls the lodge out here." "Why is that?" Neither man answered as they moved toward a black vehicle. The three of them got into a black Chevy Tahoe with tinted windows and sped off. The question was still hanging, when agent Baker shifted in the passenger seat to clarify the statement. "It's kinda hard to explain but it's because the Ops team stationed out there are the most extreme bastards you ever want to meet, sir." "Basically they live on the edge, you'll understand once you meet them, sir." *He loved hearing them call him sir, it made him feel respected.* "Fair enough, I can't wait." The Tahoe traveled for miles on the deserted two lane stretch of black top. The isolated road looked unused and newly paved. It was the smoothest dam road he'd ever remembered being on. The suits didn't talk much after the airport, and Weixel was getting anxious again. "They must keep this black top pretty well maintained from the looks of it" Weixel said. "No sir, these roads have been the same since they built the lodge out there about six years ago" the driver replied. "Then how do they stay in such good condition?" Baker and Brown looked at each and smiled. Baker answered him, "Well that's simple, no one ever comes out here. At least not by car." He continued, "You're the first transport we've ever driven out to the lodge. Most people stay clear of this place and those that do come out here, come by airlift." "So why wasn't I airlifted from the airstrip?" "That's what we were trying to tell you when you landed, there's a communications blackout. Orders came from up top just before all the lines went completely dead: no more planes or airlifts anywhere until further notice. "No one informed me of this." "Was no time to sir, lines went silent just before you landed. The last communication we received was something about an atmospheric disturbance causing problems with the radar tracking equipment." Baker answered. "Yeah all communications throughout the world has been interrupted by some kind of super magnetic energy field or something." Brown added. Weixel's thought's drifted back to the team he'd left behind. He was beginning to feel cutoff from the world, much in the way he figured they must've felt. He quickly interrupted the sympathy train and jumped off. "This mission is getting crazier by the second," he mumbled. "What's that sir? Baker asked. "Oh nothing, I was just thinking out loud; so how much further is it?" It was Browns turn in the tag team question and answer session. "Can't tell you that sir." "Why the hell not?" he said with a demanding tone. "Don't know, we've never been there before. All we know is, we're supposed to take you to the fork in the road and leave you there." "What fuckin fork in the road?" He asked angrily. "That one up ahead, sir," Brown said. He slowed to a stop at a "Y" shape junction in the road." Weixel leaned forward between the driver and passenger to see the proverbial split in the road. "Sir this is it, this is the edge" said Baker. "So what the hell am I supposed to do now?" "No disrespect intended sir but you're supposed to get out here." Brown replied. Weixel leaned back, somewhat dismayed about the situation. Suddenly the two suits had nothing more to say as they sat quietly facing ahead. Weixel took a deep breath and exhaled before exiting the cool comfort of the Tahoes leather backseat. The wide bodied SUV wasted no time skirting to the edge of the pavement and U turning back down the shimmering stretch of asphalt. Weixel watched as the suns reflections danced across the black tar strip. Heat waves crested above the isolated horizon creating the illusion that the Tahoe was sailing on a black river of tar. The glimmering reflection of metal went farther and farther, getting smaller and smaller before reaching the edge and disappearing. "How ironic" Weixel thought.

Standing alone in the middle of the junction, he suddenly realized how extremely hot it was. A look in all directions gave him a panoramic view of miles of wild and undeveloped grassland. Aside from several colonies of Yucca Trees here and there, the scenery appeared harsh and abandoned. It was definitely not club med. Weixel searched but was unable to find any sort of building or installation across the deserted terrain.

The hot relentless sun continued to beam down on him as the temperature quickly rose well above 95 F. Bewildered and unsure of things, he was about to catch the next train of paranoid thoughts, when he felt the itching sting of hot metal pressed against the back of his head. The contact pressure was firm enough that he knew not to move. Slowly he elevated both hands above his head, suddenly less than 20 ft. away a cluster of underbrush began to move toward him. Once the moving bush got within half his distance, it stopped and like magic a short Asian male appeared from within the shrubbery and trained a red beam of light on Weixel's forehead. Suddenly a man's voice came from behind him. "I'm going to ask you one question and you had better give me the correct answer. Nod if you understand?" Weixel affirmed with his head. "Who are you?" He answered slow and steady: "I'm General Weixel, *"The Office"* sent me." He felt the obtrusion relax against his cranium and the camouflaged man before him lowered his weapon to a less than ready position. That's when a large hulking Indian about 6'2 and approximately 220 lbs, stepped from behind him. "You made it; I wasn't sure you would with the communications blackout" Wolfe signaled a stand down order with his hand. "I'm The Wolfe but you can call me Wolfe for short," he said smiling. "The gentleman at your *12* is Qiox, he's our grounds keeper so to speak." Weixel greeted the small man with a slow wave but was greeted back with an unwavering stare through camouflage face paint. "Never mind him he doesn't speak much." "I can't really tell what he looks like through all the face paint." "Don't let it bother you; no one outside the Cyclops unit has ever seen his natural face." Weixel opened his mouth to speak again but he remembered what agents Baker and Brown had told him about the team. He decided to move on. "Where's the rest of the team?" "They're around." Wolfe pulled a laser pen from his pocket and pointed to a tree about 40 yards out. "You see that tree over there?" "Yeah." Wolfe handed him a pair of binoculars. "look through these and pick a spot on the tree." Weixel put the noc's to his eye and trailed along the bark of the tree. "Ok I got it" Wolfe gave Weixel the laser light and said: "Now flash the red beam on your target and lock it in." He did and almost simultaneously a .50 cal projectile bored a large smoking hole where the laser's light once laid. Wolfe turned to Weixel, "Meet Savanna. Now if you'll turn your attention to the propane canister at the foot of the neighboring tree." Weixel scanned over and down to an old rusted propane canister propped against the trunk of the tree. Weixel tried to make out the words on the canister and begins twisting the focus knob until the words: *"Death is welcome here"* appeared. Weixel saw a blue laser light pinpoint the word death and in an instant another .50 cal round pierced its center. The canister was propelled into the air as the word was replaced with a smoking gape of a hole. "Oh and that's Steele." Weixel was pumped and excited again, "Ok, I look forward to meeting them all during the debriefing." Wolfe's attitude suddenly changed like a blustering coldfront moving across a hot summer's sky. "That's never going to happen!" he said with supreme authority. "Why the hell not!' Weixel flexed. "Because I just fuckin said so!" Wolfe sneered. Must be part of the skit, thought Weixel, but he didn't see the need to act when no one else was present. Wolfe surely you got General Eiseman's orders on this, before the communications glitch didn't you?" "I sure did." Weixel sighed with relief "Well then, let's stop the break in the new guy hazing and get down to business." "I agree." "Good, I'll take it from here, call everyone in for a debriefing at the lodge; by the way where in the hell is the lodge?" Wolfe simply smiled at him. "So you are every bit as much the fuckin weasel they said you were. I just had to find out for myself, and now I know." Weixel's sunburned face lit up like a bomb had imploded inside his head. "I don't know what they teach you boys down here but there is such a thing as insubordination. In case you didn't know, failure to follow your superior's directives will get you a bonafide court marshal!" he finished. Wolfe spoke only with his eyes and in them, Weixel met his fate. Weixel continued his out of control ranting. "Now I'm willing to let you slide for leaving me in this gotdam hot sun all day, while you play your little mind games! But this is where I draw the fuckin line!" Weixel failed to notice that Quiox had faded back into the landscape and now only he and Wolfe stood on top of the scorching tar pit. Temperatures soared now above 109 F. in the shade. Wolfe finally decided to let him off the hook. "Weixel don't you think it's ironic, that you would find yourself here right now in the very same situation that you left your team in? He was too baffled by the words to see the connection. You've been setup you fuckin snake and whats worst, your head was so far up Eiseman's ass you didn't even see it coming. Now let me see if I can paint you a clearer picture. If you're a snake, then I'm a mongoose and do you know what a mongoose does to a snake? Suddenly Weixel's thoughts of grandeur were replaced by a more surreal reality. "But, what about the General's plan to get the Russians to talk? We used those Russians as the cheese in a very elaborate trap for a very large rat. Man you took the bait and swallowed it whole; besides haven't you ever heard dead men tell no tales? Tell me Weasel, what kind of man would leave his men for dead just to save his own neck? A pain in his stomach made his bowels shift and a sudden urge to visit the latrine screamed at him. Wolfe's words had exploded through him, shattering the glass menagerie of a very selfish and status ambitious man. "The difference between you and me Weixel, is when I say: *Semper Fi,* I mean it with my heart and soul and whatever fate becomes my men, becomes me. If they die, I will die beside them, no matter what the mission. So I guess your Washington connections got you out of Belarus but it seems *The Office* gave you a death sentence anyway." "Ok, that's it, I'm done taken this shit from you. I want out ... Game over!" shouted Weixel. "Yeah muthafucka . . . game over." He leaned into Weixel, placed the 45. upon his temple and pumped four rounds into his cranium before he could blink. Weixel fell like a detonated building with half his face splattered across the roadway. *"So much for loose ends. See you in hell muthafucka."*

CHAPTER 24

Slavic's Time

Kovska continued his journey south, toward the northern border of Belarus. Reaching the border would put him only a few miles from the outpost. Though, Hellena's alpha rhythms remained inactive t'was not the case with her spirit; which was actively touring the mind of a madman. She was getting to know things about him, about her and about the Fury.

Just as the hands on his Russian divers watch continued to advance with each tick, Kovska's health continued to rapidly falter. He found himself swerving and swaying the van back and forth across the winding road. With his vision blurred and distorted, he came upon a large command tent stretched across the middle of the roadway. After several doubtful blinks he still could not remove the mirage from his path. Suddenly he heard the sound of a single gunshot, followed by a barrage of gunfire. For a moment, it sounded to him as if the van had entered a meteor shower. Then time seemed to slow down as he watched the bullets penetrate and whizz about the van. Hot lead and shattered glass covered the floor. Kovska dived desperately from the driver's seat, leaving the van to plunder aimlessly down the road. "Stop shooting you fools, before you awaken her guardian!' Kovska shouted. He was attempting to reach Hellena when several bullets ripped through the van's rear tires causing it to flip and rollover. Kovska was thrown against the vans roof so hard it almost knocked him unconscious. Hellena was unscaved as her gurney seemed mysteriously held in place. Kovska watched in disbelief as an invisible shield seem to surround the gurney. The van eventually came to rest in an offroad thicket. Slavic stood in the entryway of the tent with bloodthirsty anticipation. "Welcome home comrade Kovska, I've been waiting for you." Slavic's eyes danced with approval as his death brigade mounted the wreckage. The men peeled back the metal from the wrecked van like a can opener. As the battered box revealed its contents a strange look befell them. "There's no one here!" they shouted. "Impossible, search the area, they can't have gotten far!" Slavic demanded. When you find them, do with the girl as you like but bring comrade Kovska back to me alive!" The men disappeared into the thicket of surrounding woods. Slavic accessed the situation with extreme malice. He never missed a target and no one had ever escaped him. With all his men in the field searching, he returned to the tent angry and discontented. This assignment felt strange to him. It'd been several hours since he'd heard from Drakor and now the other two death squads in Belarus had failed to report in. What was it about this mission that seemed to rip satisfaction from his grasp? He was the hand with no control over its fingers. Something or someone was stealing the satisfaction from him. Slavic though, incapable of love or having true human emotions, did feel a sort of dark comradery for his men. Much like what a swarm of vampire bats might feel for each other as they swoon and feast on the blood of their victims. Disillusioned with the failure to capture Kovska, he turned and entered the tent. Suddenly he was surprised by a sharp pain in his neck, followed by a hot burning sensation. He reached out franticly to remove the object protruding from his Jugular, that's when Kovska suddenly appeared before him. "Comrade Kovska," he grunted removing the empty syringe from his neck. "How did you get in here?" Slavic finished and fell to his knees. Kovska had little time for dialogue as he knew sooner or later the men would return. "If an explanation is your last dying wish, so be it," he said. "When your foolish soldiers shot up my van, they gave me the perfect distraction to escape and doubleback. Your idiot tactics could've gotten us all killed you stupid imbecile. Do you know how important she is to the survival of the world? No. How could you? You're just another pawn on President Aleksei's chess board of deceit. That cargo that I was carrying, in the van you destroyed, can quite possibly bring about the total extinction of every living thing on this planet."Wha., aaa ... dihhhh yuuuh givvv?" Slavic's blistered tongue was too swollen to form his words."What did I give you?" Kovska finished."Something to help you sleep ... forever." Slavic's eyes rolled like marbles in his head, before he took his last breath and collapsed on the cement. Clumps of clotting blood gushed from his gasping mouth. Kovska stepped over the bloody mess and gathered the keys to the last military transport. His head was really throbbing now, as the small pool of red syrup began to matte in his hair. He reached up to comfort the pulsing wound, only to find a very deep gash in the top of his head. He needed stitches to stop the bleeding but time would not allow it. He heard the assassins in the distance as they begin working back toward the tent. Kovska quickly grabbed a white towel from a soldiers bunk and ripped it. He then modeled the ripped towel into a large bandage. He compressed the towel tightly over the gaping gash; securing it by looping it around his chin and tieing it at the top of his head. For the moment the pressure seem to slowdown the bleeding. His prognosis had just gotten worse, he had lost a lot blood, his lung function was getting poorer and his memory was starting to lapse.

He could not seem to remember stealing the transport or stowing Hellena on it; but he was relieved to see they were on the road and moving again. The headaches continued to worsen as he increased the distance between him and the HK's.

He needed to rendezvous with his pilot at the Belarus basin but he had to pass the outpost to get there. With the Fury and the death squad on his trail his only hope was to get Hellena on that plane.

CHAPTER 25

The Hunter Killers

The smell hit him first, then the smoke. It was the unmistakable aroma of burning flesh. Death and soot filled the night time air. The combination of the two made the task of driving even more difficult for Kovska. It seemed to carry on an upwind draft that blew against a natural downwind. But as the sequence of events began to unfold it would prove that this was no ordinary night.

Kovska could see the Outpost, or at least what was left of it. The trailers were only burning empty shells now. An eerie nothingness echoed from ashes of the hungry flames. It was as if no life had ever existed before the fires came to envade. Everything was either burnt or burning. He knew only Slavic could be responsible for such dark designs. The only thing that mattered to him now was getting Hellena to safety and he needed to do it before his injuries left him crippled, helpless or worse. He had to avoid the HK's in front of him and escape the ones behind him. He reached the town entrance and pulled off road to avoid being seen. After reaching a safe location he took a moment to check on Hellena in the vehicles cargo area. She was still resting comfortably, well her body at least. Her roaming spirit had been gathering data.

Something special had happened to her during the final phase. At first she noticed a cold hollowness within her soul as if some vital part of her had been removed. A depressing feeling of loss lingered without explanation. But the library of Kovska's thoughts soon told her everything she needed to know to fill the void. She wandered hungrily through his mind picking up the lost pieces of her life. It wasn't like amnesia where, she could not recollect anything. No this was more selective. It was as if every thought, memory or emotion that involved the Fury project had been cut away. Where anger and hatred once resided, an emptiness now took its place. The dark evil inside her was gone. She felt no desire to hate anymore. She could feel things, see things and hear things impossible to a normal person. She could unconsciously travel to distant places without ever leaving her body. And then there was the *Fury*. She learned more about it from Kovska's thoughts than she ever could have through her nightmares. The nightmares were the only things that weren't erased from Helly's memories. She continued her rummage through the catacombs of Kovska's dangerous twisted mind. Only now did she begin to understand what the *Fury* was truly capable of and how Kovska had planned to use it.

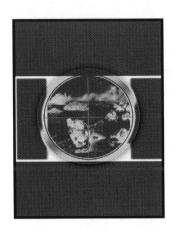

CHAPTER 26

Dead Reckoning

Tom watched as the death squad devoured all but four remaining trailers at the edge of town. Then they seemed to just disappear into the smoking wreckage. Tom turned to Mitch and said "One shot, one kill." Mitch nodded in acknowledgement and disappeared eastward into the rocky region above the remains of the raging campsite. The high ground would provide a good shot if Mitch could reach it. Tom turned to Bast and asked, "Hey where'd you plant those firecrackers we talked about earlier?" Bast pointed to an old tire about 20 feet from the towns exit. "Right over there" Tom took a long sigh before finishing. "Ok we're going to need somebody to lure them out to that old tire." "But thats suicide!" Bast answered. "Don't worry I have a plan, besides what other choice do we have?" "What do you mean what other choice? We could run, or retreat if you like that term better" Bast finished. "Not with a busted oil pan. Guess I didn't see some of those large rocks sticking out of the ground," "Whats not to see," Bast smirked attempting to get a smile from him. Tom took the ribbing in stride and laid out his plans to the rest of the team. They reluctantly decided Cin would be the bait.

The transport was large and slow but it was perfect for maneuvering through the rough terrain. Kovska steered clear of the town and started an eastwardly path along the outskirts of town. Their survival depended on his ability to remain off the grid until hitting Belarus's main road on the opposite side.

Mitch was set now, perched and ready to strike. The brilliance of the flaming town prevented him from utilizing his night vision. So he had to rely on instincts this time. He checked the wind for speed and direction. His training told him it was blowing about 10 knots northeast. The rocky hideaway put him about 700 meters from his target. This was perfect for the shot he needed to take.

Cin was already half the distance between the town and the team's position. She blended into the desert like a cameleon, one of her specialties. Like a snake she seemed to glide ever so smoothly across the cold sand. She could see the tire up ahead and just needed to get a little closer. Mitch scanned the shadows between the trailers for movement but so far there was none. "These guys are really disciplined," he thought. He almost felt a kind of mutual admiration for the dark soldiers. After all they were just like him; sent blindly into situations with not as much as a clue to why you're there. You're told to hit your objective and get out if you can, no questions asked. He thought about it for a moment longer and then settled in for a shot. He was ready to shoot anything that moved but therein laid the problem, nothing was moving.

Bast waited with detonator in hand for the signal from Cin. "Not yet," whispered Tom. He decided to check the team's status. "Cin, what's your position?" Tom looked at Bast who pointed to his ear and shrugged to confirm, nothing was coming through. Tom tried Mitch but with the same response, nothing. "What's wrong with the radio?" Bast asked. "Nothing as far as I can tell, it's like the signal is being blocked by something." Now with no means of communicating with Cin or Mitch, Tom knew things could only get worse.

Cin was near the old tire now as she'd hoped to lure them to her but no one came. She rolled left through the gritty sand till she was outside of the trailers line of sight. It was a tedious task but she managed it. "I'm about to move into flanking position." She whispered into the mic. She repeated the dialogue over and over and just like others arrived at the same conclusion. "Shit!" she thought. I wish at least one gotdam thing would go right on this mission." Tom's plan was basic and simple. It required Cin to flush the soldiers from hiding and out into the open. They were outnumbered but between Mitch's sniping and Bast's explosives they could neutralize the H.K.'s. She eased slowly up along the back of the trailer. She slipped in and out of the shadows between each trailer. She used a blitz approach to flush out the enemy. To her disappointment, she found no one. A heightened sense of danger over took her as she was hit with another premonition. She struggled with the obvious as it came to her. Her eyes widened with a gut sickening reality. She sprinted back to her original entry point behind the trailers. At first it was difficult to see but then she spotted them crawling like earthworms. They converged on Tom and Bast from different angles. Cin almost panicked as she counted seven of them maneuvering into position. There was no time to worry about the other three, she needed to act now.

Mitch saw movement behind the trailer and laid his finger gently upon the trigger. He could hear the imaginary spotter giving him the go ahead. "Take the shot," the voice said, followed by: "one shot, one kill." His finger tightened across the trigger as the metal lever began to move. "Take the shot!" it whispered again. Mitch was almost there as he followed the target to the trailers edge. A hairs pull more and it'll be over," he thought. The muscles in his finger were rigid and committed to the final distance of the triggers pull. But suddenly his target turned to face him and started to wave furiously. Mitch was within a millionth of a second from the final pull, when he realized the target he was about to execute was Cin. He gently uncoiled his finger from the engaged trigger and rolled on to his back with a groan of gratuitous relief. "Gotdamit Cin!" he whispered into the mic. "Why didn't someone tell me, you we're going to be crawling around in my kill zone. Cin?" he repeated. Mitch soon realized why no one had told him about the change of plans. He shoved his eye back to the rifles scope again. Cin was still there waving and pointing frantically in the darkness. Mitch scanned the area where she was pointing. "Nothing's there!" he exclaimed. "Cin, what are you trying to make me see?" Suddenly Cin disappeared into the darkness and

Mitch was lost. "What was she pointing at?" He tried to scan the area with his scope again but he could not see a thing. Now the blinding brightness of the burning fires was behind him so he toggled the switch. Once again the green resolve of night vision showed him the enemy's hand. Mitch saw the seven assassins converging on Tom and Bast. They had managed to get well past halfway to their targets. The smoky haze from the blazing town created the perfect ground cover for the creeping crawlers. Mitch wondered if Cin was amongst the seven but in order to proceed he had to give her the benefit of the doubt. She'd never go into the kill zone knowing he couldn't see her. Or did she know? he wondered if she even knew how close she came to dying again. He dismissed his inhibitions and took a deep breath and picked the target closest to the team. As a pelt of smoke exploded from the rifles barrel the silent killer hit its target. Seven times he expelled each spent round and inserted another. He managed the feat with mechanical precision. For that moment he had become the perfect killing machine. "Seven shots … seven kills" he mimicked with a smile. "Goodnight comrades." he said with a conquering grin. He watched as Tom and Bast sat like ducks in the darkness waiting, not knowing that death's touch had been thwarted by their avenging angel.

Mitch had been so focused on saving everyone else, he forgot to save himself and like a dark secret from his past he knew that sound when he heard it. It was the messenger, the deliverer of bad news to your next of kin. It was the piercing sound of a projectile rifling through time and space at 3500 ft. per second, only this time he was the recipient. Death came like a thief, to steal what Mitch had failed to protect: his own life. He fell off the ledge and plunged 20 ft. into the rocks beneath him. He was dead before he hit the ground and now somewhere in the dark smoky shadows the sniper reloaded and waited for his next victim.

Cin removed the blades from the dead man's throat; he'd fallen prey to the deadly *Dragon's Teeth*. She had picked him off while doubling back through the outlying areas. Knowing Mitch had a handle on the night crawlers, she moved back into the shadows between the trailers. "That leaves two unaccounted for." Cin said.

"This is some fucked up shit! How in the hell are we suppose to know what to do? Without a word from Mitch or Cin we're helpless!" Bast said franctically. "Calm down, Bast we need cool heads to get out of this. Don't go getting squirrelly on me. Besides the winds shifting, it's starting to blow north. That should lift this smoky haze so we'll be able to see whats going on!" Both men watched as the thick smog floated back toward the simmering town. Bast began to scan the areas north with night goggles. Tom did the same. Bast was the first to discover the dead men sprawled all less than 10ft. out. "Ohhhh, that Mitch is one bad son of a bitch!" Bast said smiling triumphantly. "Yeah, why's that?" "If you have to ask, something's wrong with your fuckin noc's. Tell me you don't see all those bodies out there Tommy boy!" He said the words with the jubilance of a prepubescent teen. "Well yeah I'm looking at seven dead bodies. Where's the other three and more importantly, where are Cin and Mitch?" Tom's voice was serious and a little grim. "I don't like the implications of how you said that," Bast replied. I know Cin and Mitch are fine, so don't go talking like that" "Ok, well help me find them because I don't see either one." They both stared up at the rocks where Mitch was last seen and a heavy feeling sunk inside their stomachs at the same time. "I'll go check on him, you stay here and watch for Cin," Tom said. "But you're the teams leader, we need you here to keep us sane," Bast said smiling. "Besides, like you said there's probably three of them still out there somewhere." Tom patted Bast on his back: "You guys have risked everything for the success of this team, all I've ever done is man the comm. Well this time I want to take up the point position for the team." "No Tom that's bullshit and you know it! Right now you're the teams leader and I don't know what we'd do if something were to happen to you!" "Nothing's going to happen to me." "I'm just going to go up there and check on Mitch. If he's injured I'll bring him back safely, If it's worst than that, well you know .... we'll cross that bridge ..." Bast choked up as he looked at Tom with watery eyes. Tom smiled and gazed back with confidence as he prepared to leave. Bast knew in that moment everything was going to be alright as he gave Tom a big power hug. Suddenly out of the silence he thought he'd heard a mosquito whizz by his ear as he and Tom embraced. He heard it again but this time he was suddenly splattered with an explosion of blood ...Tom's blood. Tom's body collapsed into his arms. The shock trauma kicked him like a mule forcing them both to the ground. Bast could feel the sniper's bullets ricocheting around him. He hated to do it, but knowing Tom was already dead, he was forced to use him as a shield from the snipers attack. He could feel the flaccid body recoil each time a bullet ripped through it. He knew it was just a matter of time before the shooter made the proper adjustment to hit his mark. He had to get to cover, quickly.

Cin had searched the entire outer region surrounding the remaining trailers. But so far she'd come up empty handed. There were two men left and she knew it would be their death sentence if she failed to find them. Somehow she ended up back inside the simmering remains of the Outpost. The flames were dying and the smoke was clearing but the smell of death was so thick she almost choked on it. The light from the weakening flames flickered along the backs of the remaining trailers like a floating candle. Cin could not allow her mind to drift, to think, or to wonder about the rest of the team. She consoled herself to believe that everyone would be ok, if only she could find the last two men. She found herself leaning against the back of one of the trailers again. "What did I miss?" she pondered, throwing the question out like a boomerang. And like a boomerang the answer came back so hard it almost knocked her off her feet. Suddenly she heard a noise escape from one of the vacant trailers. That's when she realized she was leaning against the answer to the puzzle. It was like a railroad spike had been driven deep inside the trestle of her skull revealing a painful revelation: "I never checked inside the trailers!" "Fuck!" she said in an excited whisper. She had no plan and no time to create one. Realizing the direct approach would be too risky and would require her to bust down one door at a time; she opted to take a more explosive approach. It was something she remembered when she first entered the gypsy town ...propane. Each trailer had its own propane gas supply tucked neatly beneath it. She'd only need to ignite one of them and the chain reaction would spread to the others. She remembered where Bast had hid the explosives and retrieved them. Quick and quietly she rolled beneath the trailer and found its propane tank release valve. The trick was to release a slow steady stream of gas, allowing her enough time to move to a safe distance. The simmering flames would do the rest.

Bast pushed Tom's bullet riddled body to the side and rolled away. He could see the van about 50 yards out but knew it would be too risky for a sprint. Another bullet tore past his head and skipped across the ground in front of him. He had to get to cover quickly before the sniper could adjust his aim. Bast looked like a lizard scurrying across the sandy terrain. He was within 15 feet of the van and a glimmer of hope rose in his heart. That was before the sniper's bullet tore a three inch hole into the thigh of his right leg. The impact knocked him into a small ravine about 10 feet from the van. "Oh shit I'm hit!" he cried. He looked down to see the perfect hole bored through his thigh. "Gotdamit I can see clear through to the other side." He almost fainted at the sight of so much blood. He removed his shirt and made a tourniquet to slow down the bleeding. Now he lay in the ditch wondering if he'd ever make it out alive. He waited with both Beretta's in his shaking hands, listening for the sound of footsteps. Minutes seemed like hours as the loss of blood began to affect him. Almost blacking out several times, he continued to drift in and out of consciousness. A crippling feeling of paranoia swept over him leaving him afraid to close his eyes. He wondered if Mitch and Cin were dead and if so, how much longer would it be before the assassins came for him. His thoughts began to revolt against him with accusations of Tom's death. If only he had insisted on doing the welfare check instead of letting Tom do it; he could've taken his place. And how did he repay Tom's sacrifice? By using him as a shield to save his own sorry neck. He was the 10 point Buck waiting to be stuffed and mounted on some wall for all to see. A small placard beneath it would read: "Here lyes an asshole who used his friend as a bullet shield." The pain in his thigh throbbed and pulsed with burning guilt. It was excruciating only to be numbed by the ache that filled his heart. He thought of Tom, Mitch and Cin and began to wail with hard gutsy tears. He had let everyone down. Now he was sure that Mitch had been the better man. In his mind he was a failure and a coward. Shamefully he wallowed in the sorrow of the moment. Then without warning his pity party was interrupted as the region was rocked by four large explosions. Suddenly the sky was filled with the remains of the last four trailers. The charred wreckage climbed high into the sky, chased off by the raging fireballs that roared behind it. Bast saw the sky turn bright orange again. There was no mistaken it . . . Cin was alive. He couldn't explain it but somehow he knew she had a hand in this. Debris rained across the outpost, sprinkling it like croutons on a salad. The effects of the massive explosions spanned far enough to reach Bast; peppering the trench with fragments of tin, wood and sheet metal. As hope returned he clawed desperately at the sides of the trench to free himself but was unable to do so. Flopping back into the trench was painful but he knew it would be just a matter of time before Cin came for him. Now he need only wait.

He looked up in time to see the silhouette of a dark figure looming over him. The loss of blood made him weak and delusional. "Cin?" He figured it had to be her but she never answered him. "Cin, is that you?" still there was no answer. He tried desperately to see the face eclipsing the moon's light above him. "Who are you?" he asked just before fading into unconsciousness.

CHAPTER 27

Hellena must survive

Cin emerged from a piece of tin metal that had fallen on her. She checked herself for injuries and was surprised to find only a few superficial lacerations across her face. She stood and knocked away the severed hand still attached to the twisted metal of the sniper's rifle. It was proof positive that the threat had been neutralized. The question in her mind was, did she get to them in time?

Her first stop of course was Mitch. She moved through the rocks like a hungry Cougar. When she arrived at the top, the first thing she noticed was Mitch's rifle, still propped and aimed at his last target. She called to him but there was no answer. Something red, stained the rocky area beside the rifle. Cin felt a sudden ringing in her head as she staggered slowly over to the perch. Like a crime scene investigator she studied the area and followed the blood trail. The spattered droplets led her to the edge of the rocky drift and disappeared. That's where she found him, at the bottom. His body was posed like a sprint runner in stop motion, except that his legs and arms were twisted and bent in opposite directions. Cin felt something pull tightly inside her mind. Layers of her soul begin to die inside as she faced the dreadful reality that waited at the bottom of the hill. Without a word she shouldered his rifle and started down the rocky slope. Her face was frigid and void of color as she reached the bottom. He was truly her best friend and she loved him as such. Cin had never been much of a crier but she knew if there ever was one, this was a crying moment. She waited for the tears to come but a dry irritated redness came instead. A blank expression of disconnection came over her as she examined his broken body. She lifted him into a fireman's carry across her shoulders yet somehow he felt weightless. She began the slow distraught walk back to camp. Tom and Bast was her next stop.

It would be dawn in a few hours and Cin needed desperately to reunite with the remaining team members. She was about two yards out when she saw the tattered body faced down in the dirt. Mitch limply rolled off her shoulders and hit the ground with a dull thud. Cin never felt him fall, she just bolted toward the riddled mass. She stood numbly above it and in one motion reached down to flip the body. That's when the cable that held all the pieces together, snapped! She felt something heavy give way inside her mind, as all the emotions, passions, and desires emptied out of her. The new void inside her was refilled with dark insane suggestions. Suddenly her body was latching on to the only thing that remained in tact: the executioner's chamber. It was her special room, where she reigned victorious over all things that dared to enter it. Now she was ready for retribution.

The seed of revenge was burrowing deep inside leaving her mind tilted with dissolutions. Reality became so painful for her to face, that she swopped it with confinement in her very own death chamber. An impression of imminent death was carved into her face like a graveyard headstone. No words or sounds escaped as her eyes grew black and shiny like glass marbles. The once white palette of her Sclera erupted with bloodshot blemishes. She readied herself and followed the pattern of logical thought. Where was Bast? Then, she had an epiphany as the mental death chamber readied itself for a new victim. Her eyes picked up the bloody trail of drag marks in the sand. The red clumps of earth had forged an undeniable path. She stood upright and snapped her head with robotic precision toward the van. Her blades seemed to automatically slide into her hands as she accelerated into a full throttle run. She shot like an arrow to the trails end. She felt another premonition but this one felt different, it felt . . . . She snatched the van's door open ready to send it's occupant to hell. Cin had stopped just short of releasing her blades of death, when she saw an old white man kneeling over Bast. "Move away from him, before I cut your fucking head off!" she demanded. "No, Cin don't hurt him! He's been helping me, he's a friend." Bast shouted the words several times before Cin finally acknowledge him. "Gotdamit, Cin where the hell have you been?" he shouted angrily. "You left us out there like sitting ducks! Why, didn't you come back to warn us, Cin . . . why?" She ignored the questions, and continued on to the stranger. "Who the fuck are you and who's that?" she asked pointing to the girl strapped to the gurney. The old man replied calmly: "I'm Dr. Kovska and this is my patient Hellena." The names blew past both of them without further inquiry. "Now that we have the formalities out of the way, explain to me why an old fuck like you would have a young girl strapped to a gurney. And of all places why out here, in the middle of nowhere?" Cin was planning to kill him no matter what he said. "I can explain that," he said calmly. "Yeah, you perverted piece of shit explain because if I don't like what I hear, you gon redecorate the inside of this van!" Bast's eyes widened, "Cin what the fuck's wrong with you? What happened to you out there?" She blocked him out and focused solely on the old man. The stares she gave him reached well beyond his eyes, piercing the protective secrets he was planning to shield from her. He recognized that gaze in her eyes, he had seen it many times before when Hellena was younger. It was revenge. He wisely decided to tell her the truth. "I know what you're thinking and its nothing like that, its far worse. We came from the village of Prypiat, where my patient and I were lucky enough to escape with our lives. Everything got out of control and I had to escape with mankinds only hope of survival. We were making our way south until we were attacked by a KGB hit squad just outside of Belarus." "Yeah we met a few of them out there earlier. We call them hunter killers." Bast said. "Shut up, he doesn't need your help!" barked Cin. "Go on," she said with the emotions of a rusty nail. "Well you see that's how I got hurt," he said pointing to the bloody sheet around his head. "And whats her story?" Cin continued. "She's in whats known as an induced coma." Cin wanted to gut him right there but curiosity dictated a few more answers before she did. "Why the induced coma, couldn't she have traveled without being drugged or restrained? You had to know she'd slow you down and make you vulnerable to attacks. It just doesn't make sense doctor. Why take the risk, what was so dam special about her?" Bast interrupted again, "It doesn't matter Cin if he hadn't come along when he did, I might have died! He patched up my leg, said the bullet went right through. Anyway, I'm lucky he came by," he finished. "Yeah you're lucky but what about her?" she replied pointing to the girl. Kovska became dizzy as he leaned back and fell against the interior sidewall of the van. He gently eased himself down and came to rest on the van's floor board. The headaches were much more severe now. His face no longer displayed the insidious treachery he'd been known for; now it was trite and worn like old leather. He was finally beginning to accept the fact that his time was running out. "Please, I will tell you what you want to know. But with this knowledge comes a dreadful responsibility." "Spit it out old man" grumbled Cin. And so he did. "I was in charge of the Chernobyl Plant experiments when" it" happened." "When what happened?" Bast asked. "When my team and I witnessed the birth of a God, which came to be known as the *Fury*." Suddenly it was clear to them both who he was. "So you're the one responsible for this big cluster of a fuck up!" Bast added. Cin toggled to Bast momentarily and gave him a look that he'd never seen before. It gave him chills. He realized at that very moment how far gone she really was. He wondered not who but what was occupying her body? She spoke to him in a calm and direct tone: "If you interrupt one more time." The statement was open ended but he knew how to draw his own conclusion. When she finished with him she turned back to Kovska again. Bast felt as if he was in a sci fi thriller and some mean ass super alien bitch had snatched Cin's body, then he remembered Cin was already a mean ass super bitch. He knew this because it was an attribute of hers he'd been secretly attracted to for years. But now, this was different, something much more intense, scary and extremely unpredictable. For all he knew she might even kill him, if he'd accidentally pushed the wrong button. Then it dawned on him, with crystal clarity that all of the emotional trauma she experienced must have triggered her battle mode. And now it would seem she was trapped there with no way of returning.

"Get to the fucking point doctor, I'm losing my patience!" she started. He continued, "We performed numerous experiments in an underground lab, miles beneath the plant." They both watched him with the agitation of someone trying to open a tightly sealed jar with slippery hands. "Get to it man, you're not looking too good." Finally he said: "The girl on the gurney is Hellena, the birth mother of the Fury." Bast started to interrupt again but Cin warned him with a cold stare, he replied with hunching shoulders. "I created the HFX-10" said Kovska proudly. Cin's voice began to fill with anger as she spoke. "I wouldn't be so fucking proud if I were you doctor! You're the cause of us being stranded in this fucking shithole in the first place. Now two of my team lay dead at the hand of your kill squads. I guess none of this means anything to you right, Dr. K?" "Who knows how many women and children died at this outpost tonight, because of your decision to play god! Oh and don't leave out all the people in Prypiat, are you even keeping up with the score? Do you know how many lives have been destroyed since your project started? I'm sure you don't, it probably never fuckin mattered to you!" Kovska raised his hand like a child seeking permission to speak and Cin eyed him with a deep, deadly hatred. She was on autopilot now and her mind was playing its favorite game: mental warfare. He was about to speak when her mind took over and like lightning she grazed his throat with one of her razor sharp blades. A dark red mist exploded from the cut spraying violently into the air. The small invisible slit grew larger as its contents began to pour from the opening. He gulped and gurgled through the pumping blood as he tried desperately to explain. The thick red sauce began to gush and rage from the cut like a busted dam but still he tried to explain. As the last drop streamed from the now gaping slit in his throat, he finally closed his mouth and eyes. Cin returned to the moment to see Kovska still there with raised hand. "You're running out of time and I'm running out of patience for your bullshit! It'll be daylight soon and I need to know what exactly are we up against here. Then I can decide what to do with you and her. Maybe I'll just kill you both. Bast watched Cin with a new respect for the psyche ward. Kovska interrupted: "You can do whatever you want with me but you cannot harm or attempt to harm her in any way. Hellena is only half of the equation! There is another part of her called the

Fury! That is what she and I were really running from. It's what's doing all the killing and destroying! I thought I would be able to control it but now I know no one can. Except . . ." He stopped and paused. "Except who?" cried Bast. "Except her." He pointed to Hellena. "How can this vegetable control your Fury?" Cin asked. "It's the other half of her psyche, if she dies it dies as long as she lives it lives." he answered. "Then it's simple we'll kill the bitch, which should destroy your monster too" she finished. "No it's not that simple, you'd be dead before you even knew you were dead. If you were to attempt to cut her with one of your knives, the Fury would appear before your blade could pierce her skin. The same holds for any weapon or threat of harm. Before any thing or person could ever get close enough to harm her, her natural instincts would alert the Fury and . . . well you do the math." "Where's this thing now and why hasn't it come for her yet?" "I'm not sure exactly where it is but I'm sure it's closing in. I believe that the weakest power the Fury has displayed thus far is its mental telepathy over distance. This seems to be its only exploitable weakness that I can tell. I can't explain how or why the Fury lost its connection with her or why I was even allowed to take her. Except that maybe, it did not feel threatened by me, knowing that I would keep her safe even in the face of my own death. But now I've come to the end of my time and surely it waits for her to awaken or for some poor fool to attempt to hurt her. Either of the two would bring them together again." Kovska grabbed his head in severe discomfort. "I take it the last option was the worst of the two" said Bast. "Yeah you could say that but no matter the circumstances anyone or anything coming face to face with the Fury will perish!"

"So what do you say I introduce this Fury of yours to my little friend!" Bast spoke while displaying a M16 grenade launcher. Kovska laughed and coughed himself into a choking frenzy at the sight of the weapon. "No known conventional weapon can stop it or affect it" he answered. "In fact anything you use to fight it, will be recycled and turned against you." "You paint a pretty dim picture doctor K." Cin said. "So is there anything that can affect this creature? Like slow it down, wound it or kill the fucker?" she asked. "Yes, aren't you listening to what I'm saying" he said looking over to Hellena again.

"Somehow she holds the key to the Fury's life or death. Find that key and you'll have a chance. Right now she is no match for it. Her body is still changing and though she is getting stronger she needs as much rest as possible. Until the process is complete she must be protected from all potential threats. Remember, if she awakens too soon it could affect the potential of her powers." Kovska paused a moment to gather himself and then continued: "You have a lot questions and I understand that but . . ." he looked serious with a touch of finality as he spoke, "All of mankind will perish, because the Fury's only desire is to kill and destroy!" he finished. "Don't direct your sermon toward us, this is your party doc." Bast said. "Not anymore, I can't protect her any longer, I'm done" he said touching the bloody sheet around his head. Cin put the blades away and took a look at Kovska's head wound. She looked over at Bast and shook her head as if to confirm that he was a goner. "How long before that thing comes looking for her, doc?" Bast asked. "It has most likely already begun the hunt. It likes the thrill of the hunt, you know." he continued. "It'll probably be here in a matter of hours." "Well I guess we're all fucked then because in case you hadn't noticed doctor we're stuck here, left behind to die! And even if we could get out of here where would we go? We're marked for death." "Yeah one way or another." Cin agreed. "Look at the bigger picture, all of mankind has been marked for death!" Kosvska said. "So now your problem's not so big anymore is it?" "Why are you trying to destroy your pet project all of a sudden?" Cin asked. He held his head down: "This is not what I wanted, the plan was to bring my country out of the dark ages and take back what had been taken from us: our dignity. At first I didn't care who it killed or how many died at its hand. But then when I realized this thing could not be controlled by me or any man it was too late to stop it. And now it could quite possibly destroy every living creature on the planet and where's the victory in that. I know it sounds a little insane but that's the truth. So I guess you could say: I'm trying to save what I once strived to destroy. It really makes no difference what my motives are now?" he finished. He looked at Cin and Bast as if there were three of each and he didn't know which one was real. Their voices began to echo inside the hollow spaces behind his eyes. He was losing the battle and his mind was starting to slip. It was frustrating having to explain every little detail to them. Didn't they realize there was no time for that? Couldn't they have known the ramifications of being caught with Hellena? The Fury would savagely slaughter them and then go on to devour the world, with not so much as a speed bump to slow it down. Why didn't they just grab Hellena, run and never look back? In the end it was the best chance they had, to simply run. How could he make them understand there was no more time for explanations? He was winding down to the one good memory cell still working. He tapped into it and purged it dry. "No more questions, time to listen now." He struggled to get the words out. First he told them where he hid the Russian transport, then he explained what to do with it. "There is a place called the Belarus basin, are you familiar with it?" They both nodded yes. "There'll be a plane there waiting to take you out of this place in approximately three hours from now. If you miss that plane you're dead. The plane will take you to Mexico. From there you're on your own. "So is that it, or do you have some more surprises for us?" Cin asked. "No that's everything I can think of," he answered exhausted. Bast started in, "I have one last question for Einstein over there since he thinks of everything. Every military unit in the country probably has orders to kill us on sight, no questions asked. So what the fuck are we suppose to do about that?" His answer was simple and to the point. "That's your problem to solve, maybe you should pray for a miracle!" he replied with a smile. "The only thing I can provide for you is a transport to Mexico and ample supplies but the rest is up to you. Hellena's sedation has been taken care for the next 24 hours." He pointed to the I.V. drip next to the gurney. If she comes out of sedation before then, just remember everyone dies. Do you understand?" Cin walked away in silence, while Bast slowly nodded in agreement.

After saying a prayer over the shallow make shift graves Bast said: "Amen." Then lifted his head and walked over to the idling diesel. Cin remained at the gravesite a moment longer and vowed to make things right but still she was unable to shed a tear for her fallen friends.

The five ton Soviet 6 x 6 pulled out leaving a sheet of sand and dust in the air. The hungry engine powered through the gears as the giant tires found the main road again. A thick black soot expelled from the trucks exhaust and thinned into the atmosphere. The heavy diesel soon faded into the distant dawn. Kovska remained behind inside the van barely alive and barely conscious.

Slavic's men had returned only to find what remained of their dead leader's body. It was a sight, they could've never imagined, for in their eyes he was immortal. Their gray hearts blackened with vengeance. Without their master they were just a bunch of ruthless assassins. The men fanned out and scattered along the trail to the outpost. The syringe they found next to Slavic's body confirmed who had killed their demigod. They wanted Kovska and they wanted him bad. The unforeseen fork in realities road left them empty and careless, so much so that they ignored the rumbling thunder off in the distant hills. As dawn awaited the arrival of the sun, something huge and black roared across the vast purple sky. It hovered only feet above the ground but climbed miles into the sky. The reluctant sun finally crested slowly along the earth's horizon. Not even the sun's ultraviolet rays could penetrate the pyroclastic monstrosity moving across the land. The dense enormous columns of death eclipsed even the sun's morning arrival. The giant super cell spawned violent winds that began destroying anything unfortunate enough to be in its path. The colossal storm contained vapor locked partitions all orbiting the storms core. It was a cyclonic rotation that was different from anything ever seen before. It was as if a series of tornadoes were all layered inside one another but each moving independently opposite of its outer stratum. The pure devastating power of the Mega super cell was unfathomable. The earth beneath was stripped, scorched and lain barren as it moved over. There at its core dwelled the ravenous ... "Fury."

The hunt had just begun and like its appetite its size had continued to grow. The Fury moved at them quickly. The distraught men felt too late the hot sweltering wind raging behind them but nothing they could've done would have mattered. They turned to see the horrific manifestation that awaited them. The sun and sky were gone, only the black thickness of the furious storm prevailed. The fear poured from them simultaneously and a rumbling moan escaped from its nucleus. And then one by one they were sucked into the massive horricane. Filled with paralyzing fear each watched the one before him vanish into the Fury's gorge. As each fell prey to the clutches of the wrathful storm, they were condemned to the grinding layers of the sandblasting winds. It was an assembly line of torture. As they progressed toward the core they were deskinned, disembowelled and ripped to peices. The demon plucked the life from them and abolished the remains to an abyss of cindered ashes. The death of a handful of men could do little to slow the monster's bottomless appetite.

The hungry and agitated Fury moved on, continuing its rampage south toward the outpost. In its wake remained a trail of scorched, lifeless earth. Every living thing above or beneath the ground had been extinguished.

The smell of burning flesh hung heavy over the outpost. The monster's agitation grew quickly as it seemed the camp had nothing to offer the hungry menace. Then a familiar scent in the air drew its attention; it was the scent of its birth mother. The hell spawn drooled at the possibility of reuniting with Hellena so soon. Though her scent was everywhere it was a familiar aroma of a different kind that drew it to the gray van sitting off in the distance.

Kovska could feel the hot air blustering around the van. He too knew that smell, a toxic cocktail of sulphuric acids, deadly poisons and volcanic ash. It was the smell of rancid rotting flesh, the Fury's calling card perhaps but all the same Kovska knew that death had finally arrived. He knew it was looming just outside the door. "Kovska!" the Fury thundered. shaking the van as it spoke. He slowly slid the van's door open, revealing his prodigal creation. He was still seeing in triplicate but it didn't matter now. The magnitude of the Furious storm was so large, that he couldn't see around it. *"Where is Hellena?"* The monster grumbled with curious pleasure. "Let me look upon your face!" Kovska shouted ignoring the demon's question. *"In due time, you'll see my face and just like the others, you'll be dying to regret it! Now, tell me! Where is Hellena?"* it growled. "She's somewhere safe and that's all I can tell you," he replied unsure of the answers ramifications. He was expecting death's hand to reach inside of him at any moment and rip his struggling heart from its cavern. But the Fury said nothing, as the storm hovered in place only feet away from the vans open door. Not even the scorching heat from the raging vortex penetrated the van's entrance. "It's toying with me" he thought. Whatever it was or was not doing, he was certain it would not continue to play nice without answers. Suddenly he felt it moving inside his head as it asked the question again. *"Where is Hellena?"* As he started to give the same answer as before, the monster sent him a painful message. It started with a rippling progression of intense throbbing pain that shot directly into his central nervous system. Kovska fell upon his back and cringed with excruciating agony as every nerve in his body cried out for mercy. The monster was squeezing his brain like a sponge looking for the cell that imprisoned his memories of her. But the majority of his brain was already dead, at least the parts that mattered. The Fury was too late, the accident had given Hellena and the team safe passage for now. The Fury scanned his remaining thoughts for any fragments of the puzzle but Kovksa's last thoughts seemed to be only of the Fury. It squeezed and squeezed until all the juices had been wrung dry and blood flowed from his ears. Kovska wasn't squirming anymore. Now his eyes blinked with synaptic impulses, as he disconnected from the world and slipped into a coma. The demon released the mush that was once his brain and as it did Kovska's comdemned soul prepared to vacate his lifeless shell. But in that moment before his last breath escaped him the furious demon erupted and ripped him to hell, sending his soul with him. Kovska's body combusted with such explosive force that the van's interior was sheeted with his remains. The Fury returned to a calmer version of hatred and gazed upon the bloody mess with bittersweet satisfaction. Kovska was dead now but still there was no Hellena.

The self proclaimed deity of death scanned the areas close and far for anything that would lead to Hellena's location. A vague familiar scent seemed to pull it toward the old Belarus airstrip.

CHAPTER 28

Mexico bound

Bast and Cin had managed to get to the Belarus basin a little after dawn. They had arrived way ahead of schedule and was pleasantly surprised to find the air transport already there. He was about an hour early and no one was complaining. At first they were skeptical about making it out of country by plane but once they arrived, it all made sense. It was a Red Cross medical supply plane. Kovska had truly thought of everything. The pilot had been flying back and forth to Mexico picking up medical supplies donated by the Mexican Government. It was all part of a worldwide effort to provide aid for the Chernobyl disaster. That was before the communications nightmare and the flying ban was imposed. Now Governments the world over had ordered attacks on anyone foolish enough to be caught in the air. With the ever present fear of a nuclear attack surface to air platoons stand ready to intercept on land or water. Cin and Bast had remained oblivious to the spiraling events occurring outside the mission. The pilot looked ancient and spoke with a thick Russian accent. He never said his name and only spoke when asked a direct question requiring a yes or no answer. He did however warn them of the no fly zones throughout the world and the risk of being shot down if they were discovered. The flight it seems only added to the already overloaded burden of keeping

Hellena safe. He seemed unconcerned that Kovska was unable to make the trip; instead he helped to load Hellena's gurney as if it were all part of the plan. That's when they noticed the enormous storm behind them. It covered the entire region over the outpost. Cin and Bast were glad they were flying away from and not into the ugly storm. "Cin, did you see the size of that fucking storm?" She answered without looking at him: "Yeah, I seen it." "Well is that all you got to say about it?" He was irritated at her lack of concern. "What do you want me to say?" "Maybe that it's the biggest and the ugliest fucking freak of nature storm you've ever seen!" "Well no need now, you just did." She was still floating between worlds unable to find her way out. Though he was more of an annoyance, Bast was the only familiar thing to her; everything else was a matter of kill or be kill. She strapped into the seat facing the pilot's cockpit. Bast sat opposite her. He was too busy licking his wounds to notice her deadly gaze through the planes cockpit. She watched the pilots movements with uncompromising focus so much so, that she hardly noticed the plane's bumpy take off. Cin was gone again, to the place she loved most and just like all the others she'd taken there: the pilot spilled himself inside her mind.

The hunger

The Fury lulled and stopped at the edge of the Belarus Basin. Its eyes were fixed on the red cross cargo plane climbing in the distant horizon. The hunger began to rise up again. The demand for more blood, more screams, and more souls kept getting bigger and bigger. And now the small isolated clusters of towns and camps it had been feeding on, would not be enough anymore.

The monster drifted in remorseful thought, not for the people it killed but for having lost the one thing that could render its destruction: Hellena. Something happened back in the room with the nurse. Whatever it was caused the break in the Fury's connection to her; It just couldn't shake the realization that, Hellena had somehow managed to suspend it in exile. **"How dare she punish me!"** it scowled. But now in retrospect the Fury vowed to end such episodes by creating a more permanent union.

Something about the tiny plane continued to draw it, a subtle hint of familiarity maybe but the sensation got weaker as the plane moved further out of range. Then a different surge of desire moved through the Fury like an enormous wave. The creature's relentless appetite had returned with a vengeance. There was no question of what would happen next: it was time to feed. Thoughts of the small disappearing blip vanished and so did Hellena's plane. The urge to devour something with more sustenance seemed more fulfilling. The monstress storm released a thunderous roar as the fires of hell began to kindle inside it again. Suddenly it was on the move again and in its path miles and miles of densely populated cities. The feast would set it on a course that would lead it right to the open sea; *and then . . . Mexico.*

"Hearing voices"

"Cin, you musn't harm the pilot," said a voice breaking the silence in her head. He is of no threat to you; besides we need him to fly the plane" Cin opened her eyes to answer but Bast was fast asleep. "How long have I been out?" she whispered. "A couple of hours." The voice answered. Cin rubbed her eyes as she turned to look behind her. There was no one there. She unstrapped from the seat and moved to the rear of the plane to check on Hellena. As she entered the cargo area of the plane, Hellena's body lay quiet, secure and in place. Cin checked her vitals and the I.V. drip and everything was fine. She returned to her seat and strapped back in. "Don't be alarmed, my name is Helly but you probably know me as Hellena." The voice said. "I know this is a shock to you but there's no other way to do this, time is running out. I will need to talk to you and Bast together, so please wake him for me." Cin thought she was really losing it now. She continued to search areas around the seat for hidden microphones or some logical explanation for the voices. "Please wake him now before it's too late!" Cin reluctantly reached over and poked Bast rigidly in the chest. He was startled and awakened to find her still jabbing her finger into him.

Cin looked at him as if being forced to speak and said: "Someone wants to talk to you." Bast thought she had totally gone mad. "What the fuck are you doing Cin, is this some kind of sick joke?" "I don't know I was hoping you could tell me" Then they both heard it at the same time: "My name is Hellena and unless you both do exactly as I ask, this trip will be a dead end for everyone." "Cin are you hearing the voice too?" Cin nodded to confirm that she heard it also. "It's the girl on the gurney!" Cin said. "But how?" he asked. "I don't know but I think we better listen to what shes trying to tell us." "Are you serious?" "What other choice do we have?"

"Now if you're both finished doubting the obvious, there's very little time to waste. I have decided to communicate with you in this unconscious state for your safety. It shields the Fury from finding me and keeps us both safe for the moment." Helly went on to explain how she had tapped into Kovska's thoughts long before he became injured. She learned of all the horrible secrets he kept. Things he burried deep beneath the conscious surface of his mind.

She explained what the Fury was and how it came to exist. She explained completing the final incubation stage could possibly give her unmeasurable powers. Her separation from the Fury had changed her hatred into a vacant emptiness. She explained that by tapping into Kovska's mind she had learned of the horrible horrible things they had done to her. She explained that as part of a failsafe system Kovska had created an antibody called the Guardian cell and implanted it inside her. The Guardian cell was responsible for alerting the *Fury* and protecting her against harm; it also rendered her incapable of harming herself. "That should rule out the suicide theory you're both exploring." she said. "I no longer have any self destructive components in my behavior" she explained.

"While I was reading his thoughts I discovered that the Fury is connected to me by some form of psychic energy. The fact is it has limited powers in this area. I have come to understand that life for me may mean death for others, and my death is unlikely as long as the Fury remains connected to me." "So basically we're fucked!" Cin said. "Not if you do as I say" Helly finished. She continued to layout her plan and explained how they could help. They agreed to follow her instructions to the letter and Helly's spiritual projection joined her in slumber on the gurney.

CHAPTER 29

Cuidad Constitucion (Mexico)

There were no shots fired at the plane as it rounded the Mexican airport. Soon they felt a firm bump as the wheels skeeted onto the concrete runway; it was a welcome sensation as they touched down at the Cuidad Cargo Service airport. Once the landing was complete two Mexican officials for the airport met the plane out on the runway. The pilot went out to meet them with a black sachel. Meanwhile Cin and Bast hid quietly inside the cargo bay. Cin listened and deciphered the dialect between them. "The pilot is telling them he has prescious cargo aboard that needs to be delivered safely to the border. Cin watched as the pilot gave the two men the large black sachel. One of the men opened it to check its contents and Cin could see that it was full of money. Now they're directing him to hangar numero nueve, that's 9 for you Bast," she whispered. "Now he's asking them about some sort of ground transportation." Bast was impressed with her translating skills stealing a romantic glance while she wasn't looking. Then suddenly with a quick jolt they were moving again taxiing to hangar #9. Helly was still safely floating in the sea of unconsciousness. She would need to remain in the vegetated state for at least another 16 hours. They could only hope for safe passage till then. It was all a gamble and the stakes were as simple as, life . . . or . . . death. The pilot stopped and secured the plane inside the old hangar. He moved back to the cargo bay and addressed them both. "Dars a vayhicle heah for juh." He pointed to an old blue battered 1950 volkswagon transporter van parked inside the hangar. He handed Bast a black duffle bag and returned to the cockpit without another word. Curiosity got the best of him as he opened it to find a surplus of tactical gear and an envelope bulging with U.S. currency. "Gottt-dam Cin there has to be at least $10,000 in here." Cin was agitated at his momentary lapse of misplaced priorities. "Bast in less than 16 hours the shit is going to hit the fucking fan! Tell me, how much that money will be worth then." "All I was saying is, it's good in case we need it, you know nothing more." He tried to recover but she'd already shut him out. Cin and Bast loaded the gurney and supplies in the van. Before they were safely inside, the plane had already returned to the runway. Bast hobbled over to the passenger side where he found a map of Mexico inside the vans glove box. Cin moved into the driver's seat and found the keys still in the ignition. "Alright, Bast how do we get the hell out of here?" Bast was about to reopen the map when they heard a car horn at the far end of the hangar. They both directed their attention to the flashing lights of a vehicle parked at the far end of the dilapidated old plane barn. "I think he wants us to come over there," Bast said. "Yeah, well lets go see what he wants to talk about." Cin replied. She started the van and gunned it toward the strange car. Bast watched helplessly as she floored the gas and converged on him. Her blades of death again fell comfortably into her left palm, while she steered with the other. "No Cin, don't do it, he may be trying to help us!" "Yeah, but what if he's not, you willing to take that chance with the cargo we got on board? Well I'm not," she added. The van's suspension came to life as she sped toward the parked car. Suddenly a short stout man stepped out in front of the oncoming van. He began to wave both hands furiously above his head. "Cin he's unarmed, slow down or you'll kill him!" She was unresponsive to him. Finally he shouted, "Cin if you cause any trauma to Helly, that thing will come!" She quickly began to pump the brakes until the vehicle pulled within a few feet of the man and stopped. Bast never took his eyes off her. He was watching the woman he had secretly loved sink into a realm he couldn't even fathom. "Cin, you have got to get a grip. What the fucks going on with you? If you don't tell me I can't help you." Cin blocked his words and thought only of the man that stood before the vans bumper. "Find out what this fucker wants, but I'm telling you if he blinks wrong, I'll squash him like a bug!" Cin's voice was filled with retribution. "Gotdamit Cin you have to listen to me!" She slowly broke her gaze with the stranger and turned to him. "What the fuck is it now Bast?" It was the first time in a long time she didn't look through him. Their eyes locked and for a brief second their souls met. It was the Cin he remembered the one he'd secretly fallen in love with. He could see her inside struggling for survival and he didn't know how to reach her. So he said the only thing left to be said: "Cin, I'm in love . . . . with you! I've felt this way for a long time and I can't, no I won't hide it any longer. Seeing you like this is killing me." At first, though she heard the words they failed to reach the depths where she hid like a scared child. Then like a voice shouting in a cathedral, the declaration slowly echoed and moved through every empty place inside of her. As his proclamation leaked beneath the cracks of her protective barrier, Bast watched her face slowly begin to change. The dark chamber opened its doors and released its prisoner and there she stood in its threshold before slowly exiting. She began the long tedious climb out of the dark hole that had swallowed her. "Cin I know you don't feel the same as I do but I can't let you self destruct like this. We're in this shit together whether you like it or not, it's just you and me now. Mitch and Tom are gone and you're gonna have to accept that and let them go." "I can't let them go and you shouldn't ask me to. What happened to us out there, I'll never forget that for as long as I live," she finished. "No, and neither will I but we can't let our hatred and revenge consume us. Because if we do, we become just like the thing we're fighting to save the world from." The old Mexican smiled and shook his head as he sat patiently on the hood of his car watching them. From his perspective it seemed like they were having a lover's quarrel. He didn't really care one way or the other as long as they were paying for his time. He sat patiently atop his gold "73 Mercury Marquis watching the soap opera unfold. Bast and Cin paused the show for a moment, as they realized the man who caused the predicament had been just sitting there enjoying their plight.

They decided it was time to see what the strange pudgy man wanted, so they joined him outside the van. "Do you speakey English?" Bast asked. "Yes, I speak good American English my friend." "Well what do you want from us?" Bast queried. "I take you to Mexican border." "Says who?" Cin barked. "I no ask who, I no care who, I only drive." "I need to know who requested for you to guide us?" she asked. "I am as you say unofficial guide for this airport," he explained. "If you come to my hangar numero nueve then you need me, you understand? No need for questions or answers my friends, we need only to go now," he finished. Bast looked at Cin and smiled, "You see everything's going to be alright." Cin did not share his optimism though. She was still slowly emerging from the chamber. One quick move from the old man in any direction could send her reeling back into the pit. They both entered the van and prepared to leave, when they noticed the old man still sitting on his car. But now his smile was gone and he seemed to be a tad pissed off. "What the fuck?" Bast shouted. Cin backed toward the edge of the pit again and waivered. The old Mexican put his right hand out in front of him and slapped it with the other. A small smile crept across Cin's face, "Bast you forgot we're in Mexico, he wants us to pay him." Bast eased into a smile and said: "Imagine that him wanting money and us by some lucky chance having some, coincidence, I think not. Maybe now you'll change your opinion of its necessity on this journey," he finished. "Ok, big boy I'll give you this one, I was wrong. Now go pay the man so we can go." It made him feel good to hear her call him that again, it was a nick name she'd only use when she was pleased with him." And that wasn't often. Bast reached in the duffle bag and grabbed a wrapped bundle of hundred dollar bills. "Hey how much are we suppose to pay him?" "I don't know go ask him, remember he speaks good American English," she said attempting to mock the man. Bast met him between the two vehicles again and asked, "How much for your help?" The old man smiled again before answering, "One thousand American dollars, is my price." Bast gestured to Cin in an effort to solicit her opinion, she hunched and conceded to the price. Bast reached into the bundle and counted out ten one hundred dollar bills to the old man. One thousand dollars and two minutes later they were moving onto a small sandy road behind the airfield.

CHAPTER 30

The first eight hours

The trip thus far was one of extreme heat and dusty back roads, through a seemingly endless desert terrain. Cin thanked god for the working airconditioner in the van. She knew the extreme heat could cause deadly repercussions if Helly were to get too hot. Kovska it seemed really had thought of everything. The van was stocked with plenty of gas, water and non perishable food items. All had been stored safely inside welded cargo bins. Everything seemed to be going smoothly. Bast and Cin had agreed to switch out every couple of hours, in an effort to battle the fatigue factor. The last thing they needed was for either of them to fall asleep at the wheel.

Helly continued to develop like a pupae inside a cocoon. Mentally it was a time for her to reconnect with who she really was. Dreams flowed through her like the galaxies milky way. She aspired of magical things. *Like*: floating weightlessly amongst the clouds and hovering above clusters of flower blossoms like a hummingbird.

Like: drinking the intoxicatingly sweet nectar from endless rows of beautiful flowers.

Like: the vision of her mom and dad walking hand in hand coming to take her to the circus. She dreamt of endless possibilities of the good fortune her powers could bring to mankind. A world without war, no more weapons of *mass destruction*, the word began to bounce inside her head like a super ball. Suddenly the glorious fantasy was fading and everything began to wither, rot and die. Something was killing her fantasy. It was that freak of unnatural disasters wreaking havoc of epic proportions. And after the last remaining remnant of life expelled itself, only *"The Fury"* was left standing amongst the stars. The nightmarish parade of events was followed by a strong feeling of guilt. Though she did not create the abomination, she still felt responsible for the part of her that breathe life into it. She tried with all the strength within her to avoid relearning the old feelings of anger and hatred. But rummaging around inside Kovska's head had proven to be a catch 22. The evil deeds she plucked from his memory banks proved to be far more devastating to her psyche than she could've imagined. The rollercoaster of emotions flooded her almost at once and immediately began to fill the empty void inside her. She knew it was an omen that her death child of Chernobyl would be coming home to her soon. The thought was so utterly terrifying that it almost ... awakened her. But a guardian inside her was preparing for the pending battle that was unfolding, between good and evil. Walls were being built and fortified, gateways, doors, cracks and crevices were all being sealed in preparation for combat. And now she loaded battle scenarios within her mind fighting and reigning victorious in each one. She had Cin to thank for allowing her the use of the mental death chamber. Helly could feel it, even see it moving across the open sea. It was closing in slowly but it had grown drastically since last she remembered it. Helly felt strange being able to probe the massive creature undetected. She was inside of it swimming against a current of black hatred and pure evil. The deadly under tow was so strong she was barely able to pull out of it. Still unaware of her presence it continued to move blindly across the open sea. She felt its hunger to kill growing like a cancer inside of it, almost consuming its every thought. She knew it couldn't wait much longer before it launched another deadly blood thirsty assault on humanity. She could only hope to awaken in time to draw the creature to her. But that was the thing, time. Too little or too much, either way it was a bad situation.

CHAPTER 31

Cin's confession

It was Bast turn to drive and they'd been on the road now for 13 hours. They had traveled well beyond the half way mark. Cin continued to monitor Hellena and keep her comfortable. Bast followed loyally behind the dusty gold mercury. He gave the old man plenty of room, in case of a sudden stop. The nonperishable food was lousy and the water was hot but it sustained them for the journey. Bast and Cin hadn't talked much since his declaration of love but he figured now was the perfect time to recap the conversation. When he made the statement earlier, she never replied one way or the other. And now his heart laid open and exposed hopelessly waiting to be crushed by her answer. But he had to know for sure. "Cin, about what I said back there in the hangar." Cin interrupted placing her index finger to his lip and replied, "No, Bast let me say something, before you start. I am not the person who everyone thinks I am. It's all a big façade. You see I don't sleep around. And I've never been bisexual nor gay for that matter." Suddenly Bast eyes refused to blink. He seemed afraid to close them for fear of missing something. "I use to put on airs that I was this tough butch bitch, that liked it both ways. But that was so that you guys wouldn't think I was weak. You don't know what its like to work for the CIA as a covert female operative do you?" Bast slowly nodded no to the question.

"Well the truth is I like men and I can use three fingers to count the actual relationships I've had. I hung out at gay bars and pretended to live on the edge as a front for my tough butch image. But all my gay friends knew what I was doing, so they all just played along. I had to make it as realistic as possible. You know just in case prying eyes came uh questioning. I think you're a good guy deep down inside but right now I don't even know who I am. My feelings are all turned upside down and nothing makes much sense to me. But if we make it through this, I'd like to redefine our relationship and see what happens. If, that's ok with you." Bast was still waiting for her to give him the friend's only line. But it never came. At first she was afraid to look at him for fear he might take her sincerity as weakness. "But how could he, after all he'd already dropped the motherload of confessions." Bast finally spoke after assuring Cin had finished. "I would love to . . . what I mean is, I would be willing to try that redefining thing you said too." Neither looked at the other as the words were being spoken but in the end Cin extended her hand and he held it for a brief moment. Then they both agreed to stick to business for now.

CHAPTER 32

The legacy of a mad man

The midday sun began to cast times shadow over the vast territory. Bast and Cin had never seen so many cacti in their lives. They had passed hundreds if not thousands of them along the way but not a single motorist was ever seen. The hot arid climate was no match for the vans cooling power. "I wonder what's under this baby's hood? Because this thing blows, like a refrigeration freezer." Bast said. "Yeah pretty deceptive, having it to look really old and shitty on the outside and inside, everything's like new," she replied. They both smiled and marveled at Kovska's ingenuity thus far. "You think he might still be alive?" he asked. "I hope not" she replied. "Why'd you say that?" "Because, he was a mad man. Just think, he had the brains to achieve the impossible and look at what he did with it. And I know you're grateful he came to your aid but he was just using you. Just like he's using us now. Screwed up huh? Think about this, here we are carrying out the dying wishes of this evil asshole to protect the very thing he created to destroy us with. That in itself makes us morons. It's almost as if he's right here inside this van with us." She finished in preparation for his usual negation of her statements. "That's all a little too deep for me" Bast responded. "I'll just stick to trying to keep us alive and leave the theorizing to you," he finished. Cin was pleasantly surprised as Bast conceded to neither agree nor disagree and for that she gave him points. After all he was confrontational by nature and loved to debate anybody about anything. He never concerned himself with being right or wrong, just on how riled up he could get the other person. She remembered Mitch use to be his favorite target. Her mind sped off in a hundred different directions.

Cin wondered if Hellena knew that they were secretly afraid of her. It was simple she was unsafe to be around. It was like carrying nitroglycerine, one small bump could blow them to bits.

The pressure was beginning to show as time seemed to speed up. With only about three hours left on Hellena's sedation, they were looking to find a safe place to stop. Bast passed an old wooden sign marked: Jicarilla Reservation 80,4672 km. "Dam kilometers, Cin how many miles is that ?" Cin smiled, "It averages out to about 50 miles." "Yeah well I'd like to meet the asshole that came up with that system" he followed. "Yeah I can see where that'd be too much for yo puny brain." she said making fun of him. "Whatever, I just know its simpler to just say 50 miles to Jocoralli." They both laughed as he purposely slaughtered the name. "It's nice to see you smile," he said as she reached to turn on the headlights. "Well, I'm still coping but at least now I'm living in the moment," she answered. Bast kept the conversation as light and upbeat as he possibly could. But under the circumstances the subject matter was limited, seems everything kept coming back to the pending destruction of the planet. "Never thought I'd see a reservation way out here but there's no tellin what you gone find in Meh hi co." he said changing the subject. "Might be a good place for a rest stop. What do you think?" "I don't see why not." she answered. They watched as the Marguis pulled to the side of the road. "What now?" Bast asked. "Who knows with this guy." Bast reached over and held Cin back in the seat. "I'll see what he wants, you check on Hellena." "Are you sure?" "Yeah, I got this, maybe he wants more money or something." Bast stepped slowly from the van and hobbled toward the silhouette by the car. "What the fuck are you stopping for?" "This is as far as I go my friend. The border is straight up this road and you don't need me for that. Just stay away from the reservation! The people there are loco the cabeza, crazy you know. I never go past there too many evil spirits in that place. "If you want more money just say so!" "Keep your money sen'yor, I go now." The old Mexican got back in his car and swung a screeching U turned and passed Cin before she reseated herself. Bast hobbled back to the van. "What the fuck just happened?" she asked. "He basically gave us the brush off, something about the people at the Indian village being crazy in the head. And this was as far as he was going, etc,etc,etc. "Good he was only slowing us down." She finished. Cin volunteered to give his leg a break and agreed to drive the rest of the distance.

CHAPTER 33

Donehogowa

(He who guards the gate of sunset)

The early evening ambience was almost upon them as they arrived at the Apache reservation. And now with just two hours before Hellena's scheduled awakening, the van pulled up to the entrance of the Jicarilla Reservation. "Look's quiet and peaceful from here," Cin said. They had expected to see teepees and animal skins scattered over the prairie with Buffalo and Bison roaming about. Instead what they saw was a small community of neatly built one story starter house's all with paved streets and signs. A large brick building stood in the center of it all. The sign on the lawn read: The Jicarilla Tribunal Chamber of Commerce and other businesses. It seemed pretty obvious this was not your normal traditional Indian reservation, thought Cin. Neither she nor Bast could see any reason the old Mexican would have been afraid of such a nice town. They needed a break to freshen up and stretch and this seemed like a safe enough place to stop.

Jicarilla seemed like one of those small communities with that cozy feeling you got when everyone knows each other, thought Cin. But the one thing they both shared in their opinion of the reservation was: the location felt somewhat out of place. There were rows of nice neat homes overshadowed by offices and small businesses. And knowing they were just sitting out here in the middle of nowhere was a weird proposition to swallow. They felt at any moment a man's voice was about to say "You have entered the Twilight Zone." "When did the Indians get so dam modern?" Bast asked. "I don't know but this is a far cry from what I was expecting," Cin added. "Let's find a spot to stop for a moment," she said driving slow and cautious. She was about to pullover and park when a enormous furry animal stepped in front of the van. "What the hell is that!" Cin shouted. Bast looked up to find an enormous Wolfe standing in the middle of the road. Cin gunned the engine to scare it but the large silver haired canine snarled and gestured with vicious intent at them. "Fuck it, I'll just run the fucker over!" Cin ordered. Bast could feel her drift a little, "No Cin wait!" But it was too late she'd already plowed over the hairy mass and stopped. No impact was felt as the van lunged forward. "That was weird" thought Bast as he eased from the van. Cin was doing the same from the driver's side. They methodically met at the vehicle's rear bumper. After an extensive search of the areas behind and beneath the van, they agreed there was nothing there. They returned to the front of the van to find a startling event taking place. Suddenly out of nowhere a large crowd of natives had mysteriously formed to block the roadway. They looked modern and out of place just like the reservation. They were all dressed up like big city folk. But their faces were very indigenous and culturally distinct. "Now this shit is really starting to get weird," whispered Bast. They both converged together along the front bumper and paused as they came face to face with the growing crowd. It was a standoff of blank stares with a strange uncomfortable silence. No one was talking so Bast felt compelled to do something. "Thank God we didn't kill that wolf," he thought. Soon they could see expressions of anger form on the faces of those who now encircled them. Bast picked his moment and words carefully, "Does anyone here speak English?" Cin couldn't help but wonder how many times had Bast used that line today. "Way to blow them away with diplomacy," she whispered. Suddenly the crowd started to open and part at the center and there admidst them stood the large silver wolf from before. It began a slow stalking stride toward them through the divide. This time it neither growled nor snarled, it only looked through them as though they were transparent. It appeared to be focusing on the van or the contents there in. They could only watch as the silver hulking canine continued its approach, then a powerful voice interrupted from behind them. "I am Donehogowa leader of the tribal council for this Jicarilla reservation. Who are you and why do you come here?" Their heads snapped around as if they had rubber necks. Upon turning to face the origin of the inquisition, they were surprised to see an old thin statured man. He was personified with silver hair and wild eyes set in a face of red eroded sandstone. Cin gazed back to cover the advancing wolf only to find he was gone again. Bast threw on a smile and addressed the tribal leader: "I'm Bast and this is Cin, we just stopped here to rest a few minutes, that's all." He held his arms out to show he had no weapons and was about to continue when suddenly the natives began to back away from them. "Was it something I said?" Bast asked rhetorically. "Yeah I guess so," Cin answered. "The time has come to fulfill the prohecy!" Donehogowa shouted. "Time for what prophecy?" Bast asked. "Time for the Great Killing," he answered. "Ok time to go." Cin sounded. "I have long prophesized of a deliverer who would travel many moons to come here to us, that is why they fear you. You bring the spirit of *Misae* with you, the goddess of the hot white sun. But she is one of two and the other we call *Nashashuki* the thunder demon of disaster. You are at impossible odds with the quest you have undertaken. For if the two should come together, they will destroy every living thing. "My people do not understand as I do, the reason you are here. It has been prophesied that you would come to us for help, he paused. Bast sighed with relief. "We finally found someone who can help us." Cin remained reserved in her assessment of the situation. "We will help you kill the girl and destroy her demon child," he finished. "You gonna help us do what?" Bast cried. Cin's fragile rubberband snapped again sending her plummeting to the deadly chamber. But Donehogowa stood with conviction and determination. The map lines in his old red face oddly seemed to plot out the trio's course and destination. His eyes were lit with a fire and passion often seen in lynch mobs. He began to flail his hands above his head in some type of ceremonial ritual. The tribal followers began returning and uncloaking themselves. They disrobed into their traditional native garb of their ancestors. War paint covered their faces and they all began to dance and chant with hands and eyes raised to the sky. Cin slipped past Bast with blades in hand. She moved toward the tribal elder and was stopped in her tracks by something. At first Bast could not see why she stood frozen in step until he moved up beside her. Both stood motionless as Donehogowa transformed into the large silver haired wolf again. The chanting began to sound like the howls of many wolves as the clan danced hypnotically around the van. The great wolf spoke to them in Donehogowa's native tongue. Suddenly it was apparent to Cin he was an Indian medicine man casting some kind of spell against them. Cin tucked Bast behind her and he in turn covered her back. They backed away in slow calculated steps, being careful not to rile the advancing wolf. Donehogowa looked up at the full moon and howled to the heaven's with a cold blood curdling moan. No sooner than Bast and Cin had reached the drivers side door a new evolution had enveloped the reservation. The entire tribal community began to evolve into large vicious wolves. The snarling pack moved around them inching closer and closer. Cin readied the blades and Bast braced his wounded leg against the van for support. They didn't talk much as there seemed little to say at this point. The pack of supersized wolves had positioned themselves like Indians surrounding a wagon train. "This is not going to end well," thought Bast. He reached in his pocket and grabbed a trinket he'd taken the liberty of pocketing from Kovska's black bag of tricks and slipped his index finger through the grenade's pin release mechanism. It would be the first time in his life he'd hope he wouldn't have to use it. Still he managed somehow to trivialize the predicament. "This shit would definitely pass the guiness book's most fucked up situation ever category, huh Cin? Imagine after all that we've been through to get this far only to be killed by a bunch of fuckin werewolves!" Cin was busy struggling at mental warfare with the nasty beasts. She was slaughtering them to the left and the right. All except for one . . . Donehogowa, who somehow managed to escape her in the dream. It was the first time she'd lost anyone inside her cerebral chamber of death. They had been thrown into a virtual reality where Donehogowa could control the outcome but only if they succumbed to his powerful night dream.

Bast and Cin stood their ground between Hellena and the Wolves. It seemed to them that the end was hinged on the events of the next 30 seconds. "Bast if any one of those wolves managed to get past us we're all dead!" "I know!" he shouted.

It'd appeared that fate was not without a since of humor. For all the trouble they'd been through only to find themselves right back at square one again. It seemed inevitable now, The Guardian would call the *Fury* to her and death would be served without limitations.

At first Bast thought maybe the creatures were Werewolves transformed by the full moon. But Cin knew from the moment Donehogowa entered her mind's chamber, what he really was. He was a very powerful medicine man and had summoned the spirit of illusions against them. "It's not real Bast he's inside our minds twisting and bending reality!" "So you're telling me these vicious, salivating wolves around us aren't real?" he asked in a ridiculous tone. "Only if you believe they are." she replied. "He's using the spirit of the wolf as a means of instilling fear in us." "Well its working!" he replied. "Can't you see that he's attacking you mentally, Bast you're going to have to fight him with your mind!" She was forcing the words out as if it was hurting her to say them. Bast knew nothing of fighting with his mind and was succumbing to Donegowa's powers of illusion. He crouched defensively as one of the circling wolves lunged into the air at him. Cin reached back and shoved him to the ground. She quickly maneurvered into position to strike before the creature could reach him. With blinding speed, she spinned into a rear thrusting kick so powerful, when it struck the hairy beast in the side of the head; it sailed back more than 10 ft. across the parkinglot. The wolf landed with a solid thump against the cement, gasping and whincing for air. A slick of bloody drool quickly rushed from its mouth. Then before their eyes the wolf transformed back into a young Indian girl. As the woman's body settled across the roadway, it was evident that she was dead. Donehogowa's howl suddenly changed into a heart wrenching whine as all the other wolves suddenly stopped in their advancing tracks. It was only then that Cin began to understand who she'd just killed. The pack looked to him for the next order of business. Then with a snarling gesture from their leader, the wolf clan gently grabbed the girl's body and carried it to him. The wounded spirits whined and howled in unison for the loss, as the body was laid gently at his feet. Cin had no way of knowing that the young girl was Donegowa's only daughter. And now she had to think fast before the clan returned the favor. There was no way she'd ever be able to fight off the whole clan. But what choice did she have?

The medicine man was chanting again and the followers listened as he prayed over the dead girl's body. "Are you ok? she whispered to Bast. "I was until you knocked me down." he said smiling. "What kinda shit was that?" he asked. "There's no time to explain, we need to get out of here now!" she said quietly. He understood and began to ease the driver's side door open. But the task did not come without problems. A loud alarming squeak resounded from the misaligned hinges. The shrill noise of the grinding metal called a warning to the pack alerting them their guests were escaping. But no one seemed to care. Instead they all stood over the body with heads hung low still mourning. Bast leaped across the drivers seat into the passenger's side and Cin followed on his heels pulling the door shut behind her. She glanced at the gurney and Hellena was still at peace with the world. "Thank God!" thought Cin. They both exhaled in relief as it appeared they'd be alright. Cin eyed the side view mirror to see the entire clan standing in human form once again. They made no attempt to move or chase the van. Instead they gazed up at the moon with a stain of permanent sadness across their faces. The van pulled away from the reservation and back to the main road.

CHAPTER 34

Brothers in arms

The stars twinkled with the sparkle of a dancing disco ball across the night sky. It was a new season, signified by the redish hue that luminated from the moon. It was a blood moon that seemed to follow them as they sped along the open road. Cin's study of Astronomy taught her that the moon could have a strange effect on people and tonight it had done just that. She tried to ignore the signs but the cratered planet promised a night of bloodshed.

"Do you know where we're going?" Bast asked. "Yeah, straight ahead." She was still struggling with the whole senseless mess back at the reservation. Bast tried to lighten the mood a bit. "You know that Mexican guide could have been just a little more detailed about that reservation, don't yah think?" "Yeah well if you don't mind I'd like to just leave that behind us, besides we have more important shit to worry about now. Like we only have about an hour before the last of that medicine wears off." Suddenly they both became quiet as the dynamic levity of the overwhelming odds they had yet to face hit home. They went about another 50 miles or so before the van sputtered and stopped. Cin managed to coast off of the main road and pulled next to a large cluster of Yucca trees. "That's it we're out of gas." "Well that makes this as good a place to stop as any." Bast marked.

Bast and Cin moved with a purpose as they began to roll out the final steps of Helly's plan. They'd been so busy talking and making preparations, that neither of them noticed the large Indian watching them from just a few feet away. He'd been following and tracking them for the last five miles.

Wolfe was alone as he approached. He hated not being able to communicate with his team because the occupants of the van would've been blown to hell already. It was a little something he liked to call, the Kmart special. One quiet flash of blue or red beamed on the target and Savannah or Steele would be already collecting their ears. But they were back at the lodge and he was alone. He tried to see inside but the old van had curtains strung around the side and rear windows. His best angle it seemed would be head on. He moved quietly to the front of the van; once in position he zoomed in on the activity inside. To his surprise it was not the scene he expected to see. "What trick is this?" he quizzed as he watched them unstrap a young girl from a medical gurney. "He counted the heads and noted their position within the van. Now it was just a matter of deciding the best way to take them out. Explosives would be too noisy and might alert any backup units they may have in the area. Who in the hell were they and why were they just sitting in his back yard. Wolfe couldn't make sense of it. "They must be decoys sent to find those red commi bastards we killed." he thought.

After pausing and scanning the entire perimeter, he concluded they were alone. He moved in closer for the killshot and repositioned himself about 10 feet from the van. Now he could hear the light murmur of conversation. "What the fuck are we doing here, Cin? Why didn't we just leave her with the old man and just let someone else do this shit?" "Because there is no one else, big guy. We didn't choose it, it chose us. Look I know you're hurt, tired and mentally fucked from all of this. But we are the last stand, Bast. Do you understand what that means? Right here and now we hold the future of the entire planet in our hands. This is the last chance for the survival of the human species" she said, embracing him tightly. Bast had become over whelmed by the grand scale of adversity they had been facing but Cin managed to level him out for the moment. "How touching." Wolfe thought.

"Cin, if I ever see that muthafucka again, it would be like a gift from heaven. I'd love to snap his head off like a crawfish!" Cin only nodded in agreement, while Wolfe continued to watch and listen. Then a strange thing happened as Bast raised his arms to stretch; the sleeve of his shirt gave way to a revelation of sorts hidden until now. The thick scarred skin of his upper arm came to form the words: *Semper Fi.* No further explanation was needed. Wolfe stood up from hiding and peered perplexed through the grimy windshield. Cin was the first to see him. "Bast, we got company and it ain't the good kind." He eyed the two Berretta's lying before him. With slow grace and caution he smoothly eased his fingers between both trigger guards. Cin bladed up and sat calm and ready but the large hulking man only stood there watching them from outside. His face was contorted with an expression of disbelief. "What's he waiting for an invitation?" Bast whispered. Cin wasn't planning to wait for his first move. "I don't know what he's looking for but that fucker came to the right place to find it!" she raged with blades in hand. They knew they were easy targets because the van provided no cover from a frontal assault. But they figured to coin the phrase: "The last stand," as they stood committed and unswerving at the front of Hellena's gurney. Wolfe continued to search his feelings as he stared directly into Bast's eyes. Suddenly the locking gaze broke into an expression of respect. Wolfe stuck his arm out and calmly pulled up the right sleeve of his shirt exposing a similar scarring pattern to that of Bast's. His bicep bore a brand which read: *Semper Fidalis Wolfpack.* And an instant brotherhood was born between the two modern day warriors. Cin wasn't sure exactly what had just happened but decided to stand down for now. She maintained her position in front of Hellena while Bast exited the van. He met Wolfe on the paved black top. They stood face to face under the sparkling stars and locked brothers in arms. "Semper Fi!" Wolfe shouted, "Semper Fi!" Bast repeated. And then they chorused: "Always faithful!" and smiled. Before Bast could dance around the truth about their identities, Wolfe had already figured it out. "You guys must be whats left of the Alpha team?" Bast instincts told him to lie but his heart told him to trust. "Yeah we're the last two of four." "And the girl on the gurney?" "Oh that's Hellena and the main reason we're here." "Well I'm Wolfe leader of strike team: Cyclops." The name gave Bast a knot in his throat. "My team is only a few miles from here. We have a lodge there and you guys are welcome to stay there till we figure out your situation." "No offense Wolfe but what do you know about our situation?" "Everything except, how you've both managed to stay alive and end up in my backyard. As far as what happened to your team over in Belarus, I know everything. Including who left you there to die. I hope you don't have any vengeful plans of finding him you know." "Finding who?" Bast asked. "That asshole . . . Weixel. No use wasting your time and energy on revenge because he's already dead." Bast looked at Wolfe with disbelieving eyes. "How can you know that for sure?" "Because I had the distinct pleasure of performing his last rites." Words could not express what Bast was feeling. It was as if a great weight had been lifted from his conscious. "What about his father's political connections?" "Not a problem the hit came from upstairs, you know the same people that ordered your . . ." He couldn't finish the sentence but Bast knew what he was saying. "Then I am certainly in your debt." "Not at all, nothing more than simply taking out the garbage." They both laughed. Wolfe had never given a shit about anyone except his team but something moved him to help them. Perhaps knowing they had cheated death and all the adversity stacked against them. But they hadn't just showed up on his door step alone, they were traveling with a very special passenger named . . . Hellena.

"I take it you've already met my people," said Wolfe. He meant the words more as a statement of fact not as an inquisition. At first Bast frowned, confused by his words and then it dawned on him. A large Indian named Wolfe about 50 miles from a Indian reservation where people just happen to turn into large wolves. "One hell of a fucked up coincidence," Bast thought. "Those were your people?" he asked. His heart dropped like an out of control rollercoaster. "Yeah I was born on that reservation, lived there till I was 9 years old. Then my family moved upstate so that I could get a good education. You know, the good ole' American public school system," Wolfe smiled. But Bast dared not, his mind was racing, wondering if the girl Cin killed had been related to Wolfe or someone he knew. Suddenly the future was looking bleak again. "What would he do if he found out they'd just killed his daughter, sister or maybe a niece? Well fuck" Bast thought, "She turned into a gotdam wolf and attacked us!" But still, the thought gave him little comfort or shelter from reality. Cin finally emerged from the van and as she did, Wolfe was instantly taken in by her beauty. Bast saw the lust in his eyes and suddenly his emotions went spiraling out of control again. Bast opened his mouth to introduce them but nothing came out. Cin saw him struggling and pulled him from jealousy's sinking ship. "Hi, I'm Cin." "Yeah, well I'm Wolfe, just like the name." Cin was immediately repelled by the insinuation of some animalistic attraction, he might have assumed he possessed. But it really wasn't his fault, Savannah had been the only women he'd seen for a little over a year now and she had no use for men. Cin neither accepted nor returned the flirtatious eye he gave her. Instead she repelled it as her face wore with the worries of the world and its uncertain future.

"So you had some trouble back there at the reservation," Wolfe said pointing to Bast leg. "No that's a little souvenir I received back in Belarus. Bast answered quickly in anticipation of the next question. "Look I know those people, you guys can be honest with me. They tried to attack you didn't they?" Bast and Cin's expressions answered before either of them could. Cin started: "Yeah, we had some trouble with the natives of your quaint little reservation." Wolfe appeared to listen with curiosity and growing concern. "So what happened?" he asked. Bast was about to put a spin on it when Cin just blurted out: "I accidentally killed a young girl at the reservation." Wolfe stared blankly at them as if he didn't understand what she had just said. Cin looked at Bast as they both prepared to deal with his response. Wolfe could tell the story was rapidly raising tension and decided to let them off the hook. "Don't worry about it, all of my relatives left the reservation years ago. Those crazy Indians probably had it coming always attacking unsuspecting strangers." he said smiling. "Did they pull the wolf trick on you guys?" "Didn't seem much like a trick to me," Bast said. "Yeah well it was real enough."

Cin added. "Well their antics are pretty well known in these parts, that's one of the reasons my family left some years back. The chief minister or medicine man if you prefer, is the one who gave me my name as a child. I remember he would tell me the spirit of the wolf was very strong inside of me, the strongest he'd ever seen. I use to respect him and looked up to him until . . . one day he just changed. He started calling himself Donehogowa: the guardian of the setting sun or some shit like that. He began preaching and prophesying about the end of the world. At first no one listened to him but then little by little the tribe began to fall under his influence. And now they're just a bunch of crazy fucking Indians who prey on the weak minded, making them believe they can change into wolves." he continued. "You, do realize it's just a mind fuck. He gets inside your head and manipulates your perception of reality. I don't know why he does it but this is the first time it resulted in death." Wolfe finished and waited for a response. "There's more to it than that," Cin replied. "He was not just inside my head, he knew things that he shouldn't have. "Like what?' Wolfe asked. "Like how he knew we were carrying a young girl with us. He also knew about the *Fury* and her connection to it. You see, he wasn't after us he was after Hellena. He wanted to kill her. In his mind he thought by doing so he could save the world. If we'd let him get close enough to harm just one hair on her head . . . we wouldn't be having this conversation" "Tell me more about this Hellena passenger." Wolfe prompted. "I'm getting to that but first I need to give you a little background info. Otherwise this shit will go right over your head." she finished. "Don't look now but you two are coming strangely close to sounding like Donehogowa." "Well lets see if you feel that way after you hear all the facts." Cin began to explain how the mission had evolved into an endless trench of death and chaos. She told him how Mitch and Tom lost their lives. The words pulled desperately at Wolfe's integrity for "The Office" and suddenly he hated Eiseman even more for sacrificing them instead of Weixel. She eased deeper into the dark chronicles explaining all the events leading up to her encounter with Kovska. Wolfe began to feel somewhat less skeptical and for the moment had agreed to help them.

CHAPTER 35

A good night to die

The Fury stoked the fires deep within its bowels and a new cloud of destruction began to form: a cloud bigger, blacker and thicker than ever before. Swirling with the soot of human ashes the crematorium glowed bright orange from beneath its impenetrable wrap. It developed quickly overtaking its previous form and within a matter of seconds stood a wall cloud about 400 ft. high and at least 200 ft. wide. The eclipsing storm boiled with hot acids and thermoclastic vapors hot enough to melt steel or anything else for that matter. A vaporizing wave of heat emitted as far as a mile in every direction ready to devour anything in its path. There deep inside the heart of the volcanic storm dwelled its queen of doom.

It searched across the open seas for some sense of direction, a scent, a trace, something new. Anything it may have missed before. There was only a minute sensation that she had crossed that way. Unlike Helly, who could teleport her spiritual presence or move objects with her mind if she wanted; the Fury lacked such powers and remained disconnected from her.

Cin was beginning to worry about the situation a little. They had no cover or protection just faith in a possibility of hope. Her tired eyes burned from the lack of any real sleep within the last 48 hrs. Bast continued to update Wolfe as he spoke quietly about the *Fury* and what lied ahead.

The three of them were standing about 10 feet from the van when Cin came to a bone chilling realization. "Oh shit, Hellena, we forgot about Hellena!" Before she could finish the words Bast was already hobbling back. Cin passed him like a stationery object. She reached the van and yanked the sliding door. "Bast!" she screamed. Wolfe caught up to Bast and helped him the rest of the way. When they arrived Cin was sitting in front of an empty gurney. "Where's Hellena?" Bast shouted. Cin never answered. Suddenly the end of the world was more than just a metaphor. Bast crouched next to her. "What happened?" Wolfe asked. He was obviously still ignorant to Hellena's relevance. He viewed the disappearance as a minor glitch. "Gone without a trace!" Bast said. "But if she was in a coma, how could she just get up and leave?" Wolfe quizzed. "There's no time to explain!" Cin answered. "We have to get to cover, now!" she finished. "Not to make light of your claims but have either of you ever seen this Fury?" Wolfe asked. "No, not really," Bast answered. "Then how do you know we don't have a chance at defeating it ourselves?" Cin turned to Wolfe and said, "You're just going to have to take our word on this one. Besides haven't you seen enough to convince you this ain't no game?" Bast interrupted: "I hate to break this up but now that Hellena's awake the Fury's gonna be on its way here. And I suggest we do more hiding and less talking."

They were surrounded on all sides by nothing but cacti plants. "Well this is great, we're sitting ducks." Bast said. Cin used the binoculars to scan the area but saw no place to hide. Wolfe grabbed Bast's arm and started north across the plain. "Hey where are you taking him?" Cin shouted. "This time you're going to have to trust me." Wolfe answered. "What choice do we have?" she murmured. They were 10 minutes in when a deep grumbling of thunder echoed from the distant sky. Bast and Cin hurried their efforts to get to wherever Wolfe was taking them. "Its just a few more steps" he plied. "There it is!" Wolfe stepped over to an old tin metal mining sign lying against a cluster of cactis. He lifted it and said: "Quickly through here."

"Through where?" Bast said. "There's nothing there but a bunch of cactis plants." "Look closer" he added. To their surprise in the middle of the prickly gauntlet was a small opening. "What the fuck is that?" cried Bast. "It's your new accommodations" He answered. "Its not the Hilton but out here, what is?" "But those pricks will be hell to pass." "Its either that or you stand out here in the open, you choose." Wolfe was tiring of Bast's whining. He'd begin to wonder if the brand on his arm was real. Cin sounded in. "Bast this is no time to worry about a small inconvenience like being stuck by cactus pricks. Believe me the alternative is much worse. Now get your ass through that opening!" she shouted. Wolfe stepped aside while Bast shrilled of discomfort as the cacti plants tasted his blood. Cin went in behind him followed by Wolfe. All bared bloody wounds from the prickly entrance. "What is this place?" Bast asked. "It's an old underground mining shaft that goes on for miles." "What did they mine down here?" Cin asked. "Coal I believe. You guys should be safe in here." "You're not thinking of leaving are you?" Cin asked. "Yeah, I have to go back and warn my team. Once I get there and explain, we'll all meet up right back here at this spot." Bast grabbed him by his arm, "Look thanks for helping us back there. Just be quick and careful because that thing will be coming with a vengeance. I know you guys are some tough hombre's but don't try to fight this thing, it'll kill you all." "Then we shall have finally found a worthy opponent" Wolfe finished. Cin thanked him again and he was on his way.

The spectacle had already started to unfold. The clear night sky had begun to fill with swirling clouds and powerful gusts of wind lifting the sands from its mystical sleep. Electric waves of lightning flowed across the sea of clouds in the distant skies. The conglomeration of elements that made up the storm was breath taking and overwhelming even in the darkness of the night.

"We'd better get a little deeper inside before that thing gets here." Bast said, and Cin agreed.

CHAPTER 36

Reunited

Donehogowa fell to his knees as the pyroclastic wall of death appeared on the horizon. His followers began to moan and shout spiritual incantations to the sky as he launched his protective spell.

It was moving quicker now, standing over five miles high and at least three miles wide. It had been traveling a path of death and destruction that was leading straight through the Jicarilla reservation. The looming superstorm moved in and ingulfed the entire reservation without stopping to enjoy it. The screams of tortured souls resonated in the vortex like voices song into a blowing fan. Now with its size, strength and momentum Hellena had to face the possibility that even she might not being able to stop it. It was as though the underworld had opened up and released its worst, vile and deadliest elements from the guts of hell.

The cool night air quickly shifted upward as temperatures soared above 100 F. and rising. Wolfe felt the change as he arrived at the lodge. Savanna, Steele and Quiox met him inside. "Where you been Sarge?" Savanna asked. "I'll tell you on the way, gear up we're going to a fight!" They had never seen him like this before. He was so pumped that he hardly noticed the streams of blood dripping from his fingertips. "Sir you're bleeding." Steele said pointing to Wolfe's bloody arms. Wolfe looked down at his bleeding wounds to find protruding cactis pricks covering both arms. Without making a fuss he began to snatch the piercing barbs from his skin. Quiox was quick to sanitize and wrap the wounds. He did so without saying a word. It was simply his way; only speaking when he had something important to say. Tonight's events didn't qualify as one of those times.

Wolfe briefed them as they prepared. He told them of Bast and Cin's story of survival against unsurmountable odds. He explained of Hellena and her strange disappearance and of the unbelievable things that he had heard tonight. But they believed whatever he believed and right now, Wolfe seemed possessed with engaging the unknown enemy.

The Cyclops team moved back into play as they jogged off into the sweltering night air. No one laughed or smiled about what they'd just heard. Instead they quickened their stride and pulsed ahead to meet the evil adversary.

As promised the enormous Fury moved across the plain like a large eraser destroying all evidence of life. Now Hellena's scent filled it with the renewed promise of reuniting with her.

Wolfe and company arrived back at the van just in time to see the advancing storm coming right for them. The amber glow of the searing clouds made it looked as if the sky was on fire. Several angry tornadoes spawned beneath the giant wall cloud. It was so large they found it hard to see where it ended. The team stood in awe of the unfightable enemy but Wolfe was unwaivered by the storm's enormous magnitude. He was prepared to die just the same as if he were fighting a human foe. "Ready yourselves!" he shouted. They took up fighting positions beside the van and waited.

Cin and Bast traveled deeper into the cool black descending tunnel. They could hear it roaring angrily above them. Each thunderboom quaked with bone rattling vibrations causing loose debris to shake from the walls of the old shaft. Within just moments of its arrival the Fury quickly changed the damp cool air to hot unbreathable vapors. The air inside the shaft suddenly reaked of putrid toxic gases. "Cin we have to move deeper, we're still too close to the surface." Bast urged. The descension gave quick relief as their breath returned to them. But the hot toxic cloud of fumes begin to follow, forcing them further in.

Steele stepped from cover to fire upon it but was quickly plucked from the earth like a common slug. The swirling winds thrusted him high above into the sky, then slammed him violently back to earth. The impact was so severe it caused an internal rupture of every major organ in his body. A burst of blood exploded from his mouth and into his face as the force ripped through him. He struggled to breathe as blood began to fill his lungs and airways. He was already as good as dead but the Fury was not finished with him. As a display of supremacy it lifted him into the vortex and pulverized his flesh and bones into hot ashes and blew them back into their faces. Savanna's eyes were burned shut as the scorching powder reached her face. She screamed of unbearable pain and wandered out blindly into the storm. Steele's ashes continued to eat holes into her face while the demon salivated to a drool. It basked in sweet anticipation of how good she'd taste. It was ready to move in for the kill when suddenly Savanna began to shout: "Wolfe don't let me suffer like this! You know what to do, just make it stop!" Savanna's call to Wolfe ordered a swift resolution from the beast; **"He can't help you now, no one can!"** Then in an instant her head was ripped from its torso. The gushing remains were sucked into the bottomless pit of death. Bloody juices overflowed at the corners of its hideous mouth but were sucked back in and savored with the rest. **"Mmmm!"** it moaned. Quiox acted swiftly to avoid the flesh eating ashes by rolling beneath the van for cover. **"There is no escape!"** it thundered. The powerful winds of the Fury slammed down heavily upon the van, flattening it on top of him. He became an inseparable part of the wreckage as freshly squeezed blood, shreds of mangled tissue and shards of crushed bones filled every crevice of the scrapped heap. The demon moaned with satisfaction as the sacrificial carnage was sucked into the core of the volcanic storm and digested. Wolfe stood powerless as his team was literally eaten alive. Everytime he tried to help them, a hot blistering hand would grip his neck and hold him down. He was purposely made to watch them die one by one. A great thunderous moan of victory escaped from somewhere deep inside the monster of all monsters.

"Where the fuck is Hellena?" Cin cried. "I don't know but we better keep moving, it'll be coming after us soon." Bast replied.

The hot vise finally released ahold of him. His neck bore horrible caustic burns where the demon had touched his skin. Wolfe slowly rose to his feet. He had relinquished his gun long ago and now he prepared to face his destiny. "Though I am unarmed I still rise to fight you! Wolfe shouted. The Fury smiled as it reached down and plucked both arms from his body. *"Now you are unarmed!"* It thundered. The Fury seemed recommitted to his horror with interest: *"I shall hear your screams now!"* it growled. The pain was beyond excruciating but made him feel more alive than ever before. He begged for more: "Is that all you got, you fuckin bitch!" he cried as he lunged his armless body out at it. The connoisseur of blood tasting was ready to savor this fine vintage of hemoglobin. He had been saved for last to sweeten the thrill of the kill. The thirsty demon could wait no longer. It lustfully dissected him, splitting his sternum and filleting him to reveal all that was inside. As the end neared, Wolfe looked up in honor to lose his life to his ungodly opponent. He imagined to himself a smile as big as Texas across his face. And then the evil she demon ravaged what remained of his body and fed it to the raging inferno. Still Hellena remained missing.

It smelled her on them as they scurried to hide in the dark shadows of the shaft. They were tiring as the endless mine seemed to go on and on. But every attempt to slow down was interrupted by the hot glowing death that hunted them. Now they knew it was not by chance that the scorching vapors had entered the mine; it had been sent to hunt them down and kill them.

A pair of fiery red eyes glowed impatiently from the depths of the raging hellstorm. It was just moments away from embarking upon the total eradication of every living thing on the planet. But first there was one last issue to deal with; locating Hellena and her protectors. Half of the equation was already being resolved but still Hellena was nowhere to be found. Frustration set in raising the demon's temperature well above 2000F. The heat surge was quickly followed by a sudden drop in atmospheric pressure. A deep earth shattering thunder roared over the entire desert region. The multi tornadic storm began to merge together to form one dark cyclonic horror five miles wide. Its rotation speed continued to rapidly increase causing the heat at the core to rise even higher. Soon the air was filled with sand, rocks, debris and human ashes. The volcanic twister was rotating now at a speed of almost 600 mph. The core temperature had climbed well above 4000 F. The sky filled with blinding streaks of atomic energy arcing inside the radioactive storm. It was an apparent build up of all the Fury's resources. Bast and Cin continued to run for their lives as the deadly vapors chased them through the shaft. It was all they could do to avoid joining Wolfe and the others in the dead zone. But where was Hellena, in their time of need?

"Hellena, I know you are here because I can smell and sense you! This is your last chance to show yourself before I devour your would be protectors! It thundered. The Fury positioned itself directly above Bast and Cin and began to drill. The cyclonic horror ripped away at the earth until the hidden mine was visible. Bast and Cin covered their faces as the demons hot breath breached the mine and singed the hair on their heads. *"I have thirsted long for your blood. No matter to me, if you cry for mercy or beg for death, your fate will be worse than the thousands before you!"* it growled. The monster began to churn up every weapon in its deadly arsenal and draw the evil mass to its core. Cin's lips cracked and peeled as blisters formed around her mouth. Bast was overtaken by the demon's toxic inferno and suddenly he was struggling to breathe. His tongue and throat began to swell closing off most of his air passage. In desperation he looked to Cin for help but she was down and unable to tend to him. His face suddenly filled with painful boiling blisters from the Fury's toxic breath. The interior of the shaft began to even look like hell. Now the monster was ready to keep its promise to them. But first it needed to know if they knew where Hellena was. Remembering the

failed attempt on Kovska It gently entered their minds searching for evidence of Hellena's whereabouts. Bast barely had the strength to move but he managed to reach Cin's hand. She had suffered severe nerve damage and could not feel anything below her neck. She was totally unaware that he was holding her hand as their final moment approached. As it opened the gate wide to release its promise of exacting vengeance, a mysterious protective barrier formed around them. At first it appeared to be some type of electro magnectic energy field but then the entity began to take form and shape. The Fury drawed on the horror from its belly and pulled it into its mouth. Suddenly just as it suspected Hellena emerged from the shield. "I am here Fury, now let them go!" The vengeful abomination embraced the moment with lustful ambition as this reunion was sure to be the beginning, of the end of days. *"Welcome to the nightmare, Hellena!"* it thundered. Helly looked like a tiny firefly in comparison to the colossal storm that loomed above her. Afterall she was still just a young girl of 17 whose youth and beauty had been magically restored. It was a fairytale rewritten. The village would be saved now as the princess delivers herself to the modern day dragon. The juices of death began to leak from the corners of its great mouth. Helly seemed unwaivered by its strength or it's monstrosity of size. *"I have fed on tens of thousands to find you and now you dare to challenge me!"* it growled as the toxic juices surged from its horrid lips. "Remember Fury, you need me to sustain your voracious existence. And it was inside my womb that you first tasted the dark nectar of hatred. For that I am responsible. But as for the senseless death and destruction, that you leave in your wake, I can not claim nor will I let it continue!" She snarled. "It All Stops Here And Now !!" Hellena's threats resounded with convincing conviction. But the words seemed only to anger the super beast even more. *"The words you speak are empty without the power to enforce them!"* it thundered. *"When this is over you shall never be seen again. You will exist only as an empty shell, residing inside of me for all eternity!"* And then the blood thirsty beast opened wide to devour her. Hellena spred her arms to embrace hatred's child that she birthed from a dark evil womb. The Fury's eyes fluttered and flashed with spastic energy as the hot raging storm totally eveloped her. Cin and Bast gasped as Hellena slowly disappeared inside the voracious vortex. "She just fuckin gave up!" Bast said. Without so much as a gotdam struggle. Cin she just gave in to it," he finished the words as if he'd used his last breath to say them. Now for first time since Belarus, tears poured from Cin's burning eyes. In some strange way that she couldn't explain, Helly had become like a bedridden kid sister to her. And now she was gone. "Nothing left to do now, but die!" Cin cried. *"And you shall!"* growled the Fury. Then for the first time it revealed itself to them. The grinding walls of the storm opened itself up to them and suddenly they were peering right into the center of hades. It's eyes were blood red now and its body was covered with dreadful crimson platelets. It grinned through stainless razor sharp teeth salivating with caustic poisons. *"My face will be the last thing you lay your eyes upon!"* it's voice cracked at them like a metal whip. The Fury began to conjer the unbridled evil again but this time something strange was happening. Its powers seem to respond with a reluctance not experienced before. Suddenly there seemed to be a struggle for control, somewhere deep inside the Fury's own psyche. The damned duo began to recover under the protection of the invisible shield. Both were relieved as the painful boils and blisters started to clear. The swelling in the lining of Bast's throat quickly reverted back to normal as Cin's nerves were renewed again with the sense of touch. It was then that she noticed for the first time that Bast had been holding her hand the entire time.

Bast was surprised to see a deceleration in the cyclone's rotation. The phenomenom was followed by a gradual calming of the deadly winds down to a mild gust. As the demon sat exposed at the core, Cin couldn't help but notice how vulnerable it appeared.

The raging inferno surrounding the beast quickly began to cool as temperatures inside began to plumet. It was as if tons of ice had been suddenly dashed into it. Huge billows of steam exploded from the demons core. The terrible black clouds were fading away into the nothingness. Only the confused and troubled creature remained at its center. Bast and Cin were the first one's ever to see such an expression form across the Fury's face. It was simple and pure, unadulterated fear. They both managed to climb to their feet as the wondrous spectacle continued to unfold. For the first time the creature could be heard crying out in pain. It was not the agonizing pain of suffering and death but more reminiscent of that of a crying enfant after a good scolding. The red scaly platelets began to cycle backward, like a reversed metamorphosis. The Fury was changing again, molding and remodeling into a disgusting heap of black gelatinous mucous. Suddenly a mysterious light ripped through the epidermal wall of the black pulsing mass exploding into a kaleidoscope of colors. The lights spectrum was so brilliant Cin and Bast were forced to look away. When they removed their hands from their eyes and faced the spectacle before them, their hearts overflowed with that feeling one only gets while experiencing a miracle. The Fury was gone now and all that remained, was a beautiful young girl with fiery red hair named Hellena. Her new skin bore the greenish hue of an olive; yet smooth and as soft as silk. Her eyes were white and pure like fresh snow. Her lips were plump and red like the richest Sangria wine. Hiding between the velvet orafice were sharp metalic fanglike protrusions. Hellena stood before them, triumphant and whole again. She had defined a new era in the struggle of good versus evil and the Fury had been returned to whence it came, back inside it's mother's womb.

The end?

AUTOBIOGRAPHY

Gregory Coleman

I was born in the small steel town of Gary Indiana. As a child I remember being somewhat moderately poor but happy. Out of three siblings I had two older sisters and one younger brother, I was somewhere in the middle. I was young, impressionable and full of imagination and life. I loved art in all its various forms: painting, drawing and even music. It was in this way that I would learn to express myself. Soon I became known for my artistic talents and the boundless imagination that fueled it.

As far back as I can remember, watching science fiction and horror movies was as synonymous as eating cereal for breakfast for me. Godzilla, War of the Worlds, Attack from Mars, Outerlimits, Twilight Zone, Star Trek, and of course Alfred Hitchcock ... to name just a few. These movies and shows added a new dimension to my already vivid imagination. Who knew these things would be the ingredients to kindle a new fire some 40 years later.